CRESCENT FIRE

ALSO BY KRISTEN MARTIN

Beyond the Stars and Shadows

THE INTERNATIONAL BESTSELLING SERIES
Shadow Crown
Renegade Cruex
Jaded Spring

THE INTERNATIONAL BESTSELLING SERIES
The Alpha Drive
The Order of Omega
Restitution

CRESCENT FIRE

BOOK FOUR

KRISTEN MARTIN

CRESCENT FIRE

For information contact :

Black Falcon Press, LLC

https://www.blackfalconpress.com

Library of Congress Control Number : 2022904929

ISBN: 978-1-7361585-1-7 (paperback)

Cover Illustration by Damonza © 2022

Map by Deven Rue © 2017

10 9 8 7 6 5 4 3 2 1

To those courageously forging their own path –
may the light continue to guide your way.

PRONUNCIATION GUIDE

CHARACTERS
Arden: Ar-den
Rydan: Ry-den
Darius: Dare-ee-us
Aldreda: Al-dray-duh
Cerylia: Sur-lee-uh
Braxton: Brax-ten
Xerin: Zer-in

PLACES
Trendalath: Tren-duh-loth
Sardoria: Sar-door-ee-uh
Vaekith: Vy-kith
Orihia: Or-eye-uh
Ipcea: Ip-see
Chialka: Key-all-kuh
Miraenia: Mur-ay-nee-uh
Lonia: Lone-ee-uh
Lirath: Leer-ath
Eadrios: Ay-dree-os

OTHER
illusié: ill-oo-see-ayy
magick: ma-jik (magic)
Caldari: Kal-darr-ee
Cruex: Crew

Vaekith
Mountains
Drakken
Isle
Rovia
Volkharn
Miraenia
Trendalath
Declorath
Crostan Islands
Ipcea
THE LAND
Athia
AERID
Sunngate

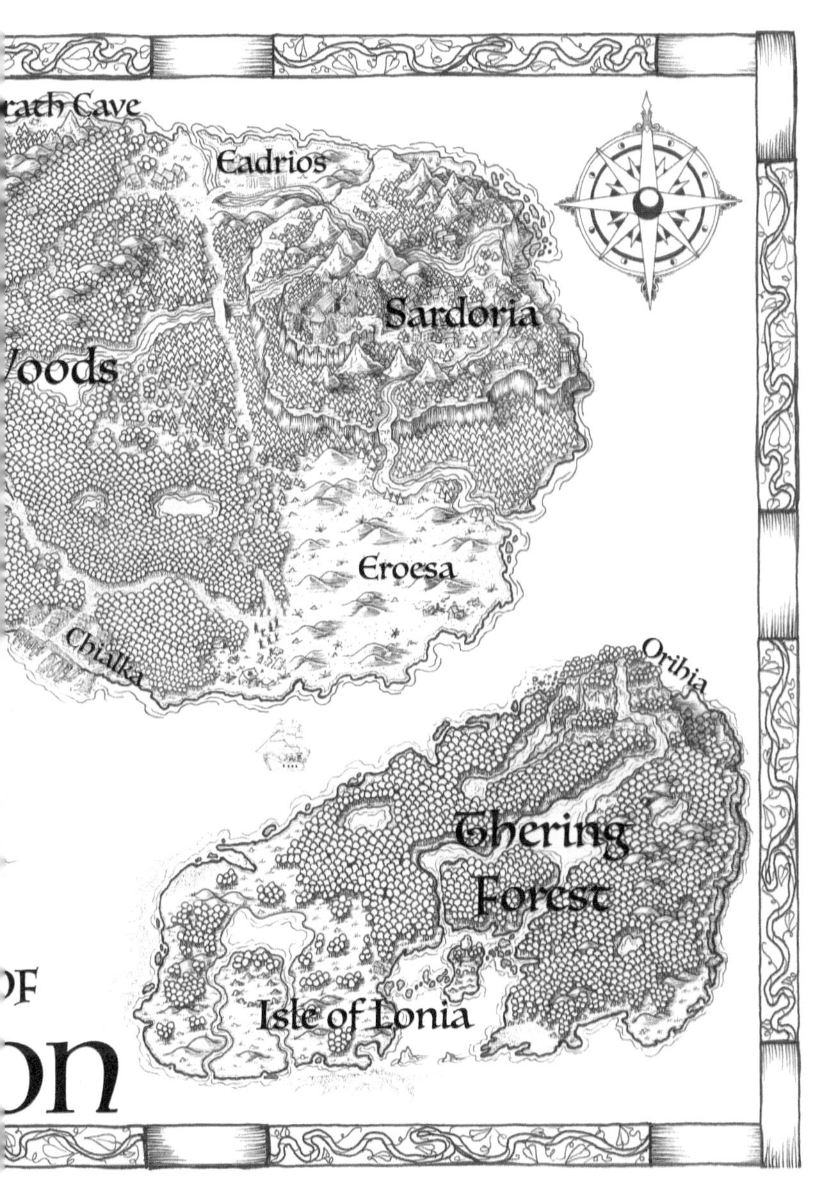

rath Cave
Eadrios
Woods
Sardoria
Eroesa
Chialka
Orihia
Thering
Forest
OF
on
Isle of Lonia

CRESCENT
FIRE

ARDEN ELIRI

FAMILIAR VOICES CARRY from just outside my window. I groan, my head still throbbing from the aftereffects of the tavern fire, then throw the blankets over my legs. A cough climbs up my throat just as my eyes are adjusting to the room, my attention shifting between the door and the rustling curtains. I take a shaky breath, hoping to push it down, but the effort is futile. Even though my breathing is shallow, and I feel the worst I've ever felt, I can't help but crack a smile. I'd be lying if I said I wasn't happy to be back here, in Orihia. I just wish it were under different circumstances . . .

From what I can remember—which is hazy, at best—Haskell had returned to the tavern with Felix in the nick of time. A moment longer and it would have been too late. After the incident there—with the Savant, with the

Mallum—I'd fallen unconscious in the fire. But, thanks to the two of them, we'd transported out of there before any real harm could be done. I don't remember much after that. The last thing I recall is seeing Felix's face again for the first time in months . . . and somehow ending up in Orihia, even though I can no longer access my healing abilities.

Oh, and seeing Rydan.

A spike of rage hits me right in the stomach, but before it can settle for good, a knock sounds at my door.

"Arden?"

I breathe a sigh of relief at the familiar voice. "You can come in—" Before I can finish my sentence, Felix comes into view.

"Morning," he says with a grin.

The sound of his voice sends a shiver down my spine—the good kind. "Did I oversleep again?"

"I was just about to wake you." He takes a seat in one of the armchairs before angling his head toward the window to indicate the time. "How'd you sleep?"

I shrug before lowering my gaze, hoping he won't see right through my lie. "Better than the night before, I suppose."

The truth of the matter is I've hardly slept since my last encounter with the Mallum. Everyone here—Rydan, Vira, Avery, Haskell, Felix . . . they're all convinced that my abilities were never absorbed because if they *were*, my being here, in Orihia, wouldn't be possible. Only illusié are capable of seeing and entering this place.

While the argument is convincing, it still doesn't explain why, despite my best efforts, I can't seem to heal anything or anyone I come into contact with. The whole thing has kept me up for days. I'm certain it's starting to show—and if it's not, it will soon enough.

"Vira's made us all breakfast."

I break from my thoughts, giving him an appreciative smile. "Afraid I don't have much of an appetite, but maybe later."

He sits still for a moment, studying me, then rises from the armchair and makes his way to the bed. Without meaning to, I pull at the blankets until they meet my chin. Gently, he picks Juniper up and sets her on the ground before sitting in her place. For that alone, I owe him a debt I can never repay.

Haskell and I had left Juniper in the Vaekith Mountains after . . . well, after *I-don't-know-what* got to her. Haskell had transported Felix back to that lords-forsaken pit and from what they'd told me, Felix had somehow been able to use his amplification abilities to round up Juniper and bring her back without any issues. Upon their return to Orihia, we've all been keeping a close eye on her. She's been acting completely normal . . . or so we've observed.

Flecked with bits of red, Felix's russet eyes blaze like hot coals as they settle on mine. I loosen my grip on the blanket, letting it fall past my chin and shoulders. A small smile tugs at the corner of his mouth as his attention shifts to my bedside table. I follow his gaze.

"Nice to see you kept it," he says, referring to the wooden carving he'd given me.

I'm reminded then of what I'd seen at the spring—the interaction between him and Cerylia, played out right before me as if I'd been in the White Room myself. I want to ask him about it, but with the way he's looking at me, I can't seem to find the words.

"You know," he says, his voice just above a whisper, "I wasn't sure I'd see you again after everything that happened in Trendalath. When I learned of Aldreda's death, I was certain Darius had sentenced you to . . ." He falters, unable to finish the thought.

"Don't," I whisper. I reach for his hand, lacing my fingers with his. "It's in the past. Let's leave it there."

A muscle feathers in his cheek. "Not for me it isn't."

I blatantly search his eyes for his meaning but come up short. My throat tightens. "Felix," I plead, "you know I didn't do it, right? I was trying to heal her." I can feel the weight of my words before I speak them. "I didn't kill her."

"I know." I wait for him to say more, but with the way he's looking at me, he doesn't need to. It's the same look he'd given me after our first dreadful encounter in the Thering Forest—what he'd been able to sense in me that no one else could.

My darkness.

My shadows.

His grip on my hand tightens before he pulls away.

"Felix," I croak, sheer desperation in my voice, "you can trust me. All I ask is that you let me in on whatever's going on. I might be able to help."

There's an edge to his tone as he says, "Even if you could, it wouldn't change anything."

I try to process the words but before I know it, he's standing by the door with his back facing me, ready to leave. I want so badly to get up, to close the distance between us, but my legs won't budge.

The silence that lingers between us is deafening.

Finally, he turns over his shoulder. He stares at me, not a flicker of emotion on his face. "See you out there."

There's no opportunity to respond as the door swiftly opens and shuts behind him. I ball my hands into fists, fighting against the perfectly rational urge to bury myself in the heap of blankets surrounding me. Try as I might, I can't come to a logical explanation for his hot and cold behavior toward me. One minute, he's the Felix I *think* I know—the one I *want* to know; the next, he's cold, callous . . . a complete stranger.

Even so, I get the sense that he's not telling me something. Whether it's out of concern for me or something else entirely, I don't know—but if I don't get some answers soon, whatever *this* is will be forced to end.

Maybe it already has.

The thought almost has me spiraling even further when I suddenly sense a flash of movement from across the room. My eyes flick to the window where a shadow is lurking just outside.

My breath catches. I blink in the hopes that I'm just seeing things, but the shadow remains. I narrow my eyes, trying to discern who or what it is, but I'm too far away.

One at a time, I throw my legs over the bed, slowly rising until I'm steady on my feet. I take a step forward. The shadow doesn't move. I take another step, followed by another, and another, until I'm clear across the room.

Standing at the side of the window, I grab the edge of the curtain and take a deep breath. I count to three in my head before flinging it open, hoping to reveal the perpetrator. I'm simultaneously relieved and dismayed to find that it's only a tree.

RYDAN HELSTROM

RYDAN'S JUST FINISHING up his breakfast when, out of nowhere, Felix storms by. He doesn't say a word as he passes, just heads straight for his dwelling.

Rydan's about to ask him what's wrong when Vira gives him a sharp nudge in the shoulder. "Looks like he just left Arden's."

Rydan scoops some more hash into his mouth, declining to comment.

Vira finishes polishing a glass on her apron before taking the seat across from him. She sets it down, then folds her hands over the table. "Dare I even ask if you've spoken to her?"

He looks up from his plate, annoyed. "I doubt she'd want to."

"You wanted to smooth things over with her," she says cautiously. "Now might be your only chance."

"How do you figure? We'll have plenty of chances, I'm sure." He gestures to the open space around them. "It's not like any of us are going anywhere."

She shoots him a knowing look. "You're delaying."

He drops his spoon onto his plate before pushing it to the middle of the table. "Wouldn't *you* after the way she reacted?"

Vira levels a steely gaze at him before pulling something from the front pocket of her apron.

Rydan recognizes it immediately. "You just carry that around with you everywhere you go?"

She ignores the jab. "You may have failed to tell Arden about her brother, but you can still tell her about her mother." She points to the piece of parchment. "You said so yourself—she should know what the Savant did."

"Might I remind you that *this* is stolen property? You took this from Haskell and haven't returned it yet?"

She seems to catch his drift. "I'll give it back to him eventually. But even if Haskell's already told her, it's still a show of good faith."

Rydan scoffs. "I'll take my chances." He's about to get up when she reaches across the table and places her hand on top of his—a quiet but unyielding demand. "I can't believe I'm about to say this but . . . you need to make things right with her. For all our sakes." She slides the parchment to him with her free hand. "This is how."

Hearing her plea loud and clear, he takes the rolled-up piece of parchment and tucks it into the waistband of his trousers. He pushes off from the table and heads toward Arden's, knowing that he can easily veer from the path where Vira won't see him—which is exactly what he does.

He makes his way around the back of Arden's dwelling, nearly forgetting to duck down as he crosses underneath the open window. In a crouched position, he runs until he's reached one of the pathways a safe distance away. Relieved to finally have some peace and quiet, he takes his time walking along the edge of the woods—but as much as he'd like a moment or two of silence, his mind seems to have other plans.

Yes, he'll eventually tell Arden about the contents of the parchment. Yes, he, Vira, and Avery will eventually tell the rest of the group about the dead illusié just outside Orihia's gates. But the more pressing item on his mind has to do with the Soames crest. Vira still doesn't know that her own brother allegedly stole it—but for what reason? The answer continues to elude him.

His thoughts scatter as he approaches a familiar setting—the entrance to Orihia. How he'd gotten all the way over here in such a short amount of time is a mystery in and of itself. He turns to head back the way he came when he suddenly stops in his tracks. His eyes land on none other than Arden Eliri, standing firm at the opposite end of the pathway . . .

It seems *eventually* has turned into *right now*.

DARIUS TYMOND

DARIUS STANDS IN the middle of the Daegrum Chambers, alone. The amethyst ring sits heavy on his index finger, a constant reminder that he still hasn't fulfilled the promise he'd made—that he's failing with each passing day. What she would think if she could see him now . . .

It's enough to make his stomach turn.

Never in his life has he felt such a loss of control, such an overwhelming sense of arbitrary chaos—chaos that is completely uncalled for—but with Clive . . . he should have known that, one way or another, it would lead to this.

Always chasing.

Always searching.

Never satisfied.

It's always felt like Clive has been one step ahead of him. A pawn in an exhausting game he'd never wanted to play in the first place. Even with the Mallum at his disposal, Clive remains a threat to his reign—but Darius cannot deny that he's also a necessary force. Without Clive, his memories are at stake—a price he'd paid to keep the soul of his beloved alive. He's searched far and wide for someone with casting abilities as potent and as powerful as Clive's to no avail. Just two pawns in two seemingly different games, they're stuck with each other, whether they like it or not.

Startled, Darius glances over his shoulder as rushed footsteps echo from just down the hall. He braces himself, half expecting Clive himself to burst through the door once again and cast yet another disenchanted illusion around him, when a gray head of hair comes barrelling in.

"Your Majesty," Cyrus pants, leaning against the door for support, "I've been searching all over the castle grounds for you."

Darius studies him in silence as he recalls his last conversation with Hugh and the empty chambers he'd stumbled upon afterward. "I could say the same for you."

Cyrus straightens a little, clearly put off by the comment, but waves it away. "I've searched everywhere for Sir Ridley—the Roviel Woods, Declorath, Miraenia—no sign of him anywhere."

Darius relaxes his shoulders as a wave of relief washes over him. And here he'd been, thinking that not only Clive, but also Cyrus, had betrayed him. His conversation with Hugh had certainly left him on edge. Although this discovery is welcome news, it still doesn't excuse his sudden disappearance.

"Why am I just now being informed of this?"

Cyrus's face falls. "You were not aware of Sir Ridley's escape?"

"I'm well aware," Darius says as he takes a step forward, "but what I'm curious about is how *you* know."

A shadow flickers in his cohort's eyes. "I'm not sure I understand your meaning."

Darius continues to walk across the room until he's standing just inches away from Cyrus's face. "There has been no formal announcement—not to the Savant, not to the King's Guard, not to the Cruex." He levels a steely look at his advisor. "How were you made aware?"

Much to his dismay, Cyrus doesn't appear to be rattled in the slightest. On the contrary, he seems more confident—empowered, even. He meets the king's gaze with equal intensity. "Perhaps you should ask your son."

BRAXTON HORNSBY

BRAXTON PEERS AROUND a corner, hoping he's disguised just enough to blend in with the castle walls. He catches a glimpse of the Cruex and breathes a sigh of relief when he realizes that they're headed down the corridor *away* from him. Given their quiet demeanor, he can only presume that they've just finished training for the day—training he hasn't attended in over a week.

Lane's come to check on him regularly, and so has Hugh, but he's managed to dodge any interaction with either of them—which isn't to say that he doesn't *want* to talk to Lane. Quite the contrary. But after what he'd witnessed in the dungeons, in the memory Clive had cast around both him and Hugh . . . well, he hasn't quite sorted out what to do about his father killing an innocent man in cold blood . . . nor Arden's involvement—or lack thereof—in Aldreda's death.

He presses his back against the wall and sighs before raking a hand through his hair. There are only so many places to hide in this castle and it seems he's run through them all. Like clockwork, Lane will be on her way to his chambers to check on him, as she always does after training, and Hugh will likely follow in her footsteps about an hour or so after that. Both will be failed attempts—so long as he can find somewhere out of sight.

What he really needs is *clarity*. It crosses his mind to go to the dungeons, to revisit Clive's old cell, but what good would that do now that Clive is gone? No, it's too much of a risk. He can't help but wonder if anyone even knows that Clive's escaped. And, if so, do they know that he and Hugh are the ones responsible? Seems his refusal to attend Cruex training has left him entirely in the dark. Surely if the king knew that he and Hugh were the ones responsible, he would have sent the King's Guard to interrogate them . . .

A door slamming shut yanks him from his thoughts. From just down the hall, his father's voice echoes—and that's definitely the *last* person he needs to run into right now. Realizing he's still somewhat out in the open, he turns on his heel and walks as fast as he can, but, without a clear destination, he may as well be running in circles. After another brisk right turn, he settles on the courtyard. Seeing as the Cruex have finished their training for the evening, it should be dark enough for him to slip across the grounds undetected.

Just as he's about to round the corner to descend the stairs that lead to a gravel pathway, he catches a glimpse of his father at the very end of the hall. Alarmed, he freezes mid-step, then begins to backtrack out of sight. Moments later, one look around tells him that he's standing in the very hallway that leads to the Great Room—which is surely where Darius is heading.

As the voices grow louder, Braxton realizes his only option is to disappear over the ledge at the far end of the hallway, which will put him on the edge of the courtyard. Without a second thought, he dashes down the hall, grabs hold of the stone ledge, and swings his legs over it, one at a time. It's not the most graceful thing he's ever done, but he manages to land on his feet, although not steadily enough to avoid a shoulder roll across the gravel.

Digging the heels of his boots into the sliding rocks, he scoots backward as quickly as he can until his back is flush against the exterior castle wall. The voices grow in volume, becoming more distinct, and that's when Braxton realizes . . .

That Darius had been walking alone.

In both of the glimpses he'd caught, there'd been no guards accompanying him. No Savant members. No one from the Cruex. *So who exactly is he talking to?*

Braxton strains his ears, but the only voice he can clearly make out is his father's. The other voice is low, hushed—although vaguely familiar. The conversation goes on for a few more minutes until Braxton hears the doors of the Great Room creak closed. He remains in the same spot, waiting to make sure that he is indeed alone before making a break for it across the courtyard. He's about to do just that when the unthinkable happens. He watches, mouth agape, as a black falcon soars through the window and into the night sky.

16

CERYLIA JARETH

CERYLIA STANDS IN the middle of Felix's chambers with her head lowered. *Another one gone.*

As if reading her mind, a faint voice echoes from behind her, "It's for a good reason."

Slowly, Cerylia turns to find Estelle in the chamber doorway. "And you know this *how*?"

As if on cue, Opal appears at Estelle's side. "Felix is safe. He's in Orihia."

Cerylia narrows her eyes at the both of them, but more so at Opal. After unexpectedly stumbling upon her undisclosed meetings with Xerin just outside the castle grounds, she has every right to be wary of anything that comes out of the girl's mouth, especially after the way she'd reacted when Delwynn had confronted her—to feign illness *over* an admission of guilt. The memory is enough to make Cerylia's blood boil.

Estelle's voice pulls her from her thoughts. "From my understanding, it seems a man arrived at the castle, well into the evening, to request Felix's assistance—"

"I don't recall extending any invitations," Cerylia interrupts, realizing that she'd been meeting with Cyrus during the aforementioned time. "Surely Delwynn would have said something, had that been the case . . ." Her voice trails off as she meets Estelle's gaze.

"He didn't need to use the entrance."

Recognition takes hold of the queen.

"The man claimed to be Arden's brother," Opal says, confirming her suspicions. "Said he needed Felix to captain a ship to Lonia."

"For what reason?"

"That remains unclear."

Cerylia studies her for a moment, searching for a flicker of uncertainty, a dash of doubt—something to indicate that she's withholding information—but much to her dismay, there's nothing of the sort. "Was Arden with him?"

Opal looks to Estelle before shaking her head. "Not at first, but then . . ."

"They're all in Orihia," Estelle blurts out.

Cerylia raises a brow. "Who exactly?"

"Felix. Rydan and Vira," Opal starts. "Someone named Avery—"

"Anyone else?" Cerylia presses, growing impatient.

"Haskell," Estelle finishes. "And Arden."

The tightness she'd felt in her chest eases. "Arden *and* Haskell are in Orihia?" This news is certainly a refreshing reprieve from the thoughts that have plagued her mind as of late.

"Yes." Another wordless exchange passes between the two Caldari. "There's something else."

"I'm listening."

Opal shuts her eyes, as if going back to the inversion itself, before saying "Prior to setting off for Orihia, Arden was in Chialka, at a tavern. Under the influence of what I believe to be the Savant, she came into contact with the Mallum—"

"Wouldn't be the first time," Estelle mutters.

"Even so," Opal says hastily, shooting her fellow Caldari a harsh look, "all of Tymond's forces have been called to duty in Trendalath. The fact that there's a rogue Savant out there is, needless to say, rather alarming."

Cerylia can't help but take a few steps backward, reaching out behind her until she finds a sturdy surface to lean against. She immediately recalls her interaction with Braxton after the Mallum had found its way into her castle—the look of sheer angst on his face when the tankard had fallen to the ground after his failed attempt to deviate; the disconcerting realization that he was no longer illusié. *Has Arden faced the same fate?*

"She's *in* Orihia," Cerylia emphasizes, "which means she must still have her abilities." She fixes her gaze on Opal. "Did you see anything in your inversion that might confirm this?"

Opal shakes her head. "It's strange. I can't quite put my finger on it, but my access to her seems to be"—she pauses, searching for the right word—"*restricted* in some way."

"If she's in Orihia . . ."

Cerylia nods at Estelle. "You're right. We can worry about that later. About the Savant—did you happen to gather any information?" She can tell just by the way Opal's face falls that her assumption is correct.

The only one in the room brave enough to say his name out loud, Estelle murmurs, "Sir Clive Ridley."

Before another word can be spoken, the bell tower chimes. Cerylia waits for it to finish before looking at the two Caldari with startling conviction. "Not a word of this to anyone else, understood? Stay close and keep your ear to the ground." She lowers her voice to a whisper. "Any news at all, find me immediately. We have the advantage here—let's not squander it."

"Understood," they say in unison.

Cerylia's about to dismiss them when Estelle asks, "Is Delwynn not to know?"

Cerylia considers this. "I'll tell him. This stays between the four of us. Agreed?" She looks to Opal in warning to not lie about any further communication with Xerin. Whether the girl catches it or not is unclear, but at least this way, she'll have her answer—even if it *isn't* the one she's hoping for.

ARDEN ELIRI

IT SEEMS PACING across this room has become my new normal. For the most part, being back in Orihia is great—much safer than being on the run or locked up in Trendalath—but I'm starting to feel a bit like a caged animal. It probably doesn't help that I've refused to leave my room, but I'd rather stare at the inside of these walls for another *week* than face Rydan.

Oh, let's be honest . . . another *month.*

By my logic, he and Vira shouldn't be here for long—really, I don't know what they're even doing here in the first place. They were so eager to leave the Caldari behind in Sardoria, not to mention Rydan's irrefutable shame of being among the illusié ranks—why, then, would he come to the one place that only illusié can access?

Only when my eyes flick to the open window do I realize I've stopped pacing. I steal a glance at Juniper, who's sitting just below it—ears alert, eyes wide. She raises her head slightly, as if to indicate her desire to go outside. Normally, I'd sigh, trudge over to my desk, and drag the chair over to the window, but I'm so happy to have her back and in one piece, that I eagerly pick up the chair and place it beneath the window. It's just tall enough for her to use—two hops and she'll be on the ledge, free to roam about Orihia and do whatever she so pleases—but she seems to sense that my plan is flawed because, well, it is. I peek over the ledge, hoping to find a pile of firewood or something else she can use to climb back inside, but the only option is a tree—and from what I can tell, it's a bit too far of a jump.

I shift my gaze to the ground to find that she's looking directly at me. "Do we have to?" She swipes a paw in the air before running it over her nose. It doesn't take much for me to submit.

I throw on a fresh shirt before pulling on my boots, all while Juniper prances in front of the door, her bushy tail swaying with each step. I can tell she's getting impatient, so I quickly grab an empty canteen from one of the cabinets. I close the doors to the armoire, then head to the window, hoping to delay our inevitable departure. I gingerly poke my head out to take a quick look around, but no one's in sight. No voices either.

"Let's make this quick," I say as I turn to head toward the door, but something in my peripheral gives me pause. My gaze lands on the gift Felix had given me.

Without a second thought, I transfer the wooden carving from the nightstand into my pocket, then proceed to finally step out the door.

A crisp spring day greets me, and I can't help but shudder with delight as a cool breeze dances along the back of my neck. I take a deep gulp of fresh air as I begin to walk along the trail, momentarily forgetting that I'm not the only one here. My gaze travels from the cerulean sky, which is dotted with an array of birds, their violet and cobalt wings soaring through the wind, to the overwhelming presence of budding trees towering over me, and finally, to the end of the stone pathway that leads directly to the entrance of this magical place. As if we'd planned it (which we most certainly did not), Rydan's standing there, transfixed.

Our eyes lock.

My first instinct is to turn and walk back to my cabin, but something in his expression piques my interest. Instead, I keep walking, slowly picking up the pace until I'm marching over to him at what I would consider to be an extremely alarming rate. It doesn't seem to faze him though—which isn't all that surprising given our past training in the Cruex. I'm just a few steps away when he extends his arm, fingers pointed at the sky, palm facing me. I swat it away, not daring to break eye contact.

He's stone-faced as he says, "Lady Eliri."

It's like he's *trying* to get a rise out of me. "Cut the formalities, Rydan," I snap. "I don't even know where to begin with you."

"Well, you're finally talking to me, so that's a start."

Normally I'd find his witty banter amusing, but given our current situation, it's just downright annoying. I clench my jaw as all the memories—*our* memories—begin to form in my head. A swell of emotions rises within me, like air bubbles finally floating to the surface of a deep, deep ocean. I'm about to let him have it when he says something that renders me speechless.

"He looks just like you." His eyes flick to the ground, a show of submission if I've ever seen one. "Your brother, I mean."

I notice my shoulders drop, but even so, my guard stays up. I decide to stay quiet, hoping he'll continue.

"I knew from the moment I met him, but I didn't want to believe it." His voice softens, but I can sense the weight of his words even before he speaks them. "I didn't want to know something so personal, so life-changing, like you having a brother—a *living* relative—with no way to communicate it to you." A long sigh, followed by an even longer silence. "I'm really sorry, Arden. I should have tried harder to find you. I should have done better. I know that."

I can't do anything except stand there, stunned. This isn't at all what I'd expected. Quite frankly, I have no idea how I feel about this vulnerable side of Rydan. It's equal parts concerning and refreshing, and honestly? I don't know what's worse—him acting this way, or me having these types of thoughts *about* him acting this way. I continue to gawk at him, hoping he'll just keep talking because finding a coherent sentence right now is near impossible.

"I need you to know that I only got confirmation that he was indeed your brother *after* he transported both Vira and me to Chialka. That's when he gave me this." He flashes Haskell's pocket watch. From the way he's looking at me, it seems like he wants to say more, but he remains silent, patiently awaiting my response.

I take a step closer before extending my arm, palm faceup. He drops it into my hand, watching as my fingers close around the metal. It isn't much, but the only words I manage to speak to him are, "What else?"

His brow furrows in confusion.

"What else do you know?" I clarify. I must admit, even I'm surprised by the strength of my tone. "Before we left Lirath Cave, Haskell was rummaging through some papers—papers about our mother he couldn't seem to find."

Rydan's face pales. "I didn't know she'd taken them until after we'd already left."

"Vira?" When he nods, I press, "What did she take, exactly?"

With a sigh, he rakes a hand through his matted hair. "The papers confirming that the Savant killed your mother."

Seeing as my brother has already divulged this information, it doesn't come as a shock. What I'm more curious about is *who*. "Do the papers mention any names?"

He angles his head as if I've lost my mind. "I just told you. The Savant."

"Yes, but *who* in the Savant?"

"No names are specified."

I try to mask my disappointment, but the effort is futile. It's then he reaches behind him to reveal a rolled-up piece of parchment. He unfurls it and hands it to me.

I take it, hastily scanning the document for something they might have missed. My frustration only grows when I discover that it's as vague as it is helpful. Just like he'd said, no names are listed. "Thanks for this," I say, not bothering to hide my exasperation. As I turn to go, his remark stops me.

"I was wrong about illusié."

Rydan saying he's sorry is one thing, but admitting he's *wrong*? I never thought I'd hear the words—certainly not in this lifetime. Slowly, I turn back around to face him. "I'd be lying if I said I wasn't pleasantly surprised."

A smirk. "Don't get used to it, Eliri. This is a one-time thing."

In that moment, I can see the cracks in the bridge between us begin to disappear, as if they'd never had the chance to form in the first place. I quickly come to realize that he's extended an olive branch—that I need to fess up and admit my wrongdoings as well.

"As intrigued as I am about your coming around to illusié, I owe you an apology." Our failed Cruex mission in Lonia flashes across my mind. My chest tightens and my mouth goes dry, but I don't let that stop me. "I shouldn't have left you vulnerable and, moreover, unconscious during our last assignment. I'm sorry."

My apology seems to stir something within him, albeit I'm not sure what—but the glimmer in his eye and the extension of his hand distracts me from asking. His hand meets mine in a firm, solid grip. "Same team?"

I give him an affirming smile. "Same team."

RYDAN HELSTROM

A HUGE WEIGHT, the size of a boulder, has finally been lifted from his shoulders. Rydan honestly never thought that he and Arden would be on the same page after everything that's transpired, but they are—and *damn*, does it feel good. Even though he'd left their conversation feeling both relieved and confident, a lingering thought proceeds to haunt him . . .

Xerin taking the fabric with the Soames crest.

Seeing as Xerin is Vira's brother and Arden just so happened to be there, at the house, during the mission, he's come to the logical conclusion that they both need to be informed—but how can he tell them what he doesn't know himself? For starters, he doesn't know *why* Xerin would have any interest in the Soames or their family crest. He's also not completely confident that Xerin was even the one who took it. It could have been Avery. Or maybe even Vira. Or perhaps a complete stranger?

Secondly, with him and Arden having just put that whole fiasco behind them, does he really want to open a new can of worms? The two things he needs most—answers and time—are luxuries he can't seem to afford at the moment.

Just as he's looking up from the table, Avery enters his line of sight. Rydan notices almost immediately that he doesn't seem to be himself, given that he's stumbling every other step he takes. Refusing to take his eye off him, Rydan reaches for a pitcher of water before filling one of the goblets. He swings his legs over the bench and approaches his fellow Ignitor, noting that his eyes are glassy and that his face is paler than usual. "Here," he says, handing him the beverage. "Drink."

Avery doesn't hesitate to take it. He downs its entire contents in record time. "Thanks, mate. I don't know what's come over me, but this is the worst I've ever felt."

"When did it start?"

Avery ponders this for a moment. "Right before we got here, I think."

Rydan takes the goblet back, studying him closely. "Was it before or after we . . . well, you know." Even though it'd happened, he doesn't care to say it out loud.

Avery seems to sense that he's referring to their incident with the dead illusié, so it doesn't take him long to reply, "It was after."

The only other people around for that unfortunate encounter were himself and Vira, and he knows for a fact that she feels just fine—no complaints from his end either. He considers taking Avery to Arden, but then he remembers that her healing abilities are allegedly gone—to which he can't quite wrap his head around because if they *are* truly gone, she wouldn't be able to access Orihia. Seeing as Avery was the one to tell him about the Mallum, he figures it can't hurt to try and get more information from him—for Arden's sake.

"Here, sit down," Rydan says, ushering him over to the table. With a grunt, Avery follows him, nearly tripping over his own two feet as he steps over the bench. Rydan waits until he's completely seated before requesting his undivided attention. "I have some questions for you about what we spoke of earlier. About the Mallum."

"I can't promise I'll be much help," Avery admits, cradling his head in his hands, "but, of course, I'll divulge any information I'm privy to."

"I certainly appreciate it," Rydan says as he refills the glass with water. He slides it over to Avery, but he's too preoccupied with what appears to be a terrible headache. "We've already covered that the stowaway on your ship was Arden and not Opal."

A slight lift of his head is the only indication he's heard Rydan.

"And you said that the Mallum visited you—the both of you—while you were at sea? And that's also when you left Arden on the shores of Lonia to fend for herself?"

"Quite the inquisition," he murmurs. "But yes, that is correct."

"Do you believe the Mallum took her abilities then?"

"That'd be my guess, although her brother seems to have a different story."

"You've spoken with Haskell?"

Avery shrugs. "Briefly."

"And?"

"He believes her abilities were absorbed just before Queen Tymond died."

Hmm. Rydan drums his fingers against the wooden table, allowing the information to sink in. "Either way, Arden shouldn't be able to be here, in Orihia. Whether her abilities were absorbed on your ship or in Trendalath, the timing is entirely irrelevant."

Avery presses his fingers against his temples before letting out a strained exhale. "Your logic is sound. If I may be frank, though, the best person to talk to about this is Arden herself. But, if you have any specific questions about the Mallum, I'd be happy to tell you what I know."

Rydan can feel his cheeks burn at the remark. "Right, of course," he stammers, trying to rephrase his question so that it's *not* directly related to Arden. "Have you ever known any illusié who have faced the Mallum and been affected, well . . . *differently?*"

At this, Avery lifts his head fully so that his eyes meet Rydan's. "In other words, is it possible that Arden's abilities *weren't* absorbed?"

Rydan puts his hands up facetiously in surrender. "You said not to ask about Arden. Just following orders."

Chuckling, Avery shakes his head, then winces. "I wish I had a better answer for you, mate, but no. The

Mallum absorbs and destroys. As far as I know, there is no other option."

Not exactly the answer he was hoping for. Rydan slumps his shoulders, racking his brain for some sort of explanation as to how Arden can see and *be* in Orihia. It's then he realizes that there's really nothing else he can ask—not with his current knowledge on the subject, anyway. Feeling defeated, he's about to get up and retreat to his cabin for the evening when a glimpse of movement grabs his attention.

Seemingly out of nowhere, Felix appears. He takes slow, steady strides until he reaches the table where both Rydan and Avery are seated but doesn't bother joining them. Instead, he reaches for the pitcher of ale and pours it into a copper tankard. "Seems you missed more than you bargained for when you fled Sardoria."

Rydan knows the comment can't possibly be directed at Avery, which means Felix is actually trying to converse with *him*. "How do you mean?"

A shadow flickers across those deep russet eyes. "I'd be remiss if I didn't disclose that Arden's been struggling with her illusié abilities for quite some time now."

Rydan *would* exchange a glance with Avery . . . if he weren't now face-down on the table. Too much ale, it would appear. So, as far as he's concerned, it's just him and Felix talking. "You've only just met."

Felix smirks, then takes a swig of his drink before setting the mug down with a bit more force than is necessary. "I suppose you could say that. But I was there, in Sardoria, when she nearly sliced Braxton's hands off and paralyzed Delwynn."

"She did *what*?"

Felix brushes past his surprise. "I was also there, in the Thering Forest, right after she'd left you behind—unconscious, alone, and with no proof of your assassination."

Although he and Arden had *just* put this behind them not even a few hours prior, hearing the words from Felix's mouth dredges up even more repressed feelings Rydan hadn't realized he had. He takes a deep inhale through his nose, hardly wanting to dignify Felix's jab with a response—but he can't help it. "I take it you were also there when she decided to come back for me? To risk everything, *including* her newfound friends in the Caldari, to break me out of Trendalath under the most impossible circumstances?"

The smirk he's worn their entire conversation vanishes almost instantly. "She went back for you out of guilt. Nothing more."

Rydan nearly scoffs out loud. "This coming from someone who's known her for a few months?" He shakes his head. "Try a decade."

Although he doesn't look surprised, he can see the wheels turning round and round in Felix's head. Rydan has no idea when this became a pissing match for who's known Arden the longest, but if a winner were to be declared, it would most certainly be him. Before this can go any further, Rydan decides to nip it in the bud. "Is there a specific reason you came over here, Barlow?"

Felix doesn't respond right away. Instead, he takes his time refilling the tankard with more ale. He sets the pitcher down, then slowly brings it to his lips, drinking every last drop. He wipes his mouth with the back of his hand, letting the mug fall to the ground with a thud. "Yes. I was thirsty."

Rydan watches in utter disbelief as Felix turns to leave, heading directly for Arden's cabin. It's only when he's out of earshot that Rydan mutters, "Can you believe that guy?"

Not surprisingly, a loud snore is his only response. He briefly considers waking Avery, then decides it's more trouble than it's worth. "Goodnight, Bancroft," Rydan says with a gentle pat on his friend's back. "Here's hoping you feel better tomorrow."

Here's hoping we all do.

FELIX BARLOW

FELIX CAN FEEL Rydan's stare burning a hole in the back of his head as he strides away from what is likely the most unpleasant conversation he's ever had. Xerin usually tasks him with putting people in their place, especially new Caldari on an ego trip—which, after what he's just witnessed, describes Rydan perfectly.

But Rydan doesn't seem to be willing to go down without a fight. Especially where Arden is involved.

The thought is infuriating.

He veers left, taking a slight detour off the path, knowing better than to engage with Arden when he's feeling triggered. *Which, apparently, is all the time, now that Rydan's here.*

"Deep breath in," Felix murmurs to himself. "And out." He repeats the breathing pattern a few more times, knowing that his incessant pacing is probably undoing any progress he's made to calm the hell down.

Back and forth.

Back and forth.

He kicks the toe of his boot into the ground, the damp soil sticking to the leather, before leaning over and raking a hand through his hair. Yes, he's aware that Arden and Rydan have a past. That they basically grew up together. So, it's no surprise that Rydan feels protective of her. But he'd assumed it'd be in more of a *brotherly* kind of way. Like how siblings joke and tease and fight, but would still protect one another at all costs; however, the sense of protection Rydan projects is . . .

Nope. Don't even think it. Don't feed the beast.

The only reason he'd even *know* the feeling is because Felix feels it himself. For Arden. And what Rydan just exhibited? Is the same level of territorialism that Felix has—he's just a lot better at hiding it.

Realizing that he's still crouched over, Felix straightens, knowing that overthinking the situation won't do him any good. It's only causing him to feel more frustrated, more angry, more territorial—all feelings that are dangerous to display in front of Arden. Not that he'd even have to *physically* display them for her to catch on.

Their unique link is to thank for that.

No, if he's going to last in this group, he'll have to remain as neutral as possible. Walk away when he needs to. Take a breath (or two). Wait for the inner storm to pass. And, hopefully, with time, this process won't be one he has to repeat.

A drop of rain hits him directly on the cheek. He looks to the sky, feeling slightly taken aback by the storm that's suddenly rolling in. Nature sure has a funny way of mirroring his emotions at times. A flash lights up the sky in a bolt of mesmerizing power. He closes his eyes as it begins to rain harder, waiting for the clap of thunder to hit next.

The deafening sound shakes the very ground he stands on, but he doesn't move. He also doesn't hear the frantic yell from the cabin across the way. Only when it gets closer does he hear her.

"Felix! What the hell are you doing?"

He opens his eyes to see Arden rushing toward him, her hair drenched and dripping from the steady downpour. He blinks through the water coating his eyelids, only to have more take its place.

"I . . ." For once, he's at a loss for words.

"Come on," she says, grabbing his arm and pulling him along with her. "The last thing we need is you getting sick. Or any of us, for that matter."

He obliges her, picking up the pace as they run toward her cabin, mud and grass flinging from their boots. She's fast, but he's faster, and so, in one deft movement, he sweeps her off her feet. She lets out a shout, then laughs before burying her face in his shoulder. It's now raining so hard that he can barely see where he's headed, but luckily, he's close enough for the cabin to come into view just a few seconds later. He bounds up the steps, Arden's arms secured tightly around his neck, until they finally reach the covered porch. He's about to set her down when she gently squeezes her arms around his shoulders, lifting her head to meet his gaze. Disheveled strands of hair stick to her forehead and the sides of her face, but the way it frames her features, most notably her eyes, is breathtaking—more so than usual.

He searches the sea of emerald before him, knowing better than to set her down, but also not knowing what to say. Instead, he presses a light kiss to her forehead, to which she lets out a small sigh. "I suppose I should thank you for saving me," he says with a wink.

"I suppose you should." The thunder rolls in the distance. "What were you doing out there, anyway?"

Even though he doesn't want to, he finally sets her down, watching as she grabs two thick linens from the bench. He graciously takes one and begins to dry off. "I see you had these at the ready." He narrows his eyes in jest. "Were you spying on me?"

She laughs. "I hate to break it to you, but I have more important things to do than worry about saving you from impending thunderstorms."

"And yet, here we are."

She wraps the now damp cloth around the bottom portion of her hair, ringing it dry. "What can I say? You got lucky with the timing."

"Sure," he says, kicking off his boots with a squelch, "let's go with that."

Her mouth drops open in mock offense. Laughing, she flings the damp linen at his face. "You still didn't answer my question."

"Which is . . .?"

She rolls her eyes. "What were you doing out there?"

Thinking about you. Worrying about you. Hoping that your past in the Cruex doesn't play into your present . . . into us.

She tilts her head as if she knows exactly what he's thinking. "Felix . . .?"

"We just . . . exchanged some words is all."

She raises a brow.

"Me. And Rydan," he clarifies, suddenly feeling the weight of his words.

"About what?"

It's almost too perfect. The rain. The thunder. The dramatic gesture. The fact that they're both soaking wet and slowly peeling off their clothes, one layer at a time. He could follow the romantic storyline and tell her the truth. But something in him doesn't want to give Rydan the satisfaction. He doesn't want Arden to be thinking about Rydan and what may or may not have transpired earlier today. He wants her to be thinking about *him.*

Only him.

"He and Avery had some questions about igniting."

"And they asked *you?*"

He forces a smile. "They didn't get very far, believe me. Not my forte."

She drops her gaze, clearly trying to hide her expression. He can't help but wonder what it is . . . *Disappointment? Indifference? Relief?* It would only take him a second to know what she's feeling. Just a brief moment to amplify. But he doesn't—because he promised her he wouldn't.

That's one promise he's determined to keep.

She shivers and looks to the door at the same time he scans the porch for some firewood. "Let's go inside. I'll make us a fire." He strips off his shirt, then his trousers, before grabbing a hefty stack of logs.

Arden pushes open the door, teeth chattering as she finishes removing her remaining wet garments. Felix sets the wood in front of the hearth, swiping a nearby fur blanket from one of the armchairs. "What was that you said earlier?" he teases as he wraps it around her. "The last thing we need is . . ."

"You getting sick," she says.

"Or anyone else, for that matter," he finishes. "That would include you, you know."

She smiles, teeth no longer chattering. "Can't argue with that, now can I?"

Grinning, Felix begins organizing the logs in the small space, briefly considering how much easier it would be if he did indeed have use of igniting abilities. Before he can chew on that thought further, Arden meets him with a mason jar filled with matches. He takes it, tipping the silver cap toward her. "It seems you've read my mind."

"Just another one of my newfound abilities."

He stops, mid-strike, unable to tell if she's joking or not.

"Calm down, Captain," she teases. "I'm not a mind-reader." She frowns. "And, apparently, I'm no longer a Healer either."

Another swift strike of the match has it blazing and, soon enough, the fire's embers are licking the sides of the wood. Felix sits back on his heels, admiring his handiwork. He'd been so focused on getting the fire started that he'd hardly registered what Arden's just said.

"I guess it's not for me to know right now," she says absentmindedly. "Confusing, to say the least."

Felix bites his tongue, unsure how to respond. He knows if he looks at her, he'll want to comfort her, but with what he knows? It'd just feel . . . *wrong*. Stacking another layer of guilt on top of the already growing pile won't do either of them any good. So, he does the one thing that always makes him feel better, in control.

He can sense Arden watching him closely as he reaches for some scrap wood. He scans the area for a small knife and, again, he's met with Arden's uncanny senses. His eyes flick to hers as he takes the knife from her outstretched hand. "You sure you can't read minds?"

She smiles, but it doesn't reach her eyes. "Believe me, I wish I could."

The fire's roaring now, the heat enough to make him sigh out loud. "Come," he says, eyes closing as he soaks in the warmth. "Sit."

It's only when she sits next to him that he realizes they're both damn near naked. The blanket falls from her shoulder, exposing her olive skin in a way that has him stirring. He can't help but watch her chest as it rises and falls—slowly, calmly—as if sitting like this is the most natural thing in the world. He supposes, with her, it is.

His gaze moves to her neck and her hair, which is slowly drying in soft, wavy tendrils. It frames her face in an ethereal way and, with her eyes closed, she looks almost idyllic. Like if he were to reach out and touch her, she'd drift away into the fleeting smoke that now surrounds them.

He stares at her for as long as her eyes remain closed but, once they open, he averts his gaze, clearing his throat as if he hadn't noticed her at all. Memories of his recurring dreams come barreling in, causing every part of his body to stand at attention. He's acutely aware that if she glances down, however briefly, she'll see exactly what kind of effect she has on him—and not just now, because of this particular situation . . . but *always*.

He shifts the position of his leg in an effort to hide the evidence, but the fact that he can *feel* her smiling at him tells him he's moved too late.

"Plan to do anything with that wood?"

He whips his head toward her in surprise before realizing that she's talking about the scrap of wood he'd picked up earlier. He clears his throat again, unable to stifle his embarrassment. "Carving things, it . . . it calms me."

Arden smirks, fixing her gaze on the fire. "From the looks of it, you could certainly use some calming."

Damn. So she had *seen.*

"Perhaps I should sit somewhere else? You know, so you can focus?" The way she says it isn't rude or condescending, but playful.

"I much prefer you right where you are, just how you are."

He isn't sure if the red in her cheeks is from the heat of the fire or from what he's just said, but there's no denying that whatever he's feeling . . . she's feeling it, too.

She lets the blanket fall off her other shoulder so that her upper chest is completely bare, leaving very little to the imagination. At this rate, there won't be a single position left for him to shift into to hide his . . . *alertness*.

She balances on her knees and moves closer to him, her scent even more intoxicating having been amplified by the rain. He's about to drop what's in his hands altogether and fill them with her and only her but, for some reason, she maintains just enough distance.

"Did you know that the first time I got to Orihia, I went to your place?"

The admission causes him to tense, which probably isn't the reaction she'd been hoping for. "Is that so?"

She angles her chin, undoubtedly noticing the shift in his demeanor. "There was a carving there, just like mine, except it was in the shape of an animal." She hesitates, but it seems intentional. "A falcon, if memory serves me."

"Quite observant, you are," he says, refusing to look her in the eye as he picks at the wood with his knife.

"It's just curious, is all."

She doesn't elaborate further, which forces him to stop what he's doing and meet her gaze. "What is?"

Her expression doesn't waver. "That your carving happens to be in the shape of the animal that Xerin frequently takes form."

He shrugs. "I carve what I know. Falcons, ships . . ."

"But mine had something inside of it." She makes a circular shape with her index finger and thumb. "And it allowed me to see things—"

"Sometimes, Arden, a carving is just a carving," he interrupts. "And, sometimes, when I'm giving it to someone I really care about, it's something more."

A blush crawls across her face.

"So, with that said," he continues, hoping to change the subject, "what would you like me to carve for you?"

She looks to her nightstand, confused. "But I already have one—"

"Well, who says you can't have two?"

Her eyes brighten. "How about a . . . fox?"

He laughs. "How about something I can finish in under an hour?" As soon as he says it, he realizes *exactly* how it sounds.

"Well, I know something you can finish in under an hour," she says, inching even closer. "And while it won't require a knife, it *will* require some wood."

The objects clatter to the floor. "I'm all ears."

DARIUS TYMOND

DARIUS STANDS WITH his right palm pressed against one of the doors that leads to the Great Room. He bows his head until his forehead is resting lightly on the iron surface. Knowing what's on the other side is enough to give him pause—and for very good reason. Between his steadily declining relationship with his son, Clive's untimely escape, and Cyrus's recent uncharacteristic behavior, Darius has every right to be concerned.

On the other side of these doors, his Savant awaits him. He still hasn't decided how to broach the subject of Clive's escape. He's almost certain by now that, at the very least, they're aware of the situation, but as far as next steps go, there's been no direction; which isn't surprising, seeing as that responsibility lies with Darius and Darius alone.

He removes his forehead from the door before dragging his hand to the middle where the bar is. He grips it tightly before thrusting it open, intentionally breezing by the Savant without so much as a passing glance. He approaches his throne more confidently than he feels, but when he whirls around, he can sense the immediate shift in the room—a shift in his favor. His concern begins to fade as he realizes that the men who stand before him seem to be more apprehensive of *his* reaction—of the reason why they've been called here in the first place—than anything else.

Darius nods at the guards, keeping his eyes on the back of the room until the doors are secured, then clears his throat before saying, "I've called you here today to discuss a rather dire matter." Although he doesn't mean for it to, his gaze lands on Cyrus. "As you may or may not be aware, Sir Clive Ridley is no longer occupying his cell in the dungeons."

"You released him?"

The question comes from the Savant's Curser, Landon Graeme. Darius shoots him a harsh look. "On the contrary"—he tries to swallow the lump suddenly forming in his throat—"he's escaped."

A low murmur rumbles amongst the group, but Darius maintains his composure.

"When?"

The king's attention travels from Sir Graeme to Julian Enfield, the one and only Multiplier he's ever had the privilege of meeting in all his time roaming Aeridon. "I'm much less concerned with the *when* as I am with the *who*."

The already palpable tension heightens.

"Surely you don't think . . ." Benson Hale's voice trails off as he exchanges a glance with both of his cohorts. "Your Majesty, I can assure you that the Savant had *nothing* to do with Clive's escape." He turns to his right, directing a sharp glance at Cyrus. "The Cruex, on the other hand—"

"The Cruex had nothing to do with this either," Cyrus interjects. "*And* might I remind you that, although I was initiated into the Cruex long ago, my true loyalty lies with the Savant, with the King himself." He takes a step forward, removing himself from the line, before bending into a low bow.

Normally, a show of such loyalty would warrant some recognition from the king, but, given his current disposition and the many unknowns of Cyrus's recent whereabouts, Darius chooses to remain silent.

It doesn't go unnoticed, however.

Cyrus looks as though he wants to say more—to out the king and reveal whatever it is he thinks he knows about Braxton—but that would certainly contradict the statement he's just made. *Walked right into that one.*

Which reminds him . . .

"How far along are our newest Cruex members?"

The question seems to throw Cyrus off, but he manages to answer without too much of a delay. "They're almost fully trained, Your Majesty. A few more days should suffice."

"A few more days?" Darius scoffs. "And what do you suggest we do in the meantime? Twiddle our thumbs? The longer we wait, the less likely we are to find him."

Cyrus's eyes grow so wide, they're on the verge of bulging. "Are you proposing that we send the *Cruex* after one of the most elite members of the Savant?"

If his intentions weren't clear before, they most certainly are now.

"Your Majesty," a young voice suddenly interjects, "I urge you to reconsider." A hush falls over the room as all heads turn to see none other than Prince Tymond standing in the doorway.

So much for securing the doors.

Without a word, Darius swiftly descends the steps of his throne to approach his son. He pulls on Braxton's arm so that they're both facing the Great Room doors, their backs to the Savant. He tries to ignore the encroaching feeling of impending doom if he doesn't squash this immediately. He lowers his voice, his tone anything but amicable. "What is the meaning of this interruption?"

"I mean no disrespect, but it's like I said," Braxton replies, not bothering to keep his voice down, "I urge you to reconsider sending the Cruex after Clive."

Darius eyes him warily. The conversation he'd had with Cyrus is pulled to the front and center of his mind, and while he has every intention of asking Braxton about it, he knows that now is not the place or time.

"He's dangerous," Braxton whispers. "There are too many unknowns. The Cruex can't possibly be prepared for what he's capable of."

It's the only confirmation Darius needs. No matter which way he looks at it, there's no other explanation.

Cyrus was telling the truth.

Braxton had something to do with Clive's escape.

BRAXTON HORNSBY

BRAXTON'S COME TO realize that if he's going to get *any* answers from this point forward, he must swallow his pride and engage with his father—which is exactly what he's just done, although he will admit, not in the most tasteful manner. Barging in on a closed meeting, especially one with the Savant, was not what he'd intended, but after what he'd witnessed in the halls—as well as what he'd seen *leaving* the halls—he knew better than to sit and sulk in the shadows.

Xerin had been in this castle—he's sure of it.

Even more perplexing, Darius had met with him.

Allegedly.

Braxton turns over his shoulder one last time to steal a glance at the guards before rounding the corner. Now that he's confronted Darius, next on the list is the

Cruex—more specifically, Hugh and Lane. Funny how he assumed he'd be *more* likely to dread the former when the exact opposite is true.

As if she'd sensed him coming, Lane, clad in her Cruex uniform, appears at the end of the corridor. They make eye contact but, much to his surprise, she stays rooted in place. Braxton holds his hand up in a half-wave, hoping that she'll return the gesture.

She doesn't.

Feeling stuck between a rock and a hard place, Braxton takes a hesitant step forward, then another, until he's nearly halfway down the hall. She's maintained eye contact with him this entire time, but the closer he gets, the clearer her expression becomes. She doesn't look pleased in the slightest. In fact, she looks downright angry.

It takes every ounce of effort he has to continue walking toward her, but he does so without stopping. Finally, he gets close enough to where if he reached out, he could touch her shoulder—but with that icy stare, he doesn't dare make the first move.

"You've missed training." Her words are empty, void of emotion. "Eight sessions, to be exact."

Her accusatory tone causes a shudder to ripple down his spine. "I . . . I haven't exactly been feeling like myself." He waits for her to say something, but she just stands there, her mouth tightening in disapproval with each passing second.

"There's just so much going on up here." He points to his head. "It's hard to explain. You wouldn't understand."

Even to his ears, the words sound callous and distant—a perfect reflection of his recent behavior toward her. He searches her face for a flicker of emotion—empathy, forgiveness, understanding of some sort—but there's absolutely nothing. What was once anger seems to have faded into indifference.

He doesn't know which is worse.

The silence between them grows longer and more pronounced. Even so, Braxton stands his ground, refusing to leave until she says or does *something*. From the looks of it, he'll be waiting all night.

When she finally does move, it's a step backward . . . *away* from him. Slowly, she continues to take small steps until she's backed up against a door. Braxton can't recall where it leads but, if he had to guess, she probably doesn't want to be followed.

Only when she turns to open the door does she break eye contact. Her words reaffirm what this interaction has already made clear. "I expected more from you."

The door shuts quietly behind her.

Even if Braxton wanted to move, to go after her, his legs wouldn't allow it. Fraught with disappointment, he hangs his head before retreating to his chambers. As much as he tries to fight it, the weight of those words stays with him from dusk until dawn.

CERYLIA JARETH

NEWS OF ARDEN'S whereabouts had arrived at the perfect time. As much as Cerylia had wanted to follow her instinct to inform Cyrus, she'd refrained from doing so. They'd seen each other not but a week ago—another visit so close to the last would have been rather precarious—a chance she isn't willing to take. He's bound to find out soon enough, whether from her or someone else, but that isn't her focus at the moment.

Today, she has other matters to attend to.

A draft sweeps through her chambers just as she's pulling a cloak around her shoulders. She fastens the button at the top but not before catching her reflection in the gold-plated mirror. Her skin is still recovering from the dry winter that's just come to pass, and her damp hair hangs limply over her shoulders. She eyes the comb on her vanity and hastily runs it through her hair, hoping that the rapid motion will cause it to dry faster. Not that it really matters, though. Where she's headed, she's unlikely to be seen.

A faint echo far down the corridor pulls her from her thoughts. Delwynn should be coming to fetch her for early evening tea any minute now. Not wanting to delay any further, she checks her pockets one last time, making sure that she has everything she needs. Her crown sits idly near her bedside, its gems glinting in the fading sunlight. A sharp pain hits her square in the chest. How she loves that crown and everything it symbolizes—and yet it's somehow lost its allure after everything she's been through. It's easy to lose touch with reality when you no longer have someone to share it with.

As quietly as she can, she opens her chamber doors and pokes her head out into the hallway. As requested, the guards are not stationed anywhere nearby—not even at the end of the corridor. She pulls the hood of her cloak over her head before heading east, toward the stairs. The Caldari—what's left of them, anyway—are nowhere in sight. As she's done so many nights before, she slips out the side entrance of the castle.

She doesn't even bother checking behind her before heading down a familiar path, one that isn't the least bit worn from months of travel. She realizes that she just might be the only person in Sardoria to head this far off the grounds.

A chill sweeps through her bones, straight to her core, as the sun begins its timely descent. She was hoping with such a nice spring day that she'd be able to arrive with *some* daylight left, but it seems she should have accounted for northern Aeridon's transition from winter to spring—until the later months, there's really no telling what to expect. Every day is a little different than the one prior. Some days feel like they drag on and on, while others pass in the blink of an eye. She debates whether to turn back, but seeing as she's more than halfway there, she decides to continue onward.

The sun is flirting with the horizon now, giving off just enough light for her to see her destination. The vines of ivy winding around the wrought-iron gate do so in such a mesmerizing fashion that she hardly notices the metal nameplate. *Bromley Burial Grounds.* Reading the name again is enough to give her pause.

As she approaches the gate, she can't help but rest her hand against one of the bars. She takes a few moments to just stand there, preparing herself for the visit she makes only once a year. How much time passes eludes her, but finally, with her eyes closed, she pushes the gate open. Even though it creaks, it gives way easily. She doesn't bother shutting it as she takes the first step, her right foot landing on hallowed ground. She can hear the riyals clinking in her pocket with each move she makes, as if Dane were walking right beside her, amber-colored coins in hand.

He'd always wanted to reside in Lonia, had always promised they'd live there someday. Perhaps when their children had grown and they'd abdicated the throne—but, sadly, they'd never made it that far. Their fate had been sealed by the Tymonds before they'd ever even had a chance to start.

With heavy eyes and an even heavier heart, Cerylia comes to a stop at the familiar headstone. She removes three riyals from her pocket, touching each one to her lips before placing them on the ground, ensuring that each individual coin is equidistant from the last. She takes a step back to admire her work in what little daylight is left, then kneels. With her head bowed and her eyes closed, she says a quick prayer, hoping she'll feel the winds change—anything to indicate that Dane is here with her—but when she opens her eyes, she feels completely and utterly alone.

She closes them once more, envisioning her beloved standing before her. Panic grips her as the images differ to a degree that she can't even recall. In one of her earlier memories, she sees a younger Dane on horseback with deep brown hair fastened into a low ponytail, eyes matching that of the mare's—hazel with a bright ring of gold around them—and the slightly puffy cheeks that propped up his elongated nose, highlighting his ever thin lips. In a more recent memory, however, his appearance had been nearly the opposite—midnight hair, cerulean eyes that could pierce the night sky, and a beard so thick, it hid his most distinguishing features.

As a Shifter, he'd begun changing his appearance at an early age. His abilities were quite similar to that of a Shaper, with one exception—he had the capability to shift into anyone at any time, including illusié *and* the use of their abilities, if only for a brief period. Unfortunately, with each shift he made, he became weaker and weaker. At first, this ability had given them an edge in combat—but oh, how the Tymonds had brought that to its inevitable end.

As quickly as it'd come, she's abruptly pulled from the memory when rustling sounds from behind her. Whirling around won't do any good, seeing as it's almost completely dark now, so instead she slowly rises from the ground. Not wanting to frighten whomever (or whatever) it is, she remains quiet, hoping that it'll reveal itself. Her eyes roam the trees, but any movement in the budding darkness is either invisible or nonexistent.

More rustling ensues until finally, a figure emerges. Cerylia watches as a cloak falls to the ground and a lantern appears. Eyes the color of lilac meet hers.

Cerylia sighs, relieved. "Well, this is unexpected."

Estelle sets the lantern down before shaking out her ebony ringlets and retrieving the cloak from the ground. She throws it over her arm as she approaches the queen. "You may think we don't notice much, but we do."

The way she says it is almost playful, as if all along she's been in the midst of some game with the Caldari she wasn't even aware of. "Care to expand on that?"

Estelle shrugs before walking over to a nearby bench, motioning for Cerylia to follow. Cerylia glances back at Dane's headstone, feeling a strong pull to stay put.

"It's not like he's going anywhere."

Normally, such a statement would have her up in arms, but the girl's right, so she joins her on the bench. "To what do I owe the visit?"

Estelle gives her a knowing look, her eyes glinting in the impending moonlight. "I think we both know the answer to that."

For the first time in months, Cerylia feels a bout of panic begin to rise, but she manages to push it back down. Her insatiable mind whirls with memories past, conversations with Cyrus, with Arden. Her face a mask of indifference, she asks, "Care to elaborate?"

"I know about the hidden chamber."

Funny how the most unexpected words can rouse the biggest sense of relief. She suppresses the small smile forming at the corner of her mouth before saying, "Seems you've been following me for quite some time."

Estelle bows her head. "Guilty." With the way her eyes flick to the queen, it seems she wants to say more, but instead, she casts her gaze back toward the ground.

"You've been inside the chamber?" Cerylia prompts.

A nod is her only response.

Without meaning to, Cerylia shifts her tone. "Why didn't you come to me sooner?"

Estelle's head snaps up. "It wasn't the right time." Cerylia hasn't the slightest inkling as to what she means, but before she can ask, Estelle says, "I've had my suspicions, but I had to be sure."

About Xerin and Opal? Arden? Cyrus? It dawns on her that perhaps Estelle knows more than she's letting on. It seems they have that in common.

"I know you've been attempting to access your illusié abilities as an Extractor."

"Oh?" is all she can muster.

"Have you been successful?"

Cerylia smirks. "Have you visited the chamber?"

Estelle returns the smile. "I think I can help."

A pleasant turn of events, Cerylia asks, "In what way?"

Estelle digs inside her cloak until she produces a pocket watch. "With this."

ARDEN ELIRI

IT'S BEEN A little over three days since Rydan and I made nice. Even though he'd been the one to show me the parchment Vira had taken from my brother, I've felt the urge to talk to Vira about it ever since.

Alone.

I'm standing behind an oak tree, with Juniper beside me, my focus on the door that leads to Rydan's dwelling. Neither of them have left this morning—if they had, I certainly haven't noticed—but my suspicions are confirmed once I see the curtains sway. I want to confront Vira without Rydan there, but getting either one of them alone hasn't been easy. They've been attached by the hip ever since arriving in Orihia.

As luck would have it, Rydan strolls out the door, giving a quick wave behind him before plodding down the steps. He heads down the stone pathway, I assume toward Avery's. I wait until he disappears behind the door before emerging from the shadows of the tree. I crouch, sneaking over to the window, although I don't know why I'm moving so furtively, seeing as the curtains are still drawn. I duck underneath it.

For some reason, I have to talk myself into knocking on the door—into facing Vira head-on. I know there's a chance she might have the very answers I seek, but it dawns on me then that perhaps I don't really want to know what happened between my mother and the Savant. Perhaps ignorance really is bliss.

Or *maybe* it's because even after spending yet another night with Felix, my subconscious feelings for Rydan have jumped to the forefront of my mind and won't go back to where they belong, no matter how hard I try. I continue to hide out of sight underneath the ledge—except I'm not at all out of sight because, speak of the devil, Felix is now approaching me with his signature half-smirk.

"Well, this is . . . *different.*"

I roll my eyes as I straighten, hoping that the curtains are still drawn because with my back to them, I can't tell. Realizing that if he comes any closer Vira will surely hear us, I put my hand up to signal to him to stop walking. He does so without question, sticking his arm out so that I can loop mine in his. Remembering which way Rydan went, I steer us in the opposite direction— away from him and away from Vira's dwelling.

"May I ask what you were doing?"

I lead us to the end of one of the pathways, where stone meets grass, and unlink my arm from his before heading into the dense forest. "I'd prefer it if you didn't."

"Does this have anything to do with Tymond's Savant?"

I whip my head around, eyes narrowed. I can't tell if he's amplifying or not—although he promised long ago that he wouldn't do that to me—but even so, I choose not to respond.

"You should know by now that I take your silence as an affirmative."

Noticing a sudden urge to be left alone, I walk deeper into the forest. He doesn't seem to catch on, though, because he follows me without hesitation. "Just . . . hold on," I stammer, trying to collect my thoughts. "How could you possibly know—?"

"I know a lot more than you give me credit for," Felix interjects.

"Is that supposed to make me feel better?"

A shadow darts across his eyes. "Regardless of the time we spend together and all the things you choose *not* to tell me, I overhear a lot, Arden, including the conversation between Rydan and Vira about the Savant— and your mother."

I place my palm against a pine tree, the bark firm and sturdy beneath my skin. "What do you make of all that?"

My question must catch him by surprise because he doesn't answer right away. *Good.*

Before he can respond, I drag my hand across the tree, making sure to keep my back to him so that he can't see my face. "I met Tymond's Savant, you know. In the Daegrum Chambers. Before Aldreda—"

"Stop," he says, clearly perturbed by my bringing up the incident. "I've met them, too."

Then and only then do I turn around. My eyes lock with his. "Who do you think it was?"

His expression mirrors my own, as if I've somehow amplified my own emotions and projected them onto him. He pauses before saying, "I think knowing the specifics might do you more harm than good."

My tone is flat. "If you know who murdered my mother, you have an obligation—as a Caldari, as my *friend*—to tell me."

His eyes don't break from mine. "A friend," he exhales, sounding disappointed.

That's *what he took away from that?* I press my mouth together, willing myself to stay quiet, to let him process whatever's rattling around in that head of his.

Finally, after an arduous silence, he says, "What I know to be true is that the Savant was indeed involved in your mother's death, but who specifically"—he hesitates, as if he has an inkling he's refusing to share—"I'm not at liberty to say." Knowing what I'll ask next, he quickly adds, "And I'm not at liberty to say because I'm not entirely convinced of my suspicions myself."

His guess is as good as mine. While this realization *is* disheartening, it only means I have more people to speak to, more research to do.

I'm completely wrapped up in my thoughts when suddenly, I feel the warmth of Felix's hand against my own. Disoriented, I look down to find that he's holding both of my hands, squeezing them tightly. I lift my head to meet his gaze, only to find that his eyes are closed. The expression he wears is anything but serene. There's conflict etched along his jawline—in every corner, in every last curve of his face. I stumble forward as he pulls me closer, watching with curiosity as he lays our intertwined hands directly over his heart. I can feel the steady *thud, thud, thud* beneath his tunic, his soft exhales of breath in tandem with each beat—a symphony of the human experience.

I don't dare move my hands. I don't dare make a sound. I remain rooted in place, deep within the forest, surrounded by nothing and everything all at once. I keep my gaze fixed on his face, watching as it alters at every interval of the emotional spectrum. Once more, how I *wish* I had the illusié ability to read minds—if such an ability even exists.

Just as I'm about to pull him from whatever has him so enraptured, I feel something. At first, it's hardly noticeable, like a single raindrop falling from the sky, but then it escalates into something grander and more visceral . . . a full-fledged storm, complete with thunder, lightning, rain, and wind—those breathtaking moments just before a hurricane forms. I try to keep my eyes open, to keep my focus on him, but the surge of power is overwhelming.

My eyes snap shut. Even though he isn't speaking, I can somehow hear his voice. His words infiltrate my mind. There's no mistaking it. *There's something here*, he communicates.

At first, it seems like he's talking to someone else—as if he's reporting his findings in some way—but then I remember that it's just the two of us in this seemingly abstract vessel of thought and emotion. *I feel it,* I communicate back, without actually speaking the words.

Arden . . .

I can only surmise that he's basing his observation on past experience, on past amplifications. There's no doubt in my mind that he's felt this before—the raw, unsettling, almost perilous side of my abilities—but there's a major distinction here. Although I can't pinpoint exactly *what* it is, the feeling flows through my veins with immense pressure. I attempt to sort through it, to give it context.

From behind my eyelids, darkness.

From Felix's embrace, warmth.

From my quivering lips, confusion.

From the depths of my mind . . . a gateway.

The realization is there until suddenly it isn't. It seems it had arrived only to turn around and leave again. A stubborn refusal that, in its wake, has left no trace, no clarity, no answers.

It's . . . it's . . .

My mind reels back to the voice that's still echoing inside my head. If I could finish his sentence, I would, but not even I can put a name, a feeling, an emotion—

anything at all—to whatever this is. My healing abilities didn't feel like this. They weren't so much a plea, but a *summoning*—and I distinctly remember the way I'd felt each time I'd called them forth. But *this . . .*

Feels desperate to belong.

Eager to be pieced together.

Uncontrollable, yet not chaotic.

Unable to fully grasp what's stirring inside me, I'm about to open my eyes—to pull us both out of whatever chasm it is we've slipped into—when suddenly, everything shifts. My body no longer feels like my own, my thoughts having drifted far, far away. In a split second, what was once mine is no longer. A new sensation compels me.

It's harsh. Unforgiving. Conditional.

Although I'm taken aback by this unexpected rush of emotion, these feelings are surprisingly familiar. Not only that, but the more I focus on their presence, the stronger they seem to get.

They feel . . . *like Felix.*

It dawns on me that I may have just crossed some sort of threshold, somewhere I'm not supposed to be. I try to convince myself it's because of our innate connection, but this doesn't feel right—like it's *invasive* somehow.

The voices in my head grow louder and louder, to an almost unbearable volume, and it doesn't take long for me to yank the tether that's binding us. As if I'm floating outside of myself, I can feel my hand lift from his chest, the warmth dissipating as my mind plunges deeper and deeper into my own gateway.

When I come back to, I stumble backward. My eyes land on Felix. He holds my gaze before bringing his hands to his face, then to his shoulders, his chest—as if checking to make sure he's still in one piece. Without realizing I'm doing it, I mimic his movements.

"Was that—?"

"—illusié?" I finish.

Seeing as it's a rhetorical question, neither of us answer out loud, but all I can think is that it *had* to have been illusié—what other explanation is there?

"I think I was . . ." I pause, not sure how what I'm about to say will come across. "It felt like I was *amplifying* somehow."

Felix studies me carefully. "On me?"

I shake my head. "No . . . like I *was* you and your feelings were somehow amplified—but *I* was the one experiencing them."

The distance between us feels infinite, and when he doesn't respond, it stretches even further. Even so, I stand my ground, eager to reel him back in.

Finally, he says, "That doesn't make any sense."

"I know it doesn't." I try to keep my voice steady, but his curt reaction isn't helping. "I'm just telling you what I felt."

"Well, I was there, too. I felt the same way I always have." He angles his head. "How could you possibly know what that feels like?"

A fiery warmth crawls up my neck. *I shouldn't have said anything.* As quickly as I can, I try to devise an exit strategy, but my mind fails me. I'm relieved to discover that he's thinking the exact same thing.

He breaks eye contact as he says, "I told your brother I'd meet up with him. He's probably wondering what's taking me so long."

Thank the lords. I nod, the words spilling out of my mouth like a waterfall, "I'll let you get to it, then."

Before he can say anything else, I swipe Juniper from the ground and walk as fast as I possibly can in the direction opposite the forest. Try as I might to shake our strange interaction, I have a feeling that this one's here to stay.

FELIX BARLOW

GUILT EATS AT him as he storms away from Arden. Yes, he's just lied to her, but it's for her own good, even if she can't see that yet.

Even if she never will.

Contrary to what he's just said, he isn't meeting up with her brother. There isn't a soul waiting for him. No, he needs to process what's just happened *without* Arden's influence, without her questions.

Having trailed deep enough into the forest at this point, Felix stops in the middle of an unusual clearing. He touches his chest again, then his arms, neck, and face. He'd sensed something in her all along, but this . . . this is beyond what he'd been led to believe was even *possible* for their kind. But he'd felt it. And so had she.

There's no denying that.

His thoughts scatter at the sound of wings flapping overhead. He can't help but groan. *Not now. Any other time but now.*

His plea goes unnoticed and unheard.

"You never seem to miss a beat," Felix grunts at the golden glow from behind the singular tree in the clearing.

"Is that so?" a callous voice counters. "You should speak with Opal more often. I drop in unexpectedly on her all the time," Xerin says, emerging from behind the lightning-scarred trunk.

"Perhaps that's because Sardoria's an easy target."

Xerin shrugs, his crimson eyes glinting. "Perhaps."

Felix scoffs, hoping that his wry demeanor will keep the self-designated head of the Caldari from asking too many questions. But Xerin's quicker than that—and has a keen eye for the peculiar.

"You're rattled," he says, circling Felix like prey. "Care to indulge me?"

"Do I really have a choice?" He doesn't bother to hide the despondence in his tone.

"I think you already know the answer to that," Xerin says with a wolfish grin. "Walk with me."

Felix obliges, taking what little time he can get to calm down and think straight, which is always difficult to do when Xerin's around. They continue to walk in silence, traversing deeper and deeper into the forest. It's the first time Felix has felt slightly uncomfortable around the Shaper, and if he didn't know why before, he's about to verify that reason now.

"Thank you for keeping an eye on her, like I've asked," Xerin finally says, his stride slowing. "The Eliri's family history is not for the faint of heart." He stops walking altogether. "Then again, I don't need to tell *you* that, now do I?"

"We've conversed, yes," Felix says, keeping his voice even. In actuality, he and Arden have done *much* more than just converse, but that little piece of information is on a need-to-know basis—and, if this interaction is confirming anything, it's that Xerin does *not* need to know. At least not right now.

"You must take me for a fool," the Shaper tsks, shaking his head. "I can feel her presence radiating from your very being. You've fallen for her."

They're eye to eye now, in the middle of the dense woods, with no clear direction to the way out. This is exactly what Xerin does—he makes his victims vulnerable and weak until they're questioning their own morals and sanity before delivering the crushing blow.

Felix is quick to respond, which comes as a surprise, even to him. 'The closer I get to Arden, the more information I have for you. Isn't that what you asked of me?" He takes a step closer, his breath misting in the crisp air. "Haven't I gone above and beyond?"

Xerin remains rooted in place, his eyes gleaming like the darkest rubies. "I suppose my answer to that depends on the information you divulge."

From inside his pocket, he grazes the wooden carving, the new one he'd planned to give to Arden . . . until they'd experienced the unfathomable. "I've already given you complete access to her, as you'd originally requested."

"Yes, in the visual sense, you most certainly have—but you now have something even more powerful than that. A connection, a *bond*. You now have access to things I never could have dreamed of."

Felix tries to hide the visible gulp that's making its way down his throat. "Our connection isn't what you think it is. The moments are few and far between—"

"But you've had moments, that much is clear." Xerin runs a hand along his jaw. "Don't you see, Felix? She's letting you *in*. She's letting you *see*. She's letting you *take*."

Felix bares his teeth, nearly growling as he says, "Whatever Arden has isn't mine to take. And it isn't yours to take, either."

"Pity," Xerin says in mock sorrow. "It's a shame that you feel that way because I couldn't disagree more."

"It's a pity that your interest in the Eliri's family history has taken you down this winding road. Tell me, Xerin, when will it be enough? Will you keep trudging along until you reach the point of no return?"

The Shaper throws his head back in jest, but the snarl that returns on his face is anything but. "If you were smart, Barlow, you'd realize we already were."

Before Felix can get another word in, Xerin's form whirls into a tangle of light, limbs, and feathers before soaring off into the distance. Enraged, Felix manages to stifle his scream, but not before removing the wooden carving of the rose from his pocket and smashing it beneath his boot—speculor and all.

73

RYDAN HELSTROM

HE'S NORMALLY NOT one to take advice, but Avery does have a point. The best person to talk about Arden with . . . is Arden herself. Lucky for him, she's headed down a pathway that leads directly to where he's sitting.

Rydan does a quick once-over of the grounds, relieved to find that no one else is around. As she draws nearer, he can tell she's completely preoccupied with her thoughts. Her expression is one he knows all too well—perplexity overshadowed by disappointment. Just as he's about to lift his hand to wave, she veers from the path. She picks up the pace and, as she passes by where he's sitting, he can see that he's read her all wrong.

She's angry. Enraged, even.

She storms past the fire, past the benches, her focus fixed on whatever is directly in front of her. Wanting to know what's put her in such a foul mood, Rydan swings his legs over the bench and jogs over. He tries to meet her in the crosshairs, but she's too fast. He picks up speed, trailing behind her, hoping that clearing his throat will catch her attention.

It doesn't.

When he's finally close enough, he gives her shoulder a gentle tap, but she hardly even notices as she continues onward. Frustrated by her lack of attention, Rydan grabs her upper arm and tugs just hard enough to get her to stop walking. She whirls around, red hot anger burning in her eyes. "What?"

Taken aback by her unforgiving tone, Rydan releases his grip, his arm dropping to his side. "You seem . . . well, I felt like I should check on you to see if you were okay." The words come out in a rush, sounding more frazzled than he'd intended. Arden studies him for a moment before turning back around.

Not one to give up easily, Rydan follows her without a second thought. "So, I take it you're *not* okay?"

She sighs, her back facing him, then runs a hand through her already tousled hair. "I don't know. I guess you could say I'm . . . *processing.*"

He takes her willingness to respond as a cue to keep going. He drifts back to their last conversation, recalling that he'd shown her the parchment about the Savant murdering her mother. Seeing as Vira knows just as much as Rydan does (in that they know hardly anything at all), a conversation with her wouldn't warrant this kind of behavior. Neither would a conversation with Avery or Haskell . . . which leaves just one person.

Felix.

Before he can confirm whether his suspicions are correct, he can't help but notice the sudden change in his surroundings. When exactly had they ventured into the Thering Forest? He'd been so deep in thought that he'd completely missed the part where they'd left Orihia behind. One look through the canopy of trees tells him exactly in which direction they're headed—and, if he's being honest, he's not quite ready to go back there just yet. Certainly not with Arden.

As fast as his feet will carry him, he sprints until he's an arm's length away from her. "Hold on," he says through labored breaths.

Much to his surprise, she stops walking, but not before crossing her arms. "What is it?"

Her attention won't be easy to keep. He's known Arden for some time and the only way to get her off one subject and onto another is to introduce another bigger, more pressing subject—one that demands her full attention. It occurs to him that now *could* be the perfect time to tell her about his discovery of the Soames crest, but since he can't quite place his finger on *why* it's so important, how can he expect *her* to?

She might know something. It's worth telling her . . .

. . . But what if she doesn't? What if bringing up anything regarding the Soames reverses all the progress we've made?

Caught in indecision, he hardly hears her when she says, "You're acting rather strange. What's going on?"

Tongue-tied, Rydan opens his mouth to speak, not surprised in the slightest when the words fail to form. She continues to stare at him with those wide, impatient eyes, but doesn't say anything. After a few moments, she sighs and glances over her shoulder. A realization seems to wash over her as she takes in her surroundings. "This wasn't my intention," she mutters.

"What wasn't?"

"Bringing us . . . *here.*" She gestures to the familiar patch of forest, to the rock-lined pathway that leads to the one place they both know all too well.

The Soames residence.

He wanted to know what her reaction would be . . . seems he's about to find out.

"We should turn back," she says brusquely. "I just needed to get some air. No need to relive the past."

She starts to walk by him but, for some reason he can't explain, he stops her. "I found something."

Her interest piqued, she retreats a few steps so that she's standing directly in front of him. "About the Soames?"

He nods, then changes his mind and shakes his head. "Never mind. I shouldn't have said anything. I don't even know what it means myself—"

"What *what* means?"

He might come to regret this later, but telling her about the crest, what he'd discovered in the cave in

Orihia, just *feels* right. "I found what I believe might be their family crest."

She turns to look at the house. "In there?"

He shakes his head. "In a cave in Orihia."

"Well," she says, brows furrowing, "as we found out the hard way, the Soames *were* illusié. I'm sure they paid a visit to Orihia every now and again."

He nods, not sure how to phrase what he wants to say next. "After seeing the crest in the cave, I came back here. I wanted to confirm that I really had seen it before."

"And?"

His eyes flick to the house before settling back on her. "I'm not sure if you remember, but there was a piece of fabric hanging from the rafters when we snuck in."

A small smile. "I was a bit preoccupied with our mission."

"Well, long story short, I came back here to retrieve the fabric and . . . the crests *do* indeed match."

She presses her lips together, studying him. "I'm trying to find the significance, I really am. Maybe if I could see it?"

"That's just it. I don't have the fabric anymore." Even though his mind screams to keep quiet, there's no stopping the words that tumble so effortlessly from his mouth. "Someone took it—and I have reason to believe that that someone . . . was *Xerin*."

DARIUS TYMOND

DARIUS STANDS IN the middle of Aldreda's secondary chambers. The scene of her hastily moving her things from their shared space is seared into his memory, something he's tried to forget to no avail. Even from beyond the grave, it seems she'll continue to torment him.

If he's to learn anything about Clive's escape, it'll be from his own son. This realization, although difficult to swallow, had dawned on him during their last interaction in the Great Room. Braxton *knows* what had transpired. Braxton was *there* when it'd happened. And, seeing as recapturing Clive is of paramount importance, Darius understands that he must take drastic measures—something he's certainly no stranger to.

Normally, he'd ask one of the guards to go through Aldreda's things, but they wouldn't even know what to look for. Not surprisingly, Braxton had asked to see his mother's chambers. He'd also asked to visit her burial site at Drakken Isle—*but* seeing as Darius had set her corpse in a canoe headed northwest . . . *her chambers it is.* However, before he honors said request, he must prep the room—and by prep, he intends to hide and *discard* anything he wouldn't want Braxton to see.

It's a task not even he feels equipped to do. Aldreda had valued her privacy above all else, so there could be *hundreds* of things stored in and around the castle that he isn't even aware of . . . things he'd certainly rather keep hidden than share with their estranged son.

After scouring the room, he's dismayed to find that he hasn't uncovered a single thing worthy of disposing or even *hiding,* for that matter. The armoire had been emptied of her gowns and robes the day he'd set her body to sea. The bedsheets are crisp, the pillows fluffed. There's nothing in the nightstand drawers, no journals on the bookshelves, no trace of her anywhere. Almost like she'd never even existed . . .

The last thing he checks is the oversize wooden chest that sits at the foot of the bed. He sorts through some old silks, scarves, and a pair of shoes before pulling out a few slats of wood that are arranged neatly at the bottom. For a brief moment, his heart races, thinking he's found something—but then he runs his hand along the walls of the chest, pressing gently against each one. No hidden compartments. No secrets. Nothing incriminating in the slightest.

He carelessly dumps everything back into the chest before doing another once-over of the room. Yes, Braxton is welcome to visit. Perhaps he'll be just as disappointed when he realizes, much like this room, just how *empty* his own mother's existence had truly been.

BRAXTON HORNSBY

AS EVIDENCED BY their strikingly cold demeanor, the Cruex don't seem to be fond of Braxton's untimely return—especially after days of no interaction, no communication, no *anything*.

Ezra certainly isn't taking it easy on him, and what's worse is that the closest person he has to calling a confidante will hardly even look at him.

Speaking of Lane . . .

Braxton steals a glance to his left, his gaze traveling in a diagonal line until he finds her. He can't help but fixate on the gentle curve of her jaw as she presses her mouth into a firm line. Moving her right foot back, she steps into a fighting stance. He watches as she draws a sword three times her size, holding it at the ready.

His eyes flick to Hugh, her training partner for the day. He unsheathes his weapon, which happens to be a sword of similar size and stature, before giving her the signal. Just as she's about to step forward, her eyes catch Braxton's. It's in that same moment that something knocks into the side of his head.

He unwillingly tears his gaze from Lane to get a good look at the perpetrator. Jedrek Easton. Hugh's *original* training partner.

"Are we just going to stand here all day?"

Braxton scowls, rubbing the side of his head with his palm. Before he can respond, another voice interjects.

"More training, less talking." Ezra marches up to them, shooting Braxton an icy glare.

Braxton holds his focus on Jedrek, trying his hardest to keep his temper at bay. If he were training with Lane, like they'd originally been assigned, this probably wouldn't be happening. To be fair, though, he hadn't exactly given her much choice. It's clear his absence had not only caused her to fall behind in her training, but had also caused a rift amongst, well, *all* of the Cruex.

The thought does nothing to curb his anger. He reaches for his chakrams, releasing them from their holsters, much like he'd seen Arden do, before crossing them in front of his chest. He's about to make the grave mistake of challenging Ezra to duel when the clearing of a throat catches the attention of everyone in the courtyard.

Slowly, Braxton lowers his weapons as his father approaches the group. Both Ezra and Jedrek fall back in line—a seemingly nonexistent one, at that.

"Come," Darius says under his breath as he breezes by. Braxton hesitates, although he's not sure why. He scans the faces of the Cruex, wondering if they're thinking the same thing he is—that he doesn't deserve to be here. That royal blood, estranged or not, will always have the upper hand, and unjustifiably so.

Instead of sheathing his weapons, Braxton tosses them onto the ground. His eyes travel to Lane one last time, but her focus is elsewhere. He sighs, kicking one of the chakrams with the toe of his boot, before leaving to meet his father at the top of the stone steps. Darius doesn't so much as wait for him to make it halfway across the courtyard before continuing along the main hallway.

Braxton jogs behind him in an attempt to catch up. When he finally does, he realizes they're standing in front of a door he doesn't recognize. Darius reaches into his robes to produce an iron key. He takes Braxton's hand, gently placing it in his palm. "Your mother's chambers." He bows his head, saying nothing more, before disappearing around a corner at the end of the hall.

Surprised at this sudden turn of events, Braxton eagerly inserts the key into the lock and turns it. It clicks, and he presses the door open.

His first thought is one he's surprised hadn't found him earlier. *Why is Aldreda's room separate from Darius's?* But it's the second thought that causes him a bit more distress. *Her room is so . . . clean. Hardly a trace of her anywhere.*

He tucks the key into his back pocket before closing the door behind him. Feeling unsure where to begin, he eyes the bed, then the armoire, followed by the nightstand and the vanity. Suddenly, he can't help but feel overwhelmed at the *underwhelming* presence of the late Queen Aldreda Tymond.

He approaches the bed first, running his hand along one of the freshly pressed linens. No indentations in the pillows. No wrinkles in sight.

The armoire is next. The doors creak as he pulls them open. He's both surprised and disappointed to find that it's completely empty. No hanging gowns or robes. No sight of her crown. Nothing folded in the drawers.

Nightstand. Empty.

Vanity. Empty.

Shelves. Full—of old, dusty books.

Hope flickers in his chest as he ventures over to them, running his fingers along the spines. He removes a few of the texts and flips through the pages, half expecting something to fall out, like another note or a piece of parchment or a map or *something*. But it seems these books haven't been touched in ages—that his hands are the first to touch them since being here in Trendalath Kingdom.

With a sigh, he flips through the last tome before placing it back on the shelf. He scans over the texts once more, willing a journal or a diary to suddenly appear out of thin air, but no such thing happens. Feeling defeated, he trudges back over to the bed and takes a seat. His gaze drifts to the door, the temptation to just leave and forget he'd ever made this foolish request imminent.

He drums his fingers against the now slightly wrinkled linens he's sitting on, then scoots to the edge of the bed, noticing that there's one thing in the room he hasn't checked yet—a wooden chest. How he hadn't noticed it beats him because it's huge, at least three times the size of a normal chest.

He hops off the bed, delighted to find that there isn't a lock securing it. With both hands, he lifts the lid until it's sitting all the way back on its hinges. Given the condition of the rest of the room, and everything *not* in it, he's somewhat surprised to see that the chest is actually quite full. First out is a bundle of scarves, all mismatched and in disarray. He gently sets them aside. A pair of dainty silk shoes is next. But that seems to be it . . .

Until he reaches into the very bottom of the chest and feels something shift. He grabs one wooden slat after another after another. He pulls them out, studying each one individually, but can't seem to find anything unusual about them. Frustrated, he sticks his head into the chest, using his right hand to feel along the edges and corners.

Again, nothing unusual.

Stumped, Braxton sighs, sitting back on his heels. He carefully examines the slats one more time before throwing them back into the chest, not even cringing as they clatter to the bottom. He tosses the shoes in there next, followed by a loose scarf, but as he goes to pick up the remaining bundle of fabric, something rolls onto the floor. If it weren't for the faint *clink*, he probably wouldn't have even noticed it.

Braxton reaches for the small object, letting the pile of fabric fall from his grip. He raises it so that it's level with his gaze, turning it round to get a better look. It appears to be a pearl of some sort. Before he can assess any further, there's a loud knock at the door.

"Prince Tymond," a gruff voice calls out. "Your presence has been requested in the Great Hall."

The King's Guard . . . with impeccably terrible timing, as per usual. Braxton tucks the pearl into his pocket, hurriedly places the rest of the scarves back into the chest, and secures the lid. He can't help but smile as he makes for the door. Even though he has no idea what the mystery object is, he knows he's just found *something*— something that undoubtedly belonged to his mother.

With a quick glance over his shoulder, he surveys the room one more time. This won't be his last visit. Not by a long shot.

CERYLIA JARETH

CERYLIA LEANS AGAINST the wall that leads to the hidden chamber, her eyes dancing back and forth from one end of the corridor to the other. Darkness surrounds her, save for the glow of the lantern at her feet. Occasionally, she'll lean forward and reach out in front of her, hoping to catch a trace of Estelle's *cloaking*, but so far, it's only empty air that greets her delicate skin.

Where is she?

She's not usually one to grow impatient, but given their original agreement, Estelle's more than a half hour late—and the girl's carrying a pocket watch, for lords' sake! Cerylia taps her foot, debating her next step. With a sigh, she swipes the lantern from the ground and briskly walks down the corridor, heading straight for Estelle's quarters. She's a little more than halfway there when

Delwynn, distraught and panicked, crosses her line of vision. He doesn't seem to see her, so she picks up the pace, making a sharp left at the end of the hall. It doesn't take long for her to realize what he's carrying in his arms.

Tinctures. Salves. Herbs.

She's been injured.

Cerylia's running so fast now that she arrives at the door at the same time as Delwynn. He looks to her, all color drained from his face. A wordless exchange passes between them before he dumps the contents from his arms onto a nearby table.

At her feet is a cloak.

Ripped.

Torn.

Mangled.

Cerylia kicks it aside before rushing across the room to where Estelle lay. Her eyes are closed and her breathing is shallow, but at least there's no visible blood from what Cerylia can see. She grabs the girl's hand, then scans her body for any abnormalities—bruises, cuts, magick-induced lacerations—but, thankfully, comes up short. Her thoughts scatter as Delwynn fumbles his way over. He's about to drop the tincture he's just made but Cerylia manages to catch it just in time.

"Delwynn," she says softly, hoping her mild tone is enough to calm him. "You've done well. I can take it from here."

Hands shaking, her advisor bows his head, nearly collasping into the chair beside her. "I couldn't understand her."

Cerylia uncaps the small glass bottle, then lifts it to Estelle's mouth, tipping her chin up at the steady flow of amber liquid. "What do you mean?"

"The moment she came stumbling into the castle, I could tell she was unwell. I tried to ask her what was wrong, what had happened, but—" His voice catches as if recalling the memory is too painful.

Cerylia doesn't press further. She simply sets the bottle on the small wooden table beside her, catching a whiff of hawthorn and ginseng. "A tincture for the mind."

Delwynn just nods.

"Well," Cerylia sighs, "there's not much we can do except wait. Her heartbeat is faint, but she's still breathing."

"I didn't want to worry you, Your Greatness."

"Worry me?" Cerylia shakes her head. "I promised the Caldari a safe haven, a refuge. Seems I haven't exactly held up my end of the bargain."

"You've done more than most."

The words are kind, even though they don't ring entirely true. "I'll tend to her."

"But Your Greatness . . ."

"I insist." She angles her head at the door. "Brew some tea. Relax. Give your mind a rest."

Delwynn gives the queen a small smile before taking his leave. Cerylia watches as the door closes behind him, then brings her attention back to Estelle. Rising from her seat, she leans closer to the girl's face, studying her forehead, her nose, her cheeks, her ears. *A tincture for the mind.*

It doesn't take many guesses to determine *who* might be responsible. If there's one illusié ability that can ravage the mind, it's casting. Pinpricks graze her neck as the image of Aldreda and her counterpart flashes across her mind.

But what had Estelle been doing out in the Roviel Woods, given that they were supposed to meet that same night? Where had she gone? Who had she been meeting?

A memory surfaces, one of her stumbling upon Opal and Xerin meeting in secret—something she still hasn't gotten to the bottom of—but Estelle *wouldn't* be . . . *couldn't* be . . .

A low groan causes her thoughts to disperse. The Cloaker stirs but doesn't open her eyes. Cerylia's about to take the girl's hand in hers again when she notices something in the other. *She's holding onto something.*

She reaches over, gently uncurling each finger. Coiled loosely in Estelle's palm is a metal chain—the same chain that *should* be attached to her pocket watch, the one she never goes anywhere without.

Cerylia searches the ground, then moves to Estelle's trousers, combing through the pockets. Nothing. Her eyes flick to the tattered cloak that's crumpled against the wall. She marches over to it, picks it up with two fingers, and searches it in its entirety. No pocket watch.

Which can only mean one thing.

Whoever did this was deliberately *looking* for that watch—the same watch that would allegedly help her retrieve her extracting abilities. The thought is jarring. If these are the lengths the Caster will go to get it . . . what might he do now that he has it?

ARDEN ELIRI

I'VE NEVER SEEN anything so beautiful—and that's saying something because Orihia is the most stunning place I've ever been to. I suppose, technically, we're still *in* Orihia, but my surroundings indicate otherwise. Orihia is mystical, almost fae-like, but where Rydan's just taken me—this cliffside waterfall—is ethereal . . . heavenly even.

I rush past him, balancing on the edge of the cliff, the crisp breeze whipping wildly through my hair. I'm so in awe of my surroundings that I hardly notice when he approaches and stands right beside me. Neither of us say a word.

Finally, after a long silence, he points down and says, "There."

I follow his gaze. It seems he's gesturing to the bottom of the waterfall, to a miniscule beach.

He surprises me by taking a few steps backward, each one slightly larger than the last. It doesn't take me long to figure out what he's about to do. I sense his next move almost immediately and step right in front of him. He's quick, though, because he slides around me, like he's made of wind and water, and goes flying off the cliff, feet first.

I run to the edge in horror. With my hands half-covering my eyes, I watch as a small splash erupts from the water below. "Are you insane?" I yell, trying to ignore the surge of adrenaline that's pumping through me. I can see him flailing, clearly trying to get my attention, but he's so far away that I can't hear anything. If I had to guess, he's probably telling me to jump.

I look to my left, then to my right, not seeing much of an option. After learning about this alleged cave, I'd said I wanted to see it—so really, this is on me. I retrace his footsteps in the damp terrain, backtracking a bit more for extra momentum. I quiet the voice in my head, the one telling me that I've completely lost it, then race forward faster than I ever have before. My feet push off the edge of the cliff and suddenly, I'm free-falling.

Down, down, down.

It feels like both an eternity and a mere instant until my body is fully submerged in the water. Coolness rushes over me and, when I come up for air, I can't help but let out a loud whoop. Rydan's floating just a few feet away with a giant grin plastered on his face. "Fun, right?"

"Hard to deny," I say through shallow breaths as we swim to the sandbank. "Honestly, I wasn't expecting that to be as exhilarating as it was."

"And why is that?"

I pull myself up onto the pale pink sand-covered ridge. Tiny rocks and shells scrape the tops of my thighs. "Because we trained together for years and years and, although you often did the unexpected, I wouldn't necessarily say that that was always a good thing."

"A curse, I suppose," he says with a wink.

I watch as he lays on his back, immediately following suit. I close my eyes and take a few deep breaths, after which the intensity of my heart thumping beneath my chest finally begins to dissipate. I bring my hands to my face to wipe away any excess water. With the sun blazing above us, the contrast of the heat on my cool skin is a welcome reprieve.

I don't know how much time passes when I hear Rydan shuffling beside me. I pop one eye open and angle my head, not wanting to move from this position. I can't help but sigh as he extends his hand out to me. Begrudgingly, I take it. He pulls me to my feet.

We walk across the shore, the residual sand flaking from our ankles with each step. I follow Rydan to what appears to be an entrance, but notice that it's covered in vines and other shrubbery. By the way he's scratching his head and pacing back and forth, I can tell he's confused.

"I'm guessing all of this," I say gesturing to the greenery, "isn't supposed to be here?"

He doesn't look at me as he mumbles, "I don't understand. It was right here . . ."

"There wasn't a door or a wall? You just . . . walked right in?"

He nods, brows furrowed.

As much as I want to question it further, the words elude me; so, we just stand there, dumbfounded. Finally, after a long stretch of silence, I say, "I don't know what to tell you, Rydan, but standing here isn't going to change the fact that there's a solid wall standing between us and this alleged *cave* of yours."

He turns to me, eyes ablaze. "You don't believe me?"

"Clearly, there's something here. But . . ."

"But what?"

I sigh. "But it's also clear that something must have happened since you last visited."

Rydan continues to place his palms against various parts of the wall, pressing his ear against it, as if that'll help him figure out how to gain access. I don't want to rile him up even more, so I spot a nearby rock and take a seat. I watch him for a few more moments—shuffling back and forth, jumping up and down—but my attention quickly shifts to something more pressing. I lift my gaze to the sky, eyeing the jutting rocks and their varying shapes and sizes. *How the hell are we going to get back up there?*

"Hey, Rydan," I say, my concern rising, "how did you get out of here last time?"

He follows my gaze, shoulders slumping, then points at the wall before slamming his fists against it. "This doesn't make any sense!"

I push myself up from where I'm seated while simultaneously considering our (quite limited) options. From my current vantage point, there *are* a few paths we can take, but they all involve climbing—and it's a pretty steep climb at that. "Come on, this way," I say, pulling on his arm before he has a chance to argue.

He follows me in silence the entire way up.

RYDAN HELSTROM

RYDAN'S COMPLETELY OUT of breath by the time he and Arden reach the top of the cliff. He's right behind her when she nearly doubles over and falls to the ground, narrowly managing to grab hold of her before she does. Together, they stumble their way to a nearby boulder, leaning on it for support. He isn't at all surprised to see that the rapid rise and fall of her chest is in sync with his own.

"Water?" she requests through ragged breaths.

Rydan shakes his head. "We'll have to head back to camp. I didn't even consider bringing our canteens."

Arden groans. "Next time let's bring Vira along with us. At least she could summon a dragon to fly us out of there."

As much as Rydan wants to chuckle, he can't bring himself to feel anything other than perplexed. He's certain that he hadn't imagined the cave. He'd found the crest—*seen* it with his own two eyes, *held* it in his own two hands. When he'd entered the cave, he hadn't passed through a wall. There'd only been a giant opening . . . and it'd been clear as day.

"Don't hurt yourself, now."

Arden's voice tugs him from his thoughts, bringing him back to reality. He looks to her, then at the long stretch of forest that awaits them. With a sigh, he pushes himself off the sturdy boulder and begins the journey back.

෯   ෯   ෯

By the time they reach camp, Rydan feels like falling into a pile of mush onto the ground—and based on Arden's glacial pace, she must feel the same way. Avery, Felix, and Haskell are sitting around the fire, with Vira at one of the wooden tables. As soon as she hears them approach, her head snaps up. Her eyes move from Rydan to Arden, then back to Rydan again. Her stony gaze is unrelenting as he takes a seat next to her.

"Where were you?"

Rydan doesn't respond right away. He watches as Arden walks past the group without so much as a wave, then proceeds to enter her dwelling, alone. Rydan shakes his head, trying to avoid eye contact with not only her, but the rest of the group. "It doesn't matter."

Vira bristles at his tone, but before she can utter another word, Rydan leans in, lowering his voice so that only she can hear what he's about to say. "The more important question that comes to mind is what your *brother* has to do with all of this."

The shift in her body language implies that she knows something, but her response indicates otherwise. "My brother is out surveying Aeridon, ensuring that the Savant steer clear of Orihia while we're here. He's keeping us safe."

Rydan grits his teeth, seeing as it's the only thing that'll keep his frustration at bay. As much as he feels obligated to tell Vira exactly what's going on, something tells him not to—at least for the time being.

"I guess I'll see you in there," he says curtly as he swings his legs over the bench. He doesn't bother to look back before making a beeline toward their cabin. It isn't lost on him that he enters it completely alone, just as Arden had done moments prior.

BRAXTON HORNSBY

BRAXTON ROAMS THE dimly lit corridors in no hurry whatsoever to make it to the Great Room. He has an inkling as to what awaits: his father; more questions; more cajoling for information he isn't willing to give . . .

However, when he rounds the final corner, he's pleased to find that his father isn't waiting for him at all—Lane is. His breath nearly catches in his throat as he takes in the sight of her. Her neatly coiffed hair is pinned up at the sides, with strands of tight ringlets framing her face. A silken floor-length gown clings to her skin, pale pink accentuating every curve, her dark shoulders bare and gleaming against the contrast. He's so used to seeing her in uniform that it hadn't dawned on him that she could look like . . . well, like *that*.

"Wow. You look stunning." His cheeks redden as soon as he realizes he's spoken the words out loud.

Her lips tilt upward in a faint smile. "The king is hosting a formal welcome dinner for the newest Cruex recruits." She looks him up and down, clearly confused. "Why aren't you dressed?"

Braxton's so mesmerized, he hardly hears the question. "I wasn't made aware."

"But he's your father."

Braxton snaps out of his daze as he remembers where he's just come from. His hand brushes the outer fabric where the foreign object is currently burning a hole in his pocket. "I suppose I'm technically not a *recruit*, seeing as I was brought here against my will." He chooses his next words carefully. "It's fine, though. I was planning on turning in early anyway."

Lane shakes her head. "I'm afraid I'm not willing to accept that." She extends her hand to him and winks. "Usually, it's the lady who has an escort, but perhaps times are changing. Who says we can't do a little role reversal?"

He'd be lying if he said that the playfulness in her tone wasn't somewhat disconcerting. After their last interaction, it'd seemed like she'd wanted space—lots of it. But how can he possibly say no, especially when she looks like *that*?

"I suppose I'll take you up on your offer." He can't help but notice the way her eyes soften when she smiles. It's comforting, warm. Reminds him a lot of his mother.

"As you so aptly mentioned, though, I should probably change."

"I have an extra outfit in my chambers."

Such a quick response. Braxton raises a brow.

Lane sighs. "Don't ask. Apparently, the guards find it off-putting that the Cruex recruits *women* assassins."

Braxton's thoughts flick to Arden, but he doesn't let them linger there for long. "Well, if you ask me, you're the best damn assassin I've ever seen—better than the whole lot of them combined."

"Thanks." She angles her head, then links her arm with his. "Best not to keep Tymond waiting. You, of all people, know how he gets."

As much as he wants to focus solely on his conversation with Lane, every step Braxton takes is a nagging reminder that he might be one step closer to deciphering his mother's note—if only he knew what that damn mystery object was. It crosses his mind multiple times to share his discovery with Lane, to ask her if she knows what it might be, if she's ever seen anything like it—but for now, he's just grateful that she's even speaking to him.

Braxton doesn't quite know what to expect when they arrive at her chamber doors, but he's certainly thrown for a loop once he steps inside. The enclosure is massive, and they haven't even reached her room yet. It dawns on him that this is where Arden—as the only female assassin in the Cruex—used to stay. Now Lane has it all to herself.

He follows her down the hallway, past the garderobe with its oversize clawfoot tub, up a set of winding iron stairs and down another hallway, until they finally reach a worn-in wooden door. She pulls an ornate key from her breast pocket and unlocks it. A pungent aroma of cherry and black licorice greets him. He watches as she vanishes behind the doors of her armoire, only to reappear with an armful of neatly folded clothes.

"Here," she says, handing the garments to him one at a time.

Braxton unfolds them, checking the length of the pants and the fit of the vest. "Well, I'll be damned. These should work."

He's about to head for the door when Lane stops him. "You can change up here. I'll be downstairs." Her gown slinks behind her as she makes for the door, slipping out without another word.

As distracting as this whole situation is, he's still very much aware of the object he'd found in his mother's room. He removes the sphere from his pocket and gently places it on the bed before removing his trousers. He slips into the pair of formal pants, then throws the vest over his shoulders. His eyes meet a gold-plated mirror. *Better*, but he should probably run a comb through his hair. He circles the room until he finally spots the vanity, which is tucked away in the far back corner of the room. Just as he's finishing up, there's a soft knock at the door.

"Are you decent?"

"Yes," he calls out, momentarily forgetting what's sitting in plain sight on the bed. He whirls around, his gaze landing on the sphere, but Lane's already entered the room—and her focus is on the exact same thing.

"What's that?" she asks as she moves closer to it.

"It's nothing," he says, meeting her step for step before quickly swiping it from the bed. "Just something of my mother's."

Lane stops walking. "That's a speculor."

While the urge to pretend he already possesses this knowledge is strong, getting *all* the facts is much more important than his pride. "What's a speculor?"

Her eyes narrow. "Well, for starters, it's of illusié origin . . . You said it was your mother's?"

Oh, lords. "Not necessarily. I, uh, found it in her chambers—recently," he adds rather quickly. "It was hidden in a chest at the foot of her bed."

"And what did you see?"

Braxton's not sure how to answer her. Clearly, she knows a lot more about *speculors* than he does. "I'm not sure what you mean. To be frank, until now, I didn't even know what it was, let alone how to use it."

The conflicted look on her face tells him that perhaps now isn't the best time for this discussion. She looks from him to the door.

"Right, the dinner," Braxton says. "We should go." It pains him to even say it, knowing that she might have the very answers he's been searching for.

Lane remains quiet as she chews on her lower lip. After an extended silence, she finally speaks. "No," she says with a shake of her head. "Forget the dinner. This is more important."

An unexpected warmth rises in his chest. Unable to help himself, he reaches out and squeezes her hand. He's never felt more seen and understood than he does right now, in this very moment.

Lane returns the gesture. "All right," she says, reaching for a leather-bound book on her nightstand, "let's see what memory it holds, shall we?"

DARIUS TYMOND

DARIUS SCANS THE room one more time, just to be sure. There's no mistaking it—Lady Devall is missing. And so is his son.

Against his better judgment, he'd started the feast right on time. It'd been more for the sake of appearances than anything else, but with this level of disrespect? It's certainly beneath Lady Devall—what he knows of her, at least.

Based on the jovial mood of the room, the Cruex, both new and old, hardly seem to notice they're missing two of their own—a bit unnerving, but not all that surprising given the amount of verdot that's been flowing. The only person not joining in the laughter is Sir Darby. The young Cruex's barely touched his food and has had his eyes locked on the king from the moment he'd entered the dining hall.

Darius doesn't allow his gaze to linger for long, knowing that any opportunity he gives Hugh is one he'll milk for all it's worth. He continues to scan the sea of faces until he lands on the oldest one in the room. Cyrus. His advisor seems to be thoroughly enjoying himself, caught up in the laughter with the rest of the group.

Without a word, Darius removes himself from the far end of the table, motioning for one of the guards to escort him out. He doesn't turn back to see if anyone's noticed—there's no need, seeing as he can still feel Hugh's lethal gaze searing into the back of his head.

He deliberates where to go first, deciding to check on Lady Devall. He commands that the guard return to his post before heading for the Cruex quarters.

An eerie silence greets him in the halls—that is, until two distinctive voices echo from just outside one of the chambers. Darius backtracks a few steps before ducking into an alcove. Seeing as he's just out of earshot, he strains to hear the conversation in its entirety. Fortunately, the voices seem to be headed toward him— and toward Braxton's chambers—when Darius hears what is unmistakeably his son's voice . . . talking about *Aldreda.*

"I think my mother left this behind for a reason, almost like she *wanted* me to find it."

"We've tried every possible avenue I know of," Lane says. "I don't know why we can't see anything."

"We need to go to my room. I might have something that'll help."

Darius can feel a knot forming in his stomach as any sense of control he'd felt shatters. Based on context alone, he'd wager that Lane and Braxton are talking about a speculor—and not just *any* speculor, but one that Aldreda had purposely left behind. The knot grows tighter when he realizes that he'd led Braxton straight into the belly of the beast . . . into Aldreda's chambers.

But he'd checked every inch of that room, had made sure there wasn't anything to find. Although, Braxton had said something else . . . that it was like his mother had *meant* for him to find it.

Darius waits patiently for them to turn the corner before stepping out of the alcove. If he wants to know what that speculor holds, he'll have to act fast. Luckily, he knows just the person for the job.

CERYLIA JARETH

CERYLIA'S VISITED ESTELLE every day for the past week. Her only reason for leaving? To catch some shuteye in the earliest hours of the morning. She's pushing the door open with her shoulder, careful not to spill her freshly brewed cup of ginger tea, when her gaze lands on something unexpected.

Opal, asleep in a nearby chair.

Of course. She'd been so distracted with Estelle's untimely misfortune—and how to regain her dormant extracting abilities—that she'd almost forgotten that Opal was still in Sardoria. *And in the castle, no less.* Perhaps the girl will be able to provide some insight as to who had attacked Estelle, who had taken her pocket watch.

Cerylia takes a seat in the adjacent chair, not wanting to disturb Estelle, but hoping to wake Opal from what appears to be a deep slumber. She gently lays a hand on the armrest, brushing the tips of Opal's fingers. She doesn't stir in the slightest. Cerylia *could* knock the chairs together, but that would undoubtedly wake Estelle and cause more of a ruckus than needed. She glances down at the cup in her hands and wafts the tea toward her. It's a good thing ginger carries such a strong scent.

With this in mind, Cerylia leans across the chair and brings the cup close to Opal's nose, moving it ever so slowly from left to right. As she'd predicted, Opal's eyes flutter open. Cerylia moves the cup just in time to avoid the potential spill from the overhead stretching that follows.

Cerylia sets her gaze forward, as if she'd had nothing to do with Opal suddenly waking. She brings the delicate china to her lips and drinks, sensing the girl watching her with those calculating jade eyes. Even so, Cerylia takes her time, only returning Opal's gaze after setting the cup down on the end table.

"Why wasn't I notified about Estelle?"

Her tone is harsh, but not nearly as lethal as the words that leave the queen's mouth. "Perhaps the question you *should* be asking is why it took you so long to notice."

Opal narrows her eyes. "What are you implying?"

Cerylia turns her head, then shrugs. "It seems you've been preoccupied with other things as of late." Her mouth presses in a firm line. "Like meeting with Xerin."

It's already tense enough between them, but what comes out of Opal's mouth next sounds like her rendition of waving a white flag. "Xerin and I—our families—we have a long history." Her voice grows quiet. "We promised we'd keep tabs on each other, no matter what. He's been the only constant in my life for . . ."

As her voice fades, Cerylia realizes that Opal's seen a lot—not only in the present day, but in every one of her traversions. Perhaps the meetings with Xerin really *are* rooted in camaraderie and nothing more.

How quick she'd been to assume.

"I understand," Cerylia says, her tone softening. "I once had exactly that in my life." Her thoughts flick to her late husband, but they don't linger long enough to disrupt her train of thought. "I hope you can forgive my insolence." She turns to look at Opal, hoping to see compassion mirrored back at her.

Even though Opal nods, her eyes are cold. "If I had to guess, you're probably wondering if I saw what happened to Estelle?"

The sudden shift in both subject and demeanor catches her off guard. "Yes, it had crossed my mind. If you know anything at all, or if we're able to travel to the night of the attack—"

"It's hard to say what's real and what isn't." Cerylia's about to ask exactly what she means by that, but Opal continues, "At first I thought it was *all* real—that is, until I found a way to separate myself from the illusion."

"The work of a Caster," Cerylia whispers.

Opal confirms with a nod.

"And the pocket watch?"

"He took it." She sets her gaze on the floor. "For what purpose, I can't be sure. I tried to follow him. Made it all the way to Orihia . . . but then it was as if he somehow just disappeared." Her voice catches. "But what I *do* know is that the illusion he draped around Estelle was so powerful, it left her like this."

The queen closes her eyes. "Memory distortion?"

"Most likely."

The words ring in her ears. The tinctures, the salves, the herbs . . . would they be enough? Already, *days* have passed without any sign of her getting better. Cerylia's mind cuts to Braxton, to Delwynn, and finally, to Arden. Could *she* heal something like this? Or have her abilities gone so rogue to the point of only making matters worse?

The possibility has her anger sharpening like a blade. She pushes herself up from the chair, not bothering to finish her tea as she makes for the door.

"Your Greatness?"

But Opal's voice is merely an echo as Cerylia heads toward the hidden chamber, more determined than ever to regain her extracting abilities—especially now that she knows exactly who her first target will be.

ARDEN ELIRI

MY EYES SHOOT open at the sound of creaking hinges. I turn my head to look at the door, simultaneously reaching for the chakrams sitting on my nightstand. The darkness plays tricks on me as shadows dance along the walls. I can't make out a figure, a shape, or *anything*, for that matter—but my focus remains steady on the door.

Footsteps. Coming from outside.

My jaw tightens as I grip the handles of each blade and spring out of bed. I rush to the window, Juniper on my heels. I peek out the opening. This time, I *do* see a shadow, and it's a familiar one. One I'd recognize anywhere.

Rydan.

Based on the direction he's heading, I suspect he's going back to the waterfall. But why? And this late at night?

I look from Juniper to the door, to my bed, then back to the door again. With a sigh, I pull on my boots and throw a cloak around my shoulders. I'm already wearing trousers, so it only takes a second to wrap my belt holster around my waist and secure my chakrams. I give Juniper a quick kiss on the head, tell her to stay put, then slip out the door into the starlit night.

A waxing crescent moon illuminates the path before me and, even in its luminescent glow, Orihia is alive with color and light. I'm so distracted by the beauty of my surroundings that I almost forget why I've ventured out here in the first place. Even though I can't physically see him, my instincts tell me Rydan can't be *that* far ahead. I continue onward, using my memory as best I can to remember the way.

When I reach the end of the path, I dig around in my cloak for my pocket watch. It's well past midnight. Even though I have the urge to turn back, I return the watch back to its place and keep going. Just as I'm starting to feel concerned that perhaps I'd taken a wrong turn somewhere, I stumble upon a familiar cliffside. There isn't a single doubt in my mind—this is it.

"Arden?"

Startled, I jump back, unsheathing my weapons.

"Whoa," Rydan says as he steps out of the shadows and into the moonlight. "On edge much?"

My arms drop to my sides. "What are you doing out here? It's late."

He angles his head. "You sound like Vira."

I sheathe my weapons before crossing my arms over my chest. "You didn't answer my question."

"I had to come back. Something wasn't right when we visited. I know what I saw. I know what I took from that cave." He walks over to the edge, his gaze traveling down the waterfall. "That wall definitely wasn't there. I needed to see it again . . . for myself." He looks to me, his gaze moving from top to bottom.

Suddenly feeling very exposed, I comb my fingers through my hair, knowing full well that I probably look like I've just awoken—and that's because prior to this little excursion, I was, indeed, fast asleep. "Well, I—I couldn't let you come out here . . . alone."

He raises a brow. "How did you know I was out here to begin with?"

I shrug. "Creaky door."

He smirks. "I forgot. You always were a light sleeper."

My cheeks burn at the remark. "At first, I thought someone had broken in, but then I heard footsteps outside."

"So, you followed me."

It isn't so much a question, but I nod anyway.

"Did anyone else see you?"

"I don't think so."

"Good." He glances over the edge again. "Ready?"

I look at him in disbelief. "Surely you're joking."

"Why do you look so surprised?" His mouth tilts in a smirk. "I just told you exactly what I planned on doing once I got here. Did you think I was just going to stand here, look over the edge, and then turn back?"

Honestly, I don't know what I expected, but the thought of jumping off this cliff *yet again*—as exhilarating as it was the first time around—is not something I'm too keen on . . . and in the middle of the night, no less. "We could just—"

"Walk down?" He shakes his head. "By the time we got down there *and* climbed back up, the sun would be rising."

Okay, he has a point, but . . .

Before I can protest the idea or try to convince him otherwise, I feel a tug on my arm. My feet stumble beneath me as I move closer and closer to the edge. I know better than to try to resist. In mere seconds, Rydan's catapulted us both off the cliff.

The fall seems shorter this time around. We both hit the water with stunning accuracy, only staying under for a moment or two before kicking to the surface for air. I'm about to scold him for his reckless behavior, but the sight before me is enough to give me pause. I blink once, twice.

From across the water, past the blush-colored sandbank, is a magnificent opening where the wall had once been. I swim closer to Rydan, grabbing hold of his shoulders to turn him around. "I'm guessing *that's* what you were talking about?"

He doesn't so much as look at me before taking off eagerly toward the ridge. I kick my legs as fast as I can, my strokes cutting through the water, but even so, he's way faster than I am. It also doesn't help that I'm wearing a heavy cloak.

By the time I've hoisted myself up onto the bank, he's already halfway to the opening. Panting, I yell for him to slow down, but he doesn't seem to hear me. I remove the cloak and begin to wring it out, checking the pockets for my watch. I pull it out, feeling disheartened to find that it's only continuing to rust, and the nondescript mark seems to be growing more prominent with each passing day. With my thumb, I press the button on the side, shaking it slightly as it flicks open. Even though no water droplets seem to have gotten in, I do notice that it's no longer ticking. I lift it to my ear to be sure.

Complete silence.

I take a deep inhale, knowing my frustration won't do me any good right now, then dart over to where Rydan's currently standing.

"Now *this* is more like it," he says, partly under his breath. "This is exactly how I remember it."

I open my mouth to respond, but the words escape me. I can't possibly explain how there's suddenly a massive opening where a giant stone wall used to be—one I saw with my own two eyes less than a day ago. I watch, dumbfounded, as Rydan digs behind some nearby shrubbery to produce two torches. He hands me one, then proceeds to hold the other out in front of him. At first, I assume he's going to close his eyes, but instead, he focuses directly on me. Surprised, I meet his gaze, the deep golden hue of his pupils searing into mine.

He raises his free hand and, just like that, it ignites in a fiery blaze. He lights his torch first, then motions for me to hold mine out. To think, how far he's come since first discovering he was illusié . . . I can't help but smile.

He returns the grin, his hand fading to a dull glow before turning to enter the cave. With plenty of light now illuminating our path, I follow him inside.

RYDAN HELSTROM

THEY'RE ONLY A few steps into the cave when Rydan feels the urge to turn over his shoulder. Just as he'd suspected, the entrance to the cave is no longer there. It's been replaced by—no surprise here—a giant wall. Not wanting to alarm Arden, he patiently waits for her to catch up, hoping that she'll continue facing forward.

"Everything okay?" she asks, her torch illuminating half her face.

He nods. "Just wanted to make sure I didn't lose you back there."

"So," she says, walking past him, "what is this place?"

"Your guess is as good as mine, but it *is* where I found the crest—multiple crests, actually."

"Multiple? I thought it was just the Soames's?"

"Well, there were a bunch of pillars," Rydan explains, "and they all had metal inserts with designated crests—except for one."

"Is that where we're headed? To the pillars?"

"It'll make more sense once we get there."

At first, he's quite certain of himself, but with each passing step along the dimly lit path, Rydan's confidence diminishes. He remembers climbing and falling, jumping and sprinting, the glow of an ubiquitous red stone guiding the way. But now? The journey is much less eventful—no climbing or sprinting. Just . . . walking.

He picks up the pace, not wanting to admit to Arden that things are starting to look less and less familiar. He stops when he approaches a fork in the path—something he definitely hadn't encountered during the first go-around. His instincts tell him to go left, but Arden seems to have another idea. She passes him without saying a word, following the pathway to the right. Rydan glances over his shoulder at the long dark corridor, still feeling an insatiable pull, but, against his better judgment, ignores it. He takes off after her, trying not to panic as the walls begin to narrow.

He's about to tell her that they should turn back, that none of this looks familiar, when a loud gasp stops him. She's up ahead, overlooking a vast darkness—arms braced at her sides, knees locked. With his torch extended as far in front of him as it'll go, Rydan runs to where she's standing. His mouth drops as a looming cavern appears in the immense nothingness.

But the cavern *isn't* empty.

As they draw closer, a structure begins to take form. At first, he hasn't the slightest clue as to what it is, but the more his eyes adjust, the clearer it becomes.

"Is that . . .?"

"No," Rydan whispers. "This wasn't what I saw. This wasn't even here."

"What is it, do you think?"

Rydan scans the cavern, starting at the bottom of the ten-story—possibly even taller—structure: its geometric order; its many peaks and spires; the gigantic walls donning plum-colored flags, as if keeping everything in place, holding it all together. And just below the monstrosity, an arched bridge that leads inside.

"There," he says, pointing.

Arden regards him with wide eyes. "How are we going to get all the way down there?"

He scans the cavern for another option, knowing that she isn't going to like his answer. "I hope you have some fondness left for our Cruex days."

She sucks in a sharp breath. "And why is that?"

"Because we just might have to relive them for the time being." He drops to his knees, rifling through his bag before producing a thick knotted rope.

"You want us to rappel," Arden eyes him dubiously, making a downward motion with her hand, "all the way down there?"

"That's the idea to beat."

She gives him a pained look before removing the sash from her cloak and tossing it to him. "Knot her up."

BRAXTON HORNSBY

BRAXTON DOESN'T TAKE his eyes off Lane as she paces back and forth across his room. The formalwear she'd given him just moments prior is somewhat constricting, especially sitting down. He pulls at the waistband of his pants to loosen his currently tucked-in shirt. *Much better.*

Finally, after a few more minutes of pacing, Lane breaks her silence. "We should be able to see *something*—a present day vision, a past memory . . ."

Speculor. Braxton wishes he could recall his mother using such an object, but such an instance eludes him. He can certainly see how it would come in handy, though. There's no doubt in his mind that his mother meant for him to find this—just like he was meant to find the note she'd left behind.

"This is what I wanted to show you," he says, hopping off the bed and making for the armoire. He retrieves the folded piece of parchment and hands it to her.

She reads it over a few times, first to herself, then out loud. "I hope you can both forgive me one day?" She turns the note over in her hands, even though the signature at the bottom indicates completion. "What do you think that means?"

"Believe me, if I knew, I'd tell you."

"The time has come to return to Trendalath," Lane whispers, reading it once more. "There is much to be said for the past, and even more to be gained for the future."

Seeing as he's read it so many times, he knows it by heart. "I hope you can both forgive me one day. Your loving mother, Aldreda," he finishes.

"There's mention of the past," Lane says slowly, "*and* the future. The time has come . . ." She trails off, deep in thought. Mere moments later, her face lights up with recognition. "I've got it! I don't know how I missed it—"

"Missed what?"

"The Veil!"

Even though he has no idea what she's referring to, he can tell it's something to be excited about. Perhaps he'll finally get some answers after all.

"We can't see anything because the memory must have occurred *inside* the Veil."

"How do we"—Braxton pauses, trying to make sense of the words—"um, get *inside* the Veil?"

She flashes him a sly smile before grabbing his arm and nearly dragging him to the door. "Looks like we're heading back to my room."

But before they can even so much as get out the door, Braxton hears a familiar sound. The flapping of wings. The scraping of talons. He turns away from Lane toward the window, blood-red eyes meeting his own.

"Xerin?" his voice is barely audible.

It's then the door to Braxton's chambers swings open, nearly knocking them both to the ground. The speculor flies from Lane's grip, rolling underneath the bed. As discreetly as he can, Braxton slips the note into one of his pockets. He turns back to the window, but the bird is gone. He has no time to feel confused as his eyes settle on the doorway.

On his father.

"I'm glad to see you're both dressed for the occasion," Darius says, motioning for one of the guards to help them to their feet. "Come," he says chillingly, "it's rude to keep the others waiting."

DARIUS TYMOND

HE CAN'T BE sure exactly what he just saw, but based on the size and shape, he'd guess that the object that had rolled underneath the bed was a speculor. And if he didn't know any better . . .

That speculor came from Aldreda's chambers.

Darius can feel the tension mounting as Braxton and Lady Devall follow him all the way to the dining hall. The corridors stretch and wind, and it seems to take forever to arrive at their destination. Even so, Darius can't help but smirk at what he's just uncovered. No longer will he doubt what he's now so painstakingly aware of—that his son is guarding dangerous secrets of his own.

Things don't stay hidden for long, though, especially in his kingdom. One way or another, Darius always finds exactly what he's looking for, regardless of timing or form.

With tremendous force, Darius pushes the doors open, standing to the side as Lane and Braxton scurry through. A hush falls over the room but, thankfully, Cyrus intervenes with an unexpected toast. He raises his glass, to which the rest of the room follows suit. "To King Tymond. Long may he reign."

Lane and Braxton halt in their tracks, glancing at each other before slowly turning to face the king. Lane keeps her head down, as she should; but Darius fixes his gaze on his son, those familiar ice-blue eyes a reflection of his own. What appears to be a snarl begins to form on the boy's lips, to which Darius merely narrows his eyes and tilts his chin upward ever so slightly.

Then, in a voice only the two of them can hear, Darius mutters, "I'd watch your back if I were you."

Lane's head shoots up. Such defiance in those hazel eyes. "Is that a threat?"

"Semantics. I'll leave it to your interpretation." His gaze tracks to his son. "Now, go take your seats."

Before another word can be uttered, Cyrus clears his throat. "Your Majesty?"

Realizing he hadn't acknowledged the toast, or the rest of the room, Darius lifts his gaze and tersely nods his head at his advisor but doesn't say anything.

Cyrus, though clearly confused by the entire interaction, doesn't miss a beat as he begins to toast the newest Cruex recruits. Thankfully, the attention shifts away from Lane and Braxton—*away* from Darius. But he remains by the door, ever silent, ever watchful, only slipping back into the halls to retrieve what is rightfully his once everyone in the room is completely and utterly preoccupied.

CERYLIA JARETH

CERYLIA DOESN'T KNOW why, but she finds herself venturing down the same hall where Braxton had lost his abilities. Carrying only a flickering lantern, she attempts to focus her eyes as she moves slowly along the side of the abandoned corridor. It's unsettling, knowing that the Mallum has been here, in her castle—perhaps even in this very spot.

One question has plagued her since then.

Is it coming for her?

Her abilities, although inaccessible at the current moment, pose an enormous threat to the Mallum. Dane had known that. So had his brother. Indeed, it would take more than just her own abilities to bring such an entity down, but extraction would play a key role in its demise—an irrefutable fact.

Her thoughts trace to Braxton, to the night where he'd shown up at her door, shaken and disheveled—the night they'd both learned his abilities had been stripped by the Mallum. When she'd asked if anyone else had been there, if anyone else had seen it . . . there'd been a slight hesitation in his response. She'd had an inkling, even back then, that he'd lied to her. But why?

Who was he trying to protect?

Who else was there that night?

She stops walking when a disconcerting realization dawns on her. Braxton had fled without any of the guards noticing, meaning he hadn't used any of the entrances— front, back, or otherwise. Furthermore, when she'd been notified of Whitley's disappearance, there had been more than one set of animal tracks headed in the same direction—which hadn't made sense, seeing as only one horse had gone missing. Unless . . . someone had turned *into* a horse; someone who possesses the abilities of a Shaper.

Xerin.

But *why* would he help Braxton flee?

For what reason?

A chill creeps down her spine.

There'd been something off about Xerin from the very start—his desire to fly under the radar, his incognito bouts of shaping, his sudden disappearances and his uncanny reappearances . . . his undisclosed meetings with Opal.

Our families have a long history. That's what she'd said in the healing ward.

Cerylia doesn't want to fall prey to these disturbing thoughts—not here, in the middle of the abandoned corridor. Her breath sharpens as she makes for the hidden chamber, a place where she can be alone for a while to think. It's just as she'd left it—messy and chaotic after multiple failed extracting attempts.

She slinks down the wall at the bottom of the stairs, curling her knees into her chest. Opal, Braxton, Xerin . . . is it possible they're all working together? And what about Delwynn? He'd rushed in with Estelle's near-lifeless body in his arms, looking as frazzled as ever. Is it possible Estelle had been a target?

What in lords' name is going on?

Unfortunately, the only person who's offered any genuine help whatsoever is unconscious—and until she wakes, Cerylia refuses to utter even one word to a single soul.

ARDEN ELIRI

IT TAKES US less time than I'd thought to arrive at the bridge in the depths of the cavern. With Rydan not far behind me, I stand at the edge, hardly able to take in the immensity of it all. I step forward, my foot landing on a sturdy iron grate. Upon further inspection, I notice that the grates are welded together to make up the long, yet narrow, bridge before me. The metal railing is cool to the touch as my hand slides along it. My gaze travels up the walls of the cavern, a multitude of rock formations jutting out at all angles. One small quake and I fear they'll all come crashing down.

Speaking of quakes . . .

Behind me, I can hear the echo of Rydan's footsteps. I glance over my shoulder before bringing my index finger to my lips. At first, he doesn't see me—it's only when I stop and he nearly runs into me that the sound of his footsteps falter. We've almost arrived at the end of the bridge—the length is quite deceiving to the naked eye—when I notice something strange just ahead.

A reflection of some sort.

I narrow my eyes as I draw closer, realizing that there's a giant plaque fixed to the main exterior wall. It appears to be made of obsidian, but even in its darkness—and in the darkness of this cavern—I can read the words clear as day.

Midvale Arcane Haven.

I absentmindedly reach for Rydan, who's finally caught up to me and is now standing at my side, before smacking him in the arm. Alarmed, he whirls toward me, mouth agape. "What the—?"

With wide eyes, I smack him again, then point forward. He follows my gaze. I watch as each word forms on his lips. "You think it's—?"

"—for illusié?" I nod my head so fast I can hardly get the words out. "Midvale. Arcane. Haven."

"Like . . . a school?"

"What else could it possibly be?"

"So, that would mean," Rydan says, his eyes growing as wide as mine, "that there are more of us. *A lot* more of us." He seems to want to say more, but for some reason, resists the impulse.

"What is it?" I press.

He waves a hand in the air. "Forget it."

"Rydan." I give him a knowing look.

He lets out a long sigh. "Before Avery, Vira, and I made it to Orihia, we sort of stumbled on something—a lot of *somethings*, actually. When we arrived at the gates," he lowers his voice to a whisper, "there were dozens of dead bodies outside. And they were all illusié."

Terror ripples through me, but I don't dare show it. "How do you know that they were illusié?"

"Because it was Avery who brought each one of them to Lonia as a passenger on his ship," he answers quietly. "And each and every one of them ended up . . . dead."

"And the bodies?" I know it's a morbid question, but I can't help myself. Surely we would have seen them—definitely *smelled* them—by now.

"Avery led us through an igniting ritual, an ancient ceremony to lay them to rest." His eyes are shadowed as they travel to mine. "One minute they were here; the next, they were mere ashes drifting into the night sky."

"Could this be what Avery was trying to find?" I gesture to the monstrosity before us. "What *they* were trying to find? You know, before . . .?" I trail off, not wanting to repeat the horrendous words he's just spoken.

He shakes his head before saying, "Avery never mentioned anything like this—at least, not that I can recall." He takes a step back, then cranes his neck upward. "As far as the . . . *fallen* searching for this place, that wouldn't make sense. They'd all been stripped of their illusié abilities."

"Well . . . so was I."

"Or so we've assumed." His eyes lock on mine. "You can still see Orihia, can see *this* place, whatever it is.

Maybe whoever's in here can give us some answers, can help us figure all of this out."

The prospect is so exhilarating that I can't think straight. "We have to go inside."

"Shouldn't we get the others?"

Well, look who's decided to be the voice of reason. "It's late and they're all sleeping," I say hastily. "Plus, who's to say this will still be here if we leave and then come back?" I make for the mahogany double doors, praying that Rydan will see reason—*my* reason—and won't do anything to squander this serendipitous moment.

I'm surprised to find him at my side without further debate. "Should we knock?"

He hardly has time to get the question out when the door clicks. I release the handle, taking a step back as the doors slowly swing inward. They lock into place at the same time my jaw hinges open. At first, I can't even process what it is I'm looking at.

Like the cavern, the room before us is massive and dimly lit—even so, what's floating above us is clear as day. Bookshelves . . . *hundreds* of them, possibly even thousands. I watch in awe as they move from one area of the room to another, some securing into the walls; others floating around aimlessly, reluctant to find a permanent home.

Even though we're indoors, any visible space is covered in climbing vines, trees, and flowers. They reach so high that I can't see what the top of the building even looks like. At our feet are small buds that have broken through the mismatched antique floor tiles, blooming in varying hues of blue and purple.

As I'm about to take a step forward, Rydan gently tugs on my arm. I glance back, waiting for him to say something, but he's just as speechless as I am, so instead, he points to something right in front of us. How had I not seen it? How was it not the *very first* thing my eyes went to?

My gaze travels along the floor, the never-ending stream of tiles seeming to turn in on each other, until finally landing on something so blinding, I nearly have to shield my eyes. Glowing plum, violet, and every other shade of purple I can possibly imagine is . . . a portal.

Like a moth to a flame, I begin to move toward it. I can sense Rydan doing the same, but he manages to snap out of his daze before I do. "Hold up. We can't just go disappearing into portals," he says evenly, his body now blocking the path in front of me.

"I'm sure it's harmless," I counter, all logic escaping me. "It's probably just a quick way to travel around the school, or whatever this place is."

"Be that as it may, we don't know for sure." He glances back at the shimmering lights. "What we need is to find someone to talk to. There has to be someone around here somewhere . . ."

As if on cue, a figure—a man—emerges through the iridescent opening. From the looks of it, he's more than a few years Rydan's senior. He's straightening the sleeves of his robe, seemingly oblivious to the fact that there are two complete strangers standing right in front of him. When he finally looks up, his already pale face drains what remains of its color.

"How did you find us?"

There's nothing accusatory in his tone. On the contrary, it's quite amicable—more curious than anything else.

"We . . . don't know," I respond, realizing that it's a terrible answer, even though it's the truth. "We just sort of stumbled upon it all."

The man shakes his head as he walks over. With each step, recognition illuminates his face. I'm even more confused when that recognition is directed at me.

"Eliri?" he says hopefully. "Arden Eliri?"

"How do you—?"

The man clasps his hands together as if he's just received the grandest news of the century. "Come, come. The timing could not be better. We were wondering how long it was going to take."

With questions forming faster than I can process them, I follow him toward the portal. Rydan exchanges a glance from beside me, and I can tell from the look on his face that he has just as many questions as I do.

"Forgive my ignorance, but I have to ask," I say, stopping in my tracks. "If I'm not mistaken, it sounds like you were . . . expecting me?"

The man only turns around once he reaches the edge of the portal. "You're who we've been waiting for. I'll explain everything, but first, we need to get you upstairs, in front of the Archmage." He beams at the statement, as if a reward of some sort awaits. "What a welcome surprise for us all."

I'm about to ask another question when, suddenly, a jolt travels through my body. My surroundings freeze—the portal, the robed man, everything . . . except for Rydan.

He grabs my shoulder. "Arden—"

But I don't hear the rest because suddenly, I'm being catapulted through space and time, moving at an unfathomable speed. Not only do my surroundings become a blur, but so does every neuron connecting my mind and body. This feeling is familiar—like when I've been plunged into a memory just to be pulled right back out—but there's something slightly different this time that I can't quite put my finger on. It's as if, somehow, I'm being reverted to a past state. A past version of myself.

I'm nearly convinced that I must be having a seizure when I suddenly land face down on a familiar shore, spitting out mouthfuls of pink sand. Next to me, I can hear Rydan coughing and gasping for air. My senses begin to return, albeit slowly, and I use my sleeve to hastily wipe the remaining grains from my tongue. I'm spitting and drooling, but Rydan is too, so at least I know I haven't totally lost it. I watch as he rushes over to the water, and only then do I realize that we're no longer in the cave—we're outside of it, wall and all.

I look up at it, flummoxed. *How did we get out here when . . . when we were just in there?*

"Did I miss the part where we went through the portal?" I hear Rydan say between labored breaths.

"Because while we were close to it, I certainly don't recall stepping *through* the damn thing."

"It almost felt like we were *pulled* out of there," I say, more to myself than to him. "Like we were forcefully yanked or cut off somehow."

"Just for the record, that *wasn't* what I saw the first time around. That was . . . well, I don't know what that was."

"Midvale Arcane Haven," I whisper, determined not to forget the name. "You know what this means, right?"

"That our sanity is in question?"

"No," I say with a shake of my head, "it means there's more to illusié than we ever could have imagined."

"You can say that again." His face turns a sickly shade of green. "I feel like I might be sick."

"You and me both." Even though I'm lightheaded, I manage to bring myself to my feet. Slowly, I walk away from him, mostly to give him privacy, and then head over to the wall. Gently, I place both hands against it. I don't know if it's just my imagination, but I swear I can feel a low pulse emanating from the stone. I can hear its hum, its vibration.

I step back, feeling more intrigued than before. I don't know when and I don't know how, but I am *hell-bent* on finding a way back in—whatever it takes.

RYDAN HELSTROM

ARDEN'S TRIED EVERYTHING in her arsenal, which isn't much, to get back into the cave, but each attempt just leads to another discouraging failure. She's tried kicking. Hitting. Bashing with rocks. Throwing of rocks. Kneeling and praying to the lords above. Cursing said lords. And everything in between.

But her best idea is yet to come.

"Light it on fire."

Rydan looks up from the boulder he's perched on. He tries to keep the amusement out of his voice as he repeats her demand back to her. "Just to clarify . . . you want me to light a *stone wall* on fire?"

Arden frowns, kicking at the sand before joining him on the rock. "You're our last hope," she teases. "I'm all out of ideas."

"And what wonderful ideas they were."

She gives him a playful nudge before sighing and turning her gaze skyward. "Would you be concerned if I told you that ever since I joined the Caldari, I question my sanity on a daily basis?"

Rydan chuckles. "You're not the only one."

"I guess we're more equipped to handle the duty of being assassins than illusié." Her cheerful demeanor fades. "I was hoping the opposite would be true."

"Well, we *did* have more time in the Cruex."

She looks at him before resting her chin on her shoulder. "Not necessarily."

"How do you mean?"

"We've always been illusié. We just didn't know it."

"Cruex by force, illusié by blood." His words hang in the air, the silence stretching between them for what feels like hours.

Arden exhales, long and heavy. "There's something I need to get off my chest." The way she looks at him is disconcerting. Her eyes are lined with guilt as she says, "What if it's the other way around? If my being in the Cruex wasn't forced? What if it's due to *blood*?"

Rydan searches her face for her meaning, but comes up short. "I'm not sure I follow."

A shaky breath. "After I met Haskell, we discovered that we . . . might share blood with the Tymonds." He can feel her pain as the words leave her mouth, as if twisting an already deeply embedded knife. "It's not something we know for sure, but the evidence is mounting and the more I think about everything—about the Cruex and the

Caldari, about Braxton, about my brother and my father"—she hesitates then, the air around them suddenly stifling—"about my mother . . ."

Rydan doesn't so much as give it a second thought before wrapping his arm around her shoulders and pulling her close. Like so many nights before, she buries her face into his chest. He can feel her trying to hold it together—the tension in her neck, the pressure of her forehead against his skin, the way she wants to heave and shake and crumble into nonexistence. But he won't let her. He needs her together and in one piece. Here.

They all do.

"Hey," he says, gently cupping the back of her head, his thumb moving in slow circles. "Even if it is true, it doesn't mean a damn thing."

She doesn't answer, but she does move her head slightly, although not enough to look up at him. She doesn't need to, though. The slight nod of her head is enough to indicate that she's heard him, that he's right.

Sitting like this reminds him so much of their time in Trendalath. Arden had been more than just a sparring partner to him—more than just a friend. He can't help but wonder . . . had their days in the Cruex *not* been numbered, where would they be? Would their spark be extinguished? Still flickering? Or spreading like wildfire?

She lifts her head all the way, pulling him from his thoughts. "I suppose we should head back before the others start asking questions."

Only when he looks up at the brightening sky does he realize that it's already well into morning. "We'll come back," he says assuredly, wishing they could stay a bit longer. "That wall can't stay there forever."

Her lips tilt in a faint smile. "Not if we have anything to do with it."

DARIUS TYMOND

HE'S LOOKED UNDERNEATH the bed at least a dozen times already, but there's no sign of the speculor. Frustrated, Darius pushes himself up off the ground, shaking the dust from the bottom of his robes. He walks to the middle of Braxton's room, scanning every inch of every surface without any luck. It's only when his gaze lands on the door of the open armoire that his breath hitches. Booted feet stand just behind it.

Before his thoughts can run away with him, the shadowed figure emerges, crimson eyes boring into his own. "Looking for this?" The speculor glints in the fading light as Xerin produces it from his pocket.

Darius levels a steely look at him. "How did you know about it?"

Xerin merely shrugs. "I didn't. Right place, right time, I suppose."

Darius wants to call foul play, but he knows better than to make an enemy of Xerin—or any of the Greys, for that matter. He's desperate to know what the speculor holds but revealing such a thing might just be the nail in his coffin. What Xerin says next surprises him.

"You have the proper viewing tools?"

Not wanting to seem too cavalier, Darius nods. "Of course."

There's an edge to the Caldari's voice. "Then I suppose you won't mind if I accompany you?"

The shadows flickering in his eyes tell Darius that, for some reason, he's testing him. Unfortunately for Xerin, the king is quick on his feet. "Seeing as the speculor belonged to my late wife, I'd prefer to view its contents alone." When Xerin doesn't respond, Darius adds, "I'm sure you understand."

But the vacancy glazing his features indicates otherwise. "So nothing has changed since we last spoke."

"I'm not sure to what you're referring." As soon as the words leave his mouth, he wishes he could take them back—and from the look on Xerin's face, the tables have just turned. *He* wants to call foul play on *him.*

The sound of voices travels down the hall. Pressed for time, Darius holds out his hand. "The speculor."

The red in Xerin's eyes has grown so dark, they're nearly black, his expression now haunted. Without saying anything, he drops the object into Darius's outstretched hand.

The voices draw closer.

Darius angles his head toward the window. "You'd best get going."

Xerin doesn't move. "I think I'll stay for a bit. I've got some catching up to do." While not unusual, the Caldari's blatant disrespect is completely unnecessary—but before Darius can counter, Xerin says, "Don't forget who got you your son back." He watches the king, his silent calm unnerving. "I'm owed at least that much."

And he's right. He is. Darius knows it's useless to try to convince Xerin otherwise, so he simply places the speculor in his pocket and makes for the door. He turns to look at Xerin one last time. The bastard is grinning, as if he knows he's won—as if he knows he now has the upper hand. *Unacceptable.* "Not a word of this to Braxton, understood?"

But Xerin's smile only turns lupine. "We've made it this far, haven't we?"

BRAXTON HORNSBY

BRAXTON SWEARS HE sees a shadowed figure turning the corner near his room, but it could just be a trick of the light. When he reaches the door, he notices it's slightly ajar, making it all the more evident that someone has indeed just left his room—which means that, more likely than not, Darius now has the speculor in his possession.

After being dragged to the Cruex dinner against his will, both he and Lane had agreed to slip out at separate intervals, hopefully undetected. Seeing as the speculor had been left in his room, they'd both agreed that he should be the first to go, with plans to meet in her chambers later that evening. He'd hoped to have better news but, by the looks of it, disappointment is in the cards—and not only that, but an element of . . . *surprise*?

He nearly trips over his own two feet at the sight of Xerin. "Lords," he says, hand flying to his chest. "What are you doing here?" And then, the more pressing question, "Why did you abandon me in the woods?"

A muscle ticks in Xerin's cheek. It's the first time Braxton's seen him at a loss for words. "I don't really have an explanation for that." His expression is cold, vacant, as he lifts his gaze from across the room. "For that, I am sincerely sorry."

"That you don't have an explanation? Or that you disappeared and didn't bother to come back?"

"Both."

"How did you know I was here?" Braxton asks, recalling the memory of Darius talking to someone in the hall before a falcon had flown out the window mere moments later.

Xerin raps his fingers against the desk. The corners of his mouth twitch before saying, "The Caster you freed."

"Clive."

Xerin nods. "We ran into each other in the Roviel Woods. I was surprised to hear that you'd been captured by the Savant—but even more surprised that *you* were the one to free him."

That last part snags on something in Braxton's mind. "Why would that surprise you?"

All color drains from Xerin's face. "You don't know."

"Don't know what?"

Xerin grimaces. "It isn't my place to say."

In a fit of rage, Braxton storms over to him and grabs him by the neck of his shirt. "You're here now. You know something. So yes, it *is* your place to say."

A myriad of unsettling emotions sweeps across the Caldari's face, but he remains tight-lipped, refusing to speak.

"Lords damn it, Xerin! Tell me *something*." It's no use trying to hide the tremor in his voice. "Sometimes I wonder why I even joined the Caldari at all. It hasn't gotten me any closer to anything or anyone."

At this, Xerin seems to soften. "I've been keeping an eye on you—and on Darius—ever since he brought you back here." His voice falls even more as he says, "He's up to something, I'm sure of it. You need to get that speculor back in your possession."

Braxton studies him, letting the words fully sink in. *How does he know about the speculor? And why is it that every time Xerin's in the picture, something seems to go awry?* His next question is answered before he even has the chance to ask it.

"I saw him from the windowsill." His throat bobs. "Your father has it."

How Xerin knows *what* the speculor contains, Braxton doesn't know—but the likelihood that he'll get any more answers today is nil.

Xerin bows his head, slipping behind the door of the armoire just before a golden glow fills the room. A falcon emerges from behind it. Braxton watches as it lands on the windowsill, its head tilting toward him. With a single flash of those beady crimson eyes, Xerin vanishes silently into the night.

CERYLIA JARETH

IF SHE WASN'T in her own castle surrounded by complete and utter familiarity, Cerylia would undoubtedly feel like a prisoner. Dodging both Delwynn and Opal had been near impossible, so the queen had struck a deal with the guards to redirect them if they got too close.

She's spent the past week traveling between her hidden chambers and the healing ward with little to steer her off course. Estelle's condition seems to be improving with each passing day, but Cerylia knows better than to try to fast-track her recovery. If her suspicions are correct, casting-related injuries are some of the most complicated to heal from. It's not so much the physical harm that is a concern, but the severe warping of the mind.

She's just left the healing ward to head back to her hidden chambers, taking all the necessary precautions as per usual. She nods at each guard in passing until she reaches a segment of the corridor where no guards are stationed. A striking sense of solitude hangs in the air. She slinks along, embracing the familiar darkness. The sliver of light from the crescent moon is all that illuminates the hallway before her. In the dim lighting, she hardly notices the shadow that moves from one end of the corridor to the other. It's only when she's halfway to the hidden entrance that she sees it.

Rightly so, a chill lodges in her chest. Her first thought is that the Mallum has returned—that it's finally come for her. It's already been here once, so who's to say it wouldn't come back, *especially* if it didn't get what it wanted the first time around?

With bated breath, she takes a quiet step backward, followed by two more—but when the shadow doesn't move any closer, she stops. Although she hasn't come into direct contact with the Mallum, all the accounts she's read or heard of mention an attack almost immediately upon encountering the entity. Why it *isn't* attacking her is fortunate but disconcerting all the same.

A soft indigo spark appears at the end of the hall, then another, and another, until the darkness is forced to fade. A mystical shower of blue and silver beams create a shimmering curtain as they highlight the walls, the ceiling, and the floor. Cerylia realizes that this is most certainly *not* the Mallum—what it is, she can't be sure.

As quickly as they appeared, the beams rush toward her at a startling speed, flashing intermittently until she's completely engulfed in light. Mesmerized by the sight, Cerylia extends her arm to the side, her fingers dancing along the sheer light-speckled curtain. Much to her surprise, there's no shock, no pulse, no electric sensation of any kind. She's so caught up in her surroundings that, at first, she doesn't notice the figure standing mere steps away. When she finally senses its presence, it's standing in plain sight. Her hand flies to her mouth as recognition sets in.

The neatly combed midnight hair.

The gentle, yet determined, cerulean eyes.

Her late husband—a former version, at least.

"Dane?" she whispers in disbelief.

A small smile plays on his lips. "My love."

Her breath hitches. "This is impossible." As much as she wants to go to him, she remains rooted in place. She can't help but take in every feature—the bushy, yet well-groomed brows, the specks of gray dotting his irises, the angular nose, the contrast of thin lips surrounded by a thick, full beard. He's just as handsome as she remembers.

Her voice cracks as she asks, "How is it that you're here?"

"It's not what you think," he says, taking a slow step toward her. "There's so much you don't know."

The sound of his voice clouds her judgment. "You're here now. That's what matters. You're back . . . you've returned." Her words jumble together as tears sting her eyes. For the first time in years, they aren't laced with despair.

"Aldreda, she . . ." His voice trails off, but the way he's just said the name sounds as though it's a remnant of a distant memory—something he's trying to grasp but can't quite seem to hold onto long enough to do so.

Hearing that name leave his lips is enough for Cerylia's blood to turn cold. An ocean of rage thrashes inside her. She nearly draws blood as she forces her teeth down on her tongue to avoid saying something she'll later regret.

Dane seems to sense her inner turmoil. "My death, I mean—it isn't what you think."

While she appreciates his attempt to clarify, it only creates more confusion. She shakes her head. "I saw you die, Dane. I saw her. With that dagger. And I saw you." She presses her eyes shut, not wanting to recall the memory Opal had shown her. "You were . . . gone."

"It isn't what you think," he repeats.

Her frustration on the rise, she's about to explain *how* she knows this—how she *saw* him die—when she hears something so heart-wrenching, it threatens to destroy every last shred of hope within her.

"It should have been you."

She's sure she's misheard. Dane would *never . . .*

A sickening realization dawns on her at the same moment her alleged husband reaches into the side pocket of his robes. A familiar blade glints in the twinkling light, his hand firmly grasping the hilt—the same blade Aldreda had used on him.

Any sense of control she'd felt shatters as panic surges through her. She swipes her hand through the faux curtain once more, but the effort is futile. Whispers push at her mind—whispers of what this *actually* is. The work of a Caster. The work of Aldreda's accomplice.

Seeing no other choice, Cerylia turns to run, although she doesn't know where to. The tunnel of light only extends so far. Even though she's now running straight ahead, the excessive flashing around her creates a dizzying effect.

She refuses to let him get close.

She turns over her shoulder, reminding herself that this isn't Dane—that this isn't *real*, isn't happening—but, in a sense, it is. And if she doesn't find a way out soon, she's going to end up just like Estelle in that healing ward—mind warped, all sense of reality distorted.

He's charging at her now, blade in hand, the fire in his gaze a stark contrast to its usual tranquil blue. She wants to scream, but it would be no use. No one would hear her. *Damn this abandoned corridor.* No one knows where she is—not the guards, not Delwynn, not the Caldari . . .

She reaches the end of the hall, desperately swiping her hand along the walls, looking for a ripple, a tear— *anything.* While she doesn't find one, she *does* notice someone standing just outside the pulsating curtain. He's so close now that Cerylia's tempted to just close her eyes and succumb—succumb to whatever the Caster wants from her, even if it means death—when, suddenly, he stops. His arm lowers, the blade dangling at his side as he looks around in confusion. Based on the actions that follow, it seems that, to him, she's . . . *vanished.*

At once, Cerylia realizes what's happened. She feels a familiar presence behind her—and all around her. There's no mistaking it. She's been cloaked.

"Let's get you out of here," Estelle whispers.

ARDEN ELIRI

BEFORE WE EVEN have a chance to say anything, I can tell by the look on our friends' faces that my nightly rendezvous with Rydan won't be received well. Avery and Vira are standing near the fire with their arms crossed; Haskell's cooking but has stopped mid-roast; and Felix is sitting at the base of a willow tree, his face almost entirely shaded by the low-hanging branches.

"Where'd you two run off to?"

While Avery's tone is playful, the vibe around the campfire most certainly is not. I shoot a sidelong glance at Rydan to see if we're on the same page. "We had some things to work out."

"In the middle of the night?"

My eyes lock on Vira's. There's ire in her gaze, but beyond that, I can see trepidation. I'm about to answer her, but Rydan beats me to it.

"There were a few things from our Cruex days we needed to clear up." Not exactly a lie, but not entirely the truth either. "It seems we may have wandered a little farther than we originally intended."

The conversation carries on, but I'm no longer listening. My attention is on Felix—what I can see of him, anyway. The leaves rustle at the same time he lifts his hand and motions to his dwelling. With my head down, I silently slip away from the group and follow him. Neither of us speak until we're inside with the door shut securely behind us.

"He's lying." His eyes search mine, hungry for answers. That makes two of us.

I can tell his urge to amplify is strong, so I quickly turn away. I pull one of the chairs out from under the table and offer it to him. In usual Felix-fashion, he spins it around before taking a seat. With his elbows propped against the back of the chair, he waits for me to sit.

I slink into the chair, unwilling to make eye contact with him. "It isn't a lie," I finally respond, feeling put on the spot. For some reason, I feel a new level of discomfort I haven't felt with him before—and that's saying something, seeing as his steady gaze usually makes me feel anything but.

"How many times do we have to go over this?" He runs a hand down his face, clearly frustrated by my ambiguity. "You can tell me *anything*, Arden."

My blood heats at the remark, and I'm certain the war waging inside me is etched all over my face. I know what he's saying is true. I know I can confide in him. I've done it before—and I *want* to do it again. But the time I've just spent with Rydan, what we'd discovered in that cave underneath the waterfall . . .

I'm not so sure it's something I want to share just yet. It feels private somehow, like that decision doesn't belong to only me, but to the both of us.

I look down, realizing that Felix has moved his chair closer. His hands are now placed gently over mine. Only then do I recognize that *this* is what I've been afraid of. Our undeniable bond—the one that extends beyond the physical. I slip my hands out from under his and place them in my lap. As I do so, I can see the confusion, and then the hurt, play out in his eyes.

"What's changed?"

It's merely a whisper, but the weight of his words burrows deep inside my chest, like an anchor clinging to shore. As much as I want to reassure him that everything is fine, I don't know that it is. I'm beginning to doubt everything I know, everything I've been told. The Caldari had made it sound like illusié were a dying breed—a pulse cut off so long ago that those who still have magick pumping through their veins are few and far between. And yet, Rydan and I have just discovered a place where the opposite might be true. Yes, we'd witnessed only one person inside Midvale Arcane Haven, but such a massive structure being unoccupied?

Highly unlikely, if you ask me.

I don't realize how long I've been silent until my gaze lands on the empty chair in front of me. Felix has made his way to the door, a look of pure torment ravaging his face. It's unsightly to see him so distraught, but I don't know what to say to make things right. I don't want to lie—his ability to amplify will see right through that. And I don't want to tell him the truth because . . . well, I don't even know what the truth is myself.

He doesn't say anything as he opens the door. Just as I think he's about to leave, Haskell walks in, followed by Avery, then Vira and Rydan. I'd been so wrapped up in my own thoughts that if they'd knocked, I hadn't heard it.

Being crammed together like this reminds me of when I'd awoken in Orihia, surrounded by this very group of people—the same group who'd questioned how I could be here after allegedly losing my abilities to the Mallum. A question none of us knows the answer to . . . still.

Being the only one sitting, I feel like the odd person out, so I push off the back of the chair and stand, deciding to lean against it instead. I scan their faces, wondering who's going to speak first. It certainly won't be me—not with all this tension hanging in the air.

Brave soul that he is, Haskell grunts, "Are we just going to stand here or are we going to talk about it?"

"We need to talk about it," Avery says. "And we need to figure out how you got there in the first place."

I can feel Felix's heated gaze from all the way across the room, but he's not the one I'm looking at. My focus is set on Rydan. *He told them?*

"The truth of the matter is, we don't know." It's then I realize he's completely unaware of his actions, of what he's just done. "Right, Arden?"

His voice cuts through me like glass. "Right," is all I can manage to say. At my response, I notice Felix's shoulders drop and his head lower in disappointment.

Looks like we're sharing something after all—even if it's for different reasons.

"We need to know everything you know about this place," Avery says. "Where it is, how you got there, the time of day, *everything*."

Rydan glances my way, as if silently asking for permission. Oh, so *now* he wants to make a decision as a team?

"I guess now would also be the time to tell them about the fallen illusié," I say, failing to fight my budding anger. "Should you do the honors or should I?"

RYDAN HELSTROM

SEEING AS THERE'S more room at his and Vira's place, the group unanimously decided to migrate from Felix's. Rydan's gone over the details of his rendezvous with Arden at least four times and repeating himself is getting real old real fast. Perhaps if Arden would chime in every now and again, it'd help—but she's perched in the corner, refusing to say a word.

"To me, the most confusing part is how it wasn't there the first time around," Avery says, "but then you went back and . . . voila?"

"No shit," Felix mutters.

Avery cuts a sharp glance his way.

"What I can't believe is how you *chose* not to tell us about the fallen illusié."

"You're right, poor judgment on our part," Vira says in an effort to diffuse the mounting tension. "But now that we're all on the same page, we can move forward."

The innocence in her voice is only a stark reminder of the guilt piling up inside—of all the things he still hasn't told her. Rydan makes a mental note to bring her up to speed sooner rather than later.

"Look, they're probably exhausted. They've been up all night." Felix's eyes land on Rydan, lethal in every aspect of the word. "Let them get some rest and we'll reconvene later this evening." And then, under his breath, he mutters, "We could all use a little time to think anyway."

Rydan bows his head, watching out of the corner of his eye as Felix walks to the door. His focus flits to Arden, whose gaze happens to be on Felix as well.

"Felix is right," Haskell says as he grabs Avery by the arm. "We'll let you get some sleep."

At that point, only Rydan, Vira, and Arden remain—and from the looks of it, she doesn't seem to be leaving anytime soon. She buries her face in her hands.

"Can I make you some tea?" Vira offers.

Rydan can tell by the way she directs the question *only* at Arden that she's upset with him. Honestly, she has every right to be. He'd snuck out, with *Arden*, of all people, and hadn't uttered a word to her about it.

Arden responds with a nod and a forced smile.

Once Vira's out of earshot, he says, "I suppose that went over as well as could be expected."

A muscle ticks in her jaw. "I thought we were going to keep quiet. You know, until we figured things out?"

He studies her—the straight face, the stiffness in her shoulders, the crease along her brow. It dawns on him that perhaps he'd spoken too soon. For the first time in months, they'd shared something, just the two of them, and he'd paraded it around for all the world to see.

"No point griping about it now," she says, brushing some invisible lint from her pantleg. "What's done is done. They know. We know. Like one big, happy family."

Before Rydan can try to make amends, Vira returns with the tea. She sets the tray down next to Arden before pouring her a cup. The scent of lemongrass and mint fills the room.

"Thank you," Arden says as Vira hands the steaming mug to her. Before she so much as takes a sip, she leans onto her left hip, then pulls a rolled piece of parchment from behind her.

Vira's eyes grow wide as recognition sets in. "Is that what I think it is?"

Arden nods as she sets it on the tray. Even though Rydan knows she's already looked it over dozens of times, she scans the document in its entirety, her eyes darting every which way.

Vira says what they're all thinking. "I know it doesn't tell you much—"

"Much?" Arden retorts. "It doesn't tell me *anything*."

"You want to know who." The words are soft-spoken, but assured all the same.

Rydan's just as surprised at the remark as Arden seems to be. They both turn to look at Vira.

"Getting involved with the Savant is a dangerous endeavor," she continues. Her expression indicates that she knows more than she's willing to say. "My own mother would be the first to tell you that."

Rydan can't help but feel a stab of remorse. He's immediately taken back to when he'd first met Vira in the dungeons in Trendalath—the way she'd finally opened up to him after the delivery of many, many silent meals. Even as a prisoner, she'd seen his innocence. Even though they'd only known each other a short while, she'd trusted him enough to flee Sardoria for no other reason than to protect his own fragile ego.

His thoughts scatter as Arden says, "I know it's dangerous. The Savant nearly killed me." Her tone is flat.

The look in her eyes is one Rydan knows all too well, so before things can get too heated, he interjects, "Haskell made a good point. We're all tired and should sleep on it. Trying to figure all of this out now won't do us any good."

Arden doesn't bother making eye contact with him as she finishes her drink. She sets the mug down with a loud *thunk*, but leaves the scroll exactly where it is. "Thanks for the tea." And with that, she pushes off from the chair and flings the door open. Rydan braces himself, assuming she'll slam it shut, but surprisingly, it closes quietly behind her.

"I don't blame her," Vira says with a sigh.

"What do you mean?"

Tray in hand, Vira angles her head toward the door. "I understand why she's upset. About her mother. About the Savant. I'd want to kill them, too." And then, with a shrug, "Perhaps we should."

Her suggestion is entirely unexpected. No longer does Rydan see the meek and harmless girl he'd met in Trendalath, but someone with a vengeance. Someone looking for answers. Someone who'll stop at nothing to get what she wants . . . Perhaps she and Arden are more alike than he thought.

DARIUS TYMOND

STEERING THE CARRIAGE is the last thing Darius thought he'd be doing and yet, here he is. After retrieving the speculor from Braxton's room—and unexpectedly speaking with Xerin—Darius had gone straight to the stables. No Cyrus. No King's Guard. No Savant.

He will admit, he's a bit on edge being out here alone, especially with Clive on the loose. But he's ridden this same path hundreds of times before . . . even if he *had* been the passenger, he still knows it by heart.

Darius follows the winding trail up the side of the mountain, his staff tucked securely beneath his lap. The carriage bounces and bobs behind him as he moves into slightly rockier terrain. He reaches a good stopping point, pulling tightly on the reins to bring the steed to a halt. He checks to make sure the speculor hadn't dislodged during the latter part of the ride, then hops down, staff in hand. He's about to start the final leg of his ascent into Volkharn when something rustles in the trees. He's used to traveling at night, so he's sharp enough to know the difference between an animal and his own kind.

He twists the amethyst ring round his finger, narrowing his eyes in the hopes that they'll adjust to the darkness. He considers readying his staff and using its emerald glow, but drawing attention to himself is the last thing he wants. He can already feel eyes on him—no need to make the target even bigger.

Had Cyrus perhaps followed him? He thinks back to earlier that evening. Unlikely—the last time he'd seen Cyrus was at the Cruex dinner. He hadn't so much as caught a glimpse of him afterward. Thereby, he can eliminate the Cruex as well. They'd all been at the dinner, both new and old.

As for the Savant? More specifically, an *ex*-Savant who's escaped imprisonment? As much as it pains him to admit, that is *highly* likely.

Although the carriage serves as weak camouflage, he slinks around the back of it before drawing closer to the dense brush. Unlit staff in hand, he creeps along the trail, making sure not to accidentally snap any twigs or fallen branches along the way. The rustling in the distance ensues.

With his back pressed against a cedar tree and his focus directed at the branches above, he doesn't detect any movement—in fact, the forest is the most peaceful he's ever seen it. If it *is* Clive, he'll have to show himself sooner or later. Without a direct target to cast on, his attempted illusions are meaningless.

Darius stays put for a few minutes, his gaze still directed skyward. When he sees a squirrel jump from one branch to another and scurry off, he can't help but roll his eyes. Although it'd sounded much larger than a squirrel, he knows from experience that this forest, in particular, tends to amplify everything in (and around) it.

With a shake of his head, he treks back to the carriage, checks on the spooked mare, and finally begins the last leg of his journey on foot to the jaded spring.

BRAXTON HORNSBY

IT'D BEEN A risk to stow away in the carriage, but Braxton's idea had paid off. *Big time.*

He motions for Lane to duck as Darius once again moves past the sheer curtained windows, their backs pressed against the wall, just as Darius's back had been pressed against a tree just a few moments prior.

"What is this place?" Lane whispers.

Braxton waits until his father is a good distance away before peering over the velvet-lined seats and out the front window. "I'm not sure. All I see are trees, a trail, and some more trees."

"A trail?" Lane joins him at the window. "Where do you think it leads?"

"Guess there's only one way to find out." He reaches for the carriage door when he feels his arm suddenly being yanked back.

"Are you insane?" Lane hisses. "If he sees us, we're done for."

Braxton raises a brow. "I think you're forgetting that I'm his *son*."

"Yeah, his son who discovered something *invaluable* that he obviously wanted to keep you in the dark about," she counters. "We should stay here. Wait until he comes back."

"Then you stay. I'll go." This time, when he reaches for the door, she doesn't stop him. He pushes it open and steps out. Just as he's about to shut it, her hand smacks the side, forcing it back open.

Lane gives him a wry smile. "If you think I'm going to sit here and wait while you have all the fun, you have another thing coming." She breezes past him, patting the horse on the nose before taking off down the trail.

Braxton suppresses the urge to shout after her. As stealthily as he can, he jogs to catch up—but when she stops suddenly in her tracks and jumps into the bushes, Braxton immediately follows suit. Cautiously, they part the shrubbery leaves. It's not the clearest view, but it'll have to do.

Darius is stopped near an alcove in the mountains, the early spring winds rustling the bottom of his robes, as he switches a tall object between his hands.

A wooden staff.

Affixed to the top is a clear glass sphere. At first, it doesn't seem to be glowing, but, within the blink of an eye, a pale light appears, casting a sickly green shadow against the darkness. Darius then pats his chest pocket—which no doubt holds the speculor—before journeying farther on his skyward hike.

❧ ❧ ❧

Braxton and Lane have been following Darius for what feels like hours. Each time he stops, Braxton feels as though his heart might leap from his chest—but he can't tell if that's because he's winded and needs to rest, or if it's because he's anticipating what they're bound to discover whenever they *do* arrive. If it weren't for the glow of the staff, they would have lost his trail a *long* time ago.

"We have to be getting close, right?" Lane whispers breathily. "I can't imagine he does this often. Traveling at this altitude at his age can't be healthy."

She has a point. Although Braxton was quite young when he lived in Trendalath castle, he certainly doesn't recall his father leaving for hours on end. On the contrary, he never left Aldreda's side—and if not there, he could usually be found in the Great Room. Then again, if he had partaken in nightly escapades into the earliest hours of the morning, such as this one, Braxton would have been fast asleep and wouldn't have been the wiser.

He's beginning to think his father might just be out for a midnight hike, however unusual that might be, when he *finally* reaches something: a gate. And not just any gate, but a towering metal structure that stands three times his height. There's another glow, of faint purple, and Braxton quickly realizes that it's the amethyst ring—the same one Cerylia had previously tasked him with retrieving.

It seems the ring is the key to unlocking the entrance because, ever so steadily, the gates creak open. He and Lane glance at each other, knowing that if they want to see what's inside, they'll have to make a run for it.

Once Darius has left their sight, they rush out of the bushes, sprinting toward the now closing gates. Lane's ahead of him by more than a few paces and easily slips through. She reaches her hand out, impatience flaring in her eyes as she motions for him to hurry up. He doesn't know how, but he makes it just in time.

Lane grabs him by the wrist to pull him the rest of the way in. His boot nearly gets caught in a spire at the bottom of the gate, but he shakes it loose before it can do any real damage. Up ahead, they can still see Darius, but he's fading from view rather quickly.

"All good?" she asks, almost completely out of breath.

Braxton nods, angling his head at the sound of rushing water. "Hear that? It should mask our footsteps."

"I'll follow you," she says, crouching behind him.

The glow of the staff disappears as Darius turns a corner. "Stay close," Braxton whispers. "If I know my father, whatever we're about to find isn't going to be pretty."

CERYLIA JARETH

CLOAKED, THEY'D MANAGED to make it through the castle completely undetected. The library had seemed like a safe bet and, although not as spritely as usual, Estelle had led them to safety without a second interference from the Caster.

Cerylia paces along the bolted-down desks. She's considering her next move, with Estelle watching quietly from one of the suede-lined armchairs. Her footsteps echo in the enormous space and she can't help but feel like the shelves, housing thousands upon thousands of books, are watching her as well. She tries to ignore how *exposed* she feels, but after being in the presence of her late husband again—even though it *was* only an illusion—she's convinced herself that there must be some truth to his words.

It's not what you think, he'd said. *There's so much you don't know.*

Even if it *had* been the Caster talking, she'd be remiss to not at least consider the possibility that there might be a remnant of truth lingering in those words.

Cerylia's attention shifts to Estelle, who's digging in her pocket for a small vial. She removes the cork before tipping it to her mouth. It's one of the tinctures Delwynn had made. She'd probably swiped it on her way to the abandoned corridor . . .

Which brings Cerylia to her first question—how had Estelle known that she was in danger? She stops pacing and takes a seat in the chair across from the Caldari. Not wanting to start the conversation off too inquisitively, she says, "I've visited you every day in the healing ward."

Estelle studies the queen, her expression wavering between emotions. Finally, she says, "I know."

"You're feeling better?"

"These have certainly been helping." She shakes the vial for emphasis. "I suppose I have Delwynn to thank for that."

"He was the one who carried you back into the castle after . . ." Not wanting to pry, her voice trails off.

Estelle casts her eyes at the ground. "The illusion he wove around me . . . it felt so *real*." Her voice cracks. "I lost almost everyone. Felix. Xerin. *All* of the Caldari. So, I gave it to him. Handed it over. Just like that." She shakes her head at the memory. "I should have known better, should have been able to see right through it." She's crying now, her voice muffled by a steady stream of tears.

The weight of what she's just confessed is palpable. Cerylia goes to her, kneeling next to the chair. "Never blame yourself for wanting to protect your family." At this, Estelle looks up with tear-stained cheeks. "I thought I *was* seeing my family again, my sweet Dane—and look what almost happened to me. If it hadn't been for you, who knows where I'd have ended up."

"While that may be true, I'm afraid I have failed you in another way, Your Greatness. I cannot apologize enough." She inhales a shaky breath. "He took the one thing I promised I could help you with."

Cerylia knows exactly to what she's referring.

The pocket watch.

"It was our only way to enter the Veil. And now it's gone." Estelle forces the words through gritted teeth. "And it's all my fault."

Downtrodden, Cerylia slinks away from the chair. Although she knows she won't find answers here, in the library, she still scans the packed shelves, the cluttered desks, the intricately carved beams that run parallel across the ceiling. "There's always another way," she murmurs, her eyes landing on one of the globes.

The moment ends abruptly as someone pushes open the library doors. Delwynn enters and, from the frazzled look on his face, it's obvious what he's searching for. When his gaze lands on Estelle, he exhales a loud sigh of relief. "I'd thought the worst," he says as he rushes over with another tincture.

Estelle lifts her half-empty vial. "All good here, but thank you, Delwynn."

As Cerylia watches him—how easily he glides and moves across the floor—an idea begins to take root. Even though he's now directing the conversation at her, she doesn't hear a word that leaves his mouth. Her mind is on one thing, and one thing only:

The Eliris.

They're going to enter that damn Veil . . . and Cerylia knows exactly *how* they're going to do it.

ARDEN ELIRI

FROM UP HERE, the sky seems to extend for miles. In the waning light, I can see every constellation, every star, the outline of the crescent moon—a world of infinite possibilities. And yet, I feel chained by my circumstances. Trapped by my past.

Immobilized by my future.

More than I've ever seen it, Orihia is alight with color and music. The birds sing as if dawn were just breaking, the crickets chirp their harmonious melodies, and the frogs croak back and forth, joining the symphony with their own unique chorus. Even though I'm floating above the treetops, I can hear them clear as day, as if they're putting on a performance just for me.

Unfortunately, something has to interfere with the tranquility of this moment. I can sense him beside me before a word is even uttered—and here I thought I was the only one who cared to use the shimmering walkways.

"Who's spying on who now?" I murmur, just loud enough for him to hear.

Felix chuckles, stretching his legs out so that his back is flat on the platform, hands cupping the back of his head. I pretend not to notice and continue stargazing, but he decides to join in on that, too.

"See that?" he says, pointing directly in my line of vision. "That's the Chiron constellation."

I narrow my eyes, making out a horse-like shape.

"It's been said that some illusié abilities originated in the stars," he goes on. "Shapers, for instance, draw a close parallel with centaurs. Half man, half horse. The ability to shape into an animal and then back into human form is thought to be largely influenced by Chiron."

"You didn't answer my question."

"I assumed it was rhetorical."

"Hmm, I suppose it was." I close one eye, raising my arm as I begin to trace the constellation. *Damn my curiosity for always getting the better of me.* "Have you met any other Shapers besides Xerin?"

Felix doesn't miss a beat. "Can't say that I have. But with Xerin? He can shape into any creature under the sun. You name it, I've seen it."

I let out a small laugh. In testing the waters between us, it seems he's willing to press the reset button and resume a status I wasn't sure we'd ever get back to. "You know, Xerin was the first dragon I ever saw—outside of books and paintings, of course—which makes me wonder if it even really counts?"

I can feel him smiling next to me. "I think it does."

"What about the other illusié abilities?" I ask as I turn to face him, propping my head up on my shoulder. "Does amplification have an origin story in the stars?"

From the side, I can see his eyes twinkle. "I'm sure it does, but I don't know it. Never thought about it, really. Now *Healers* on the other hand . . ."

I wait for him to continue until I realize he's trailed off on purpose. With my free hand, I nudge him in the shoulder. "What about Healers?"

"Ophiuchus," he says, meeting me upright. He points out another constellation, this one less defined in its shape. "Ophiuchus was a master healer. It's believed he was actually taught by Chiron." He doesn't take his eyes off of me as he says, "It was Ophiuchus who learned how to bring people back from the dead."

Unease ripples through me as I begin to draw the evident parallels. *Me, a Healer. Xerin, a Shaper.* My voice grows quiet. "Why would anyone want to do such a thing?"

"For power. Eternal life. Control." The vacancy glazing his features is unsettling. "To many, it's the ultimate feat." He pauses. "Immortality, that is."

I don't like where this conversation is heading, but I'm not sure how to change the subject. My mind whirls with different possibilities—and, suffice it to say, the outcomes are bleak. Am I bound to end up like Ophiuchus? Darkness has already overpowered my healing on more than one occasion. With Delwynn, Braxton, Aldreda—and knowing that that power now lies with the *Mallum*?

Guilt coils in my stomach. *What have I done?*

I'm certain Felix can read my every thought, can sense every emotion thrashing against the shores of my relentless mind. I meet his gaze again, not wanting to pry any further, even though I'm desperate to know more. But with one look into those deep russet eyes, the tightness I'd felt in my chest disappears. A wordless exchange passes between us.

He slowly trails his fingers along the side of my arm, which, quite honestly, surprises me. I never know what I'm going to get with him. Sometimes it feels like I'm dealing with two completely different people.

Any train of thought I had dissipates as his touch moves up the side of my arm, past my shoulder, straight to my neck. A shiver of pleasure cascades down my spine, and, as much as I try to conceal it, I know he's felt it, too. His mouth rigs to the side in confirmation. I want so badly to close the distance between us, but it seems I won't have to. I can see it in his eyes. He's seconds away from destroying me, but in the best possible way.

Without even the slightest hesitation, he pulls me close, our legs intertwining. Even though we're laying on our sides, I can feel the length of him against me. His mouth grazes my neck, my blood heating even more at the familiar scent of sandalwood and myrrh. Any and all resistance I've felt up until this point falls away instantaneously.

I dip my head so that it's level with his, our lips meeting in feverish anticipation. My mouth parts and he eagerly takes the opportunity to explore. Locked tightly in his embrace, I lean against him even more, tightening my hold around his neck. A guttural groan passes between us, the urge to ravage one another growing more apparent as he cradles my lower back and slides over me.

He only pauses when I release my grip to run a hand through his hair, my fingers lightly following the curve of his neck. I can feel his skin prickle beneath my touch, his breath warm against my cheek. He lifts his head so that he's directly above me now, his eyes so dark, I would think his pupils have been swallowed whole.

All logic and reason leaves me. Suddenly, I don't care what may or may not have been said between us. I don't care what he may be hiding—what I'm certainly hiding from him. *No one* has looked at me the way he is right now—yearning, terrified . . . but certain.

No one's ever been certain of me. Not even myself.

I halt the lazy circles I've been tracing along the back of his neck as I bring my hand to his chest. His heartbeat rages beneath my palm. I study his face—every contour, every angle—desperate to capture every detail of this moment. The one I've been in denial about ever since I met him.

My grip shifts to his arms, my nails digging into the rippling muscles beneath his shirt. His fingers graze the inside of my thighs. Taunting me.

What happens next is a blur. His shirt comes off, and so does mine. He stands above me, removing his pants as I shimmy off my own, until we're both completely bare. He towers over me, his searing gaze scanning every inch of my skin.

I'm certain that the feral look in his eyes is merely a reflection of my own. With a wicked grin, I sit up and pull him to me, our bodies meshing fully for the first time. I take his hand, guiding it exactly where I want it to go, but it seems he has plans of his own. His breath shudders as he moves against me, slowly at first. I move my hips in response, urging him not to withdraw, but to go even deeper.

He does.

His hands press against my shoulders, his mouth finding mine once again. My body aches with each thrust, but only because I know this will end far too soon. With every movement, the tether that binds us grows even stronger—and with every shared breath, we entangle our fates as one. I let out a soft cry as my core tightens then releases, just as he stills.

He lingers inside me, sweat gleaming along his brow, before planting a tender kiss on my forehead, then my temple. He rolls to the side but keeps me close. Even though we're both panting, I bury myself in his chest anyway, relishing the feel of his skin on mine. We remain there, tangled together, underneath a canopy of stars in the waning night sky.

FELIX BARLOW

That night in her cabin had been one thing, but this? This is a death sentence . . . for them both.

Felix shifts his position beneath Arden ever so slightly, his chin resting atop a tangled mess of chestnut hair. She's fast asleep, her breath releasing in tiny wisps before floating into the steadily dropping temperature of the night. He wants to wake her, to take her into the warmth of either of their cabins . . . but he can't bring himself to disturb the absolute perfection of this moment.

Because who's to say how many more he'll get?

His recent conversation with Xerin pushes against the barriers of his mind, desperate to reinforce just how selfish he's being. And that might be so, but truthfully, it doesn't matter. For so many years, he'd given up on the idea that anyone could understand him—could *really* understand him. And even though they'd gotten off to a rocky start, Arden had been this shadowed spark in a world of painful absolutes. He'd recognized in her the very things he'd known, and had been forced to hide, about himself.

She stirs beneath him, curling even further into his warmth, and even though he promised her he wouldn't, amplifying is the only way they'll be able to stay up here for the remainder of the night. Otherwise, they'll be defrosting by a fireplace for a large portion of the day tomorrow, and that's something he isn't willing to risk.

He brings his gaze to their tangled limbs, letting it drift to all the places where his skin is touching hers. Heat begins to collect in every cell of his body until it rises to his chest, and only when he feels like a furnace does he allow it to disperse. His eyelids grow heavy and, as much as he wishes he could drift off, without his focused intent, the cocoon of warmth around them wouldn't last. He can feel Arden's body as it begins to uncurl, limbs loosening as the heat radiates between them. As long as he can stay awake through the coldest part of the night, he can drift off in the hours just approaching dawn without jeopardizing their health.

Felix stifles a yawn as he tilts his chin to the night sky, the stars winking against the cobalt canvas. His eyes catch the very constellations he'd shared with Arden earlier. As cryptic as the message may have been, she'd seemed to connect the illusory dots he'd drawn for her.

Let's just hope it's enough.

Arden turns away from him then, but she doesn't get far. She murmurs sleepily, pressing her backside into him. Felix smiles as he turns onto his hip and pulls her in close, admiring how seamlessly she fits into the curve of his chest and lower stomach. It seems the heat has done its job, which means he can finally get some shuteye. Not that he's complaining.

He nuzzles his face into her hair, whispering a quiet *goodnight* before sleep rushes in to take him.

RYDAN HELSTROM

RYDAN WAKES TO sunlight streaming through the windows, his eyes still heavy from the night before. He turns over to see that Vira's sound asleep next to him. With a yawn, he stretches his arms overhead, then throws on a shirt and some trousers. Barefoot, he makes his way through the kitchen, grabbing a ripe red apple before heading out the door.

He isn't surprised to see everyone in their usual meeting place, at the wooden table by the cooking fire. They'd agreed to reconvene yesterday in the later hours, but his afternoon nap had morphed into a full night of restful sleep.

Avery's the first to see him and waves him over. As if reading his mind, he says, "Don't worry. You aren't the only one, mate."

Rydan nods as he helps himself to the tray of hash Haskell's just set on the table. "I figured." His eyes travel to his left before landing on Arden. She's sitting next to Felix—rather closely, at that. A coy smile touches her lips as Felix leans in to whisper something to her, completely oblivious to his late arrival. "Morning," Rydan says brusquely, not bothering to hide the edge in his voice.

Arden's face falls as she looks down the table. "Good morning," she and Felix say simultaneously, sounding more annoyed than anything else.

Rydan decides to ignore it—and the warning glance from Felix that follows—by digging into his plate of hash. The scent of smoked salmon fills the air as Haskell joins them at the table, passing around the final tray of food. Rydan takes a heap of that, too. He can't help but notice that Felix seems to have worked up quite an appetite.

Arden as well.

"Where's Vira?" Avery asks, interrupting his thoughts. "I can't imagine she's still asleep?"

Rydan shrugs. "Seems we were all a bit tired."

At that, Felix's lips twitch upward. "Happy to see you're well rested." It seems like he wants to say more, but Rydan's view becomes blocked as Arden stands and reaches across the table. She takes her time locating the pitcher of fresh-squeezed orange juice before filling her glass.

"You prepared all of this?" she says to Haskell, clearly wanting to change the subject. "You should have woken me. I would have helped."

"It was no problem, really. As you might imagine, transporting makes cooking a hell of a lot easier." He pauses, debate warring in his eyes, then says, "Not to mention, I *did* come to wake you, but you weren't there."

Her cheeks turn crimson at the insinuation. Even so, she deftly counters with, "I couldn't sleep."

Rydan looks around the table, wondering if anyone else is picking up on this, but before he can say anything, Avery slides along the bench until he's standing at the edge of the table. "I suppose I'll go get Vira, now that we're all here—and *awake*." He adds that last part mockingly. "Anyone need anything?"

"You stay, I'll go," Rydan says, scooping the last bit of hash from his plate. "I should have woken her anyway." His plate now empty, he leaves the table in a rush, hoping to shake off the strange vibe, but it only lingers, following him all the way to the cabin.

When he arrives, Vira's already up. She doesn't so much as look at him, and that's when Rydan notices what's on the table. His leather-bound journal, flipped open to the page where he'd drawn the Soames's crest from memory.

"What is this?" she asks, her tone flat.

Rydan approaches the counter, turning the page toward him. He runs a finger over the symbol he'd drawn, following the gentle curve of the rising flames. "Just something I drew." The minute the lie leaves his lips, he wishes he could take it back.

Her mouth presses into a firm line. "Where did you see this?"

The way she's phrased the question . . . it's as if she *knows* what it is. He regards her with wide eyes, spinning the image back in her direction. "It's something I found."

"Where is it?"

"Not here."

"Where is it?" she repeats.

His curiosity piqued, he says, "As a matter of fact, I have reason to believe that your *brother* took it the last time he was here."

She remains stone-faced as she processes the information. A long silence stretches between them before she finally says, "It's the crescent fire."

"The crescent what?"

Mimicking his movements, she turns the page back to face him, although not all the way. From the side, Rydan can clearly see the shape in which he's drawn the flames. In a backwards C.

A crescent. Obviously.

"What does it mean?" he asks. "What is it?"

She hesitates. "I'll tell you what I know, but first you need to tell me *everything* that happened in that cave."

Rydan searches her face, confused. "We've already talked about it, multiple times—"

"Not what you told all of *them*," she interrupts. Her lethal gaze could snap someone in half. He's not sure he's ever seen her like this. "But what you saw when you found *this*." Her finger lands on the middle of the page.

"Okay," he agrees, blowing out a long breath through his nose. "I'll tell you everything I saw, exactly as I saw it."

She takes a seat at the table, gesturing for him to do the same. "And after this?" Her expression darkens yet again. "No more, Rydan." She gives a solemn shake of her head. "No more damn secrets."

DARIUS TYMOND

THE RUSHING WATER is even more deafening than Darius remembers. With great caution, he steps onto the floating stones that'll take him into the depths of Volkharn. He places his hand on the vine-covered wall, his ring pulsating from the contact, carefully stepping through it once it disperses.

The cavern is darker than usual—so dark that he can hardly tell the difference between the rocks and the water. The usual cerulean tint beneath him is now a deep navy—and, if it weren't for the steady ripples from the waterfalls pouring into the spring, he would have easily mistaken this place for somewhere else. The pale green glow of his staff doesn't illuminate much, only a few paces or so ahead, but it's enough for him to do what he came here to do.

As he's done many times before, he leans his staff against the cavern wall, removes his robes, making sure to pull the speculor out first, then locates his tried-and-true triangular-shaped stone. He's about to step onto it when . . . *footsteps*. He freezes in place with one foot on the stone, the other on the bank. He squints in the dim light, wishing now more than ever that tonight's lunar event would have been a full moon, but that's more than two weeks away.

After a few moments, he decides he's probably just being paranoid and steps onto the stone with both feet. As expected, the waterfalls cease. He carefully pivots back toward the shore as the stone carries him out into the water, taking one last look at every corner, every crevice of the cavern—but he doesn't see anyone or anything.

It's a swift arrival to the center of the spring. The stone stops, the jolt nearly throwing him off balance, before securing itself into place just below the water's surface. He opens both of his palms, side by side, and places the speculor right in the center. He closes his eyes as he feels the sphere-shaped object leave his skin, the amethyst in his ring pulsing once more. His eyes shoot open, the speculor hovering just above his head. He watches as it floats away from him, deeper into the cavern, moving closer and closer to the emerging black mist. He kneels, readying himself for the red cloak to appear, but just as he's about to plunge his ring into the water, a deeply disturbing hiss stops him. Alarmed, he lifts his gaze. The speculor is no longer floating, but, instead, is in between the spindly fingers of the Mallum.

"Release it," Darius orders, his chest tightening at the sight. "At once."

The Mallum tilts its cloaked head, bringing the speculor closer to its invisible face, as if observing it more closely. Darius rises, his hands fisting at his side. "I will not ask you again."

The Mallum hisses once more. *Not for you.* The words are so quiet and yet seem to bounce off every surface in the cavern.

"Release it," he says again, through gritted teeth.

The Mallum's crimson cloak flutters in a phantom breeze as its skeletal fingers wrap around the glowing sphere. It remains in place—floating, lingering—with only its head moving from side to side, as if somehow scanning the contained memories itself. And then . . .

It opens its fingers.

Darius doesn't wait another second. He plunges his ring into the water, the speculor mimicking the movement. Immediately, the Mallum fades into the background, the red cloak disintegrating, leaving only a glowing black orb in its wake.

Suddenly, Darius is pulled away from reality—away from time and space entirely—and is thrust into something so blinding, he's forced to shield his eyes. When he's finally able to open them, he's no longer in the vast cavern, but is instead surrounded by tall grass and a blazing sun. The setting is vaguely familiar. Even through his pounding headache, he's able to conclude that he's in a meadow . . .

A meadow from his memories.

BRAXTON HORNSBY

BRAXTON'S BREATH HITCHES as his surroundings fade. He looks to his left. Lane has disappeared. When he looks up again, the spring is no longer there, and neither is his father—but something strangely familiar, yet simultaneously *unfamiliar*, stands in its place. A small cottage that backs up to a meadow.

Something rustles in the distance. Not wanting to be out in the open, he darts over to the small dwelling, pressing his back against the side of the house as he peers around the front edge. His eyes follow the trail that leads to the front door before landing on two figures at the far end—one tall and one short. A woman and a child.

There's no mistaking the delicate sway of her hips as she walks, the deep-set cobalt eyes, the braid of white-blonde hair that so clearly matches his own. It doesn't take long for him to realize that the speculor is showing him a memory. *His mother's memory.*

Which means that the child walking next to her . . . is *him.*

Braxton's heart nearly leaps from his chest as the younger version of him reaches for his mother's hand, interlocking his fingers with hers. She glances down at him with a warm smile, stopping briefly to fix his hair. Once she's smoothed down one of the sides, they climb the steps to the cottage and knock on the door. Although muffled, the voice on the other side of the door sounds like a woman's, but he can't be sure. He only steps out into the open once he hears the door shut. There's an open window nearby that he rushes over to, crouching just underneath the overhang. When he realizes he can't hear much, he rises just high enough to see past the ledge.

His mother is talking to another woman as his child-self sits on the rug with another young boy. The back of his shaggy russet head catches in the afternoon light. Although he can't see the other boy's face, he senses that they're roughly the same age and, from the way they're playing, have known each other since birth. Braxton shifts his attention back to his child-self as a squeaky voice roars, then lifts a small toy to make it fly.

It's a gold dragon figurine.

The same one Braxton had found in his room.

A lump forms in his throat as he watches the two boys play, breaking into fits of laughter every few seconds or so. He only averts his gaze when he sees his mother move to follow the other woman into the kitchen. He inches to the far right of the ledge, not wanting to miss a thing. From this angle, he has a clear view of them both. The first thing his eyes land on is the woman's protruding stomach—but the higher up he goes, the more certain he is he's seeing double. The shoulder-length wavy chestnut hair. The piercing emerald eyes.

As if to confirm his thoughts, Aldreda reaches out and lays a hand on the woman's stomach. "It won't be much longer now, my sweet niece," she coos.

The woman smiles. "We'll finally have a girl in the family."

Aldreda nods, her eyes brimming with anticipation. "Tell me, sister, have you decided on a name?"

Braxton knows exactly what she's about to say. He watches as the woman beams from the inside out. "Her name is Arden . . ."

Without warning, the image before him fades from view. Suddenly, he's left the cottage behind and is now standing on the outskirts of the Roviel Woods. He glances left, then right, before taking in the castle before him. He's in Trendalath now, there's no doubt about that—but based on the sparseness of the forest alone, he can tell it isn't present day . . . that he's still in the past.

Feeling completely and utterly exposed, he ducks into the woods, running along its edge until he spots something unusual. He crouches behind a giant oak tree, then peers around the trunk. The flaps of a brown tent sway in the breeze, muffled voices coming from inside.

He remains in a crouched position for so long that it feels like his knees are on fire until, finally, two cloaked figures emerge from the tent. Equipped with a bow and quiver, they speak to one another in harsh undertones. It's near impossible to hear what they're saying, but if Braxton moves any closer, they'll surely see him. He stays put, waiting for some clue as to who these two people are.

His discovery is cut short when he's unwillingly pulled from the memory and plopped back into the present, back at the spring. From his left, Lane grips his arm, her chest heaving. They remain as quiet as they can, realizing that Darius has snatched the speculor from the water. He curses loudly, his voice echoing in the massive cavern.

"Did you see any of that?" Braxton whispers.

Lane's eyes are so wide, he can see the white around them. She just nods.

"I'll explain everything," he says, glancing over his shoulder, then back at Darius. "But first, we need to get the hell out of here."

CERYLIA JARETH

CERYLIA BURSTS INTO the White Room with Estelle just steps behind her. She surveys the vast emptiness until her eyes settle on the only other person in the room.

Delwynn.

He's standing at the tea cart with a sachet of herbs in one hand, a jar of honey in the other. Startled, he glances up from the porcelain set of dishes. He frees his hands the moment he sees the queen, then bends into a low bow. "Your Greatness"—he looks behind her then, his expression shifting to one of shock—"and Lady Chatham. You seem well," he says, fumbling over his words. "This is quite a surprise, but a welcome one at that. I thought you would be resting."

Estelle gives him a polite nod. "Your tinctures have worked wonders," she says with a wink. "I haven't felt this good in years."

"I'm happy to hear it." He looks from her to the queen. "May I be of assistance, Your Greatness?"

"Opal," Cerylia says, her tone flat. "Where is she?"

"Last I saw her, she was walking the gardens."

Cerylia goes to the window and, sure enough, Opal's sitting on a bench, her silver hair gleaming in what little moonlight remains.

"Follow me," she instructs both her advisor and Estelle.

"Should I bring the—?"

"Leave the tea," Cerylia says, answering his question before he can finish asking it.

Even with the gravel crunching loudly beneath their feet, Opal doesn't so much as turn in their direction. Her gaze remains fixed on the far end of the courtyard, as if lost somehow, in a faraway trance.

Cerylia's about to shout the girl's name when she feels a gentle hand on her shoulder. Estelle brushes by the queen with a reassuring look—a look that says she has this handled—then kneels in front of her fellow Caldari.

Cerylia stops walking, extending her arm to block the path so that Delwynn knows to do the same. His chest nearly collides with her arm, but he catches himself just in time. Cerylia leans in slightly, listening closely to their conversation.

"I couldn't see him," Opal says, her voice barely audible. From the sound alone, it seems she's been crying. "I've tried everything imaginable, but the casting is just too strong."

Estelle leans forward so that she's nearly eye level with Opal, her hands pressed firmly on her knees. "I don't blame you," she says gently, her tone reminiscent of a cooing dove. "It's not like you could have seen him coming anyway."

Opal averts her gaze then. Her lips part as if she wants to counter, but she remains quiet. From the side, she could be the poster child for sheer suffering—the wind dancing through her hair, framing her almost too-perfect mask of torment. The sight alone is nearly enough for Cerylia to want to shake some sense into the girl, but she remains where she is, a silent observer.

"He took something very valuable to me," Estelle goes on. "Something I need to get back. I know finding him is proving difficult, but can you give some direction as to where he might be?"

Opal only sighs. "Like I said, I've tried. I can't seem to get through, *especially* not now." She tilts her head, her eyes suddenly brimming with curiosity. "What did he take?"

Estelle shoots a sidelong glance at Cerylia, who's now moving a few steps closer, but remains crouched on the gravel as she answers, "My pocket watch."

A flicker of hope darts across Opal's eyes. "I may not have anything to worry about then. Perhaps I've been overreacting."

"How so?"

"I've been worried that my abilities may be growing weaker the more I use them." She shakes her head sadly. "Time may be a construct of the mind, but it's a ruthless master, nonetheless. Merciless to all who abide by it, especially those who dare to manipulate it."

"Perhaps you should get some rest. Come," Estelle says, as she rises to her feet. "Delwynn's made tea in the White Room."

"Tea does sound exceptionally lovely . . ."

At first, Cerylia doesn't know why, but Estelle shoots her another glance, this one full of warning—but once Opal stands and turns to head inside the castle, her reasoning is clear as day. No longer does a young, spritely girl stand before her, but a tired, old crone with wrinkled skin. Speechless, the queen steps aside, watching as Delwynn and Estelle assist a nearly unrecognizable Opal inside the castle.

RYDAN HELSTROM

VIRA GLANCES OUT the window of their cabin, brows furrowed. "We'd better hurry. They're looking more restless than usual."

"You're telling me," Rydan says, thankful for the noticeable change in her tone. "They all seem to be in on some sort of inside joke, something I don't care to know about." He recalls the way Felix had looked at him, the hint of victory that had lined his smile. He pushes the thought away, choosing instead to focus on the sketch in front of him.

Vira joins him at the table, eyeing the page. "I was so young when I first heard of the crescent fire. Avery's father used to tell us stories about it when I lived in Chialka. Not exactly a bedtime story, if you ask me."

The pained look on her face is enough to make him reach across the table and place his hand on hers.

She gives him a small smile, but it doesn't reach her eyes. "Centuries ago, families with Draconian heritage were given special crests by the Council, one of many illusié-established authorities. Forged from the finest metals known to Aeridon, and fire-breathings of the dragons themselves, each crest contains the unique ability to wield a crescent fire, so long as the one wielding it is of said Draconian bloodline."

While it's a brief explanation, it's loaded with information. It takes him a moment to process it. Finally, he asks, "So, what does the crescent fire *do*?"

"It's the only thing known to destroy illusié-made creations." She leans forward, lowering her voice as she says, "The Council's goal was to maintain balance in the magickal realm, but, as with all governing structures, sometimes the most obvious solution isn't the best one."

He glances at the sketch on the page. "So, theoretically speaking, could the crescent fire destroy the Mallum?"

The question seems to catch her by surprise. "I suppose it *could*. It's certainly possible. But who's to say the Mallum was made, or even conjured, by illusié?" She shudders. "If you ask me, it seems like the Mallum is something else *entirely*—something from another realm."

That crest had belonged to the Soames. Rydan had confirmed as much when he'd revisited their home after finding it. His mind travels back to the joint mission he'd shared with Arden, the one where he'd killed Radelle and

Erle Soames. Darius had been so adamant about it being a dual mission—had wanted proof of the assassination—that he can't help but wonder if what the king had *really* been after all along . . . was the crescent fire.

"I haven't even gotten to the most intriguing part."

Rydan lifts his eyes from the page, the intensity of her gaze matching his own. "And what would that be?"

"Those with Draconian blood running through their veins are few and far between, but the majority of them happen to be . . . Ignitors."

He sucks in a sharp breath before asking, "Avery?"

She shakes her head. "Believe me, I would know. It's all Avery used to talk about when we were growing up. His family never received a crest from the Council." Her eyes grow wide with excitement. "But what about you, Rydan? What about *your* family?"

His mind flits to what little information he has. He shrugs, suddenly feeling reluctant to even entertain the thought and what that might mean for him . . . and his family history. Much like Arden, his family growing up had been the Cruex and King Tymond—but with the way Vira's currently looking at him, he'll say anything to keep the spark in her eyes from fading. "It may take some digging," he says, forcing his most sincere smile, "but with the way things have been going as of late, you might just be onto something here."

ARDEN ELIRI

I'M STARING AT the closed door to Rydan and Vira's cabin when Felix grabs my hand and pulls me away from the table. Avery's so concentrated on his meal that he doesn't seem to notice, but Haskell, whose plate is completely clean, does. There's a mischievous gleam in his eye as he says, "Don't stray too far, you two."

A warmth rushes up my cheeks, but I turn my head before he can see it. Seemingly unbothered by my brother's insinuation, Felix gives a small wave, tugging me along toward one of the winding dirt trails. I follow him without saying anything, although I am a bit curious as to where we're headed. We stay on the edge of the woods, not far enough out to completely lose sight of the others, but just out of view from their vantage point.

A blur to us, a blur to them.

When we reach a spot that he deems appropriate, Felix turns toward me. He takes both of my hands in his until our fingers are interlacing. He leans in to brush a gentle kiss to my cheek, his lips softly grazing my jaw until they reach my mouth. The gesture wholly consumes me, just as it had the night before. I remember the way his skin had felt on mine. The way we'd moved together with such synchronicity, such ease. When he pulls away, it's much too soon and, even though the thought crosses my mind to take a fistful of his hair to bring him back toward me, I manage to fight the urge.

He guides me to a nearby willow tree before sliding his back against the trunk. He motions for me to sit in the space between his legs, and I can't help but give him a coy smile, happily obliging him. His arms wrap around me then, and the weight of his embrace around my shoulders is more than welcome. With his chin atop my head, I can feel his gaze roving my body, his fingers tracing lazy circles in the small space just above my navel. I take a deep breath in, then sigh deeply before closing my eyes. I allow my head to roll to the side, relishing the feeling of being held like this for what feels like the first time in my life.

"Glad to see last night wasn't just a figment of my imagination." His voice is low as he teasingly nips at the back of my ear. "Seems like some of the group is onto us, though. Especially your brother."

I stifle a yawn, hoping that he'll keep talking. I don't know what it is about the sound of his voice, but I could listen to him for hours on end. I can't remember if it's always been like this, or if I'm just overtly aware after our unexpected . . . *well, you know.*

When I don't respond, he gently shakes me. "Don't go falling asleep on me, now."

"I'm right here," I whisper absentmindedly. And I am. There's nowhere else I'd rather be.

"As fun as last night was, have you given any more thought to Midvale?"

The way he says it is so casual, as if it's been a part of our everyday conversation for months, even though it hasn't. I roll to the side, momentarily breaking our embrace until I'm facing him, my arms folded across his stomach. Given the angle he's leaning against the tree, I'm more than pleased with the view—with each slight shift, his muscles ripple beneath his tunic. I divert my gaze, not that his face is any less enticing. Perhaps I shouldn't have turned around at all . . .

"Are you going to answer my question, or are you just going to sit there and ogle me all day?" He raises a brow in jest.

I inch my way up to his chest so that I'm nearly laying on top of him. I set my chin against the back of my folded hands, trying to remember his original question. *Oh, right. Midvale.* "Seeing as I've been a bit preoccupied, I haven't given it much thought."

He studies me before gingerly brushing a wavy tendril from my face. "Rydan seemed to do most of the talking."

I knew that, at some point, my fellow ex-Cruex was bound to come up, but lords, how I was enjoying this moment between us. I try to hide my annoyance as I say, "From what I recall, he covered everything pretty thoroughly—not much to add when everything's already been said."

Felix seems to read the emotion in my eyes. "I'm sure he missed something. Something only you could catch."

His words strike a chord in my mind. I lift myself up just enough to reach into the pocket of my trousers. He watches me closely as I bring my arm back around, the tarnished watch dangling from my fingers.

Recognition flashes in his eyes. "You had *that* with you?" When I don't object, he begins to sit upright, his spine stiffening, shoulders tense. I shimmy my way back down so that I'm sitting on my knees, my posterior flush against my calves. He takes the watch in his hands, turning it over a few times before clicking it open. "We need to find Estelle. Immediately."

I search my memories for a reason why, daring to go back as far as our first chance encounter in Lonia, in the Thering Forest—when Estelle had shown me *her* pocket watch. I regard Felix with burning curiosity. "What does it mean?"

"That somehow, without even realizing it," he says, lifting the watch just high enough for it to catch the light, "you were able to enter the Veil."

DARIUS TYMOND

DARIUS ISN'T THE least bit surprised that one of the memories Aldreda had concealed in the speculor was that of her sister, before everything had been turned upside down. For years, Aldreda had wanted their son to know the truth, but Darius had refused, relaying his multitude of excuses—the boy wasn't old enough, the boy wasn't ready—perhaps it'd been *he* who hadn't been ready. But when Braxton had fled, it'd only magnified the already colossal divide between them.

Surely she'd left this speculor in the hopes that her son would one day find it. Even in death, it would seem she's still fighting for the upper hand. But until Darius can regain control of his kingdom, of Aeridon as a whole, no such knowledge can be revealed.

He'd intentionally pulled the speculor from the spring early, not caring to relive her affair with now ex-Savant Clive Ridley, even if they *had* killed Dane in the memory. It only serves as an aching reminder of the many transgressions that would follow.

It's early enough in the morning where he manages to slip into the Daegrum Chambers undetected, speculor in hand. On his way back from Volkharn, he'd considered numerous places to hide it where Braxton would never find it. He'd finally settled on the Daegrum Chambers, since only the Savant have access to it—and, seeing as the only member of the Savant he'd ever worried about is no longer strolling the grounds, there's no foreseeable threat.

Darius digs through drawer upon drawer in the rear of the chamber until he finds a small lockbox, maybe the size of his hand, tucked in the very back of one of the cupboards. He opens it to make sure it's empty before nestling the speculor neatly in its plush, velvet-lined interior, the miniature sphere gleaming against the burgundy fabric. Gently, he closes the lid, making sure to secure the antique lockbox with its brass-plated skeleton key. He considers hiding it in his own chambers but, seeing as where he'd found it is indeed the most inconspicuous place in the entire castle, he decides to leave it there. Try as his son might, Braxton's search for answers will *not* be fruitful—not if Darius has anything to do with it.

BRAXTON HORNSBY

BRAXTON CAN FEEL Lane watching him from the boulder she's perched on at the edge of the Vaekith Mountains as he paces back and forth. They'd fled Volkharn in a hurry, mostly out of shock and confusion at what they'd witnessed, as well as from growing concern that Darius would eventually spot them. They'd raced past the parked carriage, nearly spooking the horse, knowing it was too risky to hitch a ride both to *and* from Volkharn.

Although completely unintentional, he'd hardly spoken a word to Lane as they'd delved deeper into the Roviel Woods. She'd rightfully pointed out that they were heading in the wrong direction—*away* from Trendalath—but given what he's just found out? That Arden is his cousin? That she has a brother? That their mothers are *sisters*? Well, *were* sisters, seeing as his mother is no longer living—it's a *hell of a lot* to process.

When he feels like he's finally got his wits about him, he looks up to start talking to Lane, but she's no longer sitting on the boulder. *Had he really been caught up in his thoughts for that long?* Confused, he turns in a circle, scanning the perimeter until he spots her off in the distance. She seems to sense that he's looking for her because she raises a hand high in the air, giving him a wave to head over. Probably smart, seeing as they're basically sitting ducks, *way* more out in the open, at the base of the mountain.

Braxton trudges through the forest, stepping as quietly as he can over twigs and fallen branches. Silver-haired bats, having just emerged from their winter hibernation, fly overhead in search of their next meal. When Lane finally comes into full view, he realizes that she's doing something similar—foraging for food. He's been so wrapped up in trying to figure this all out, he can't remember the last time they'd eaten.

Her hands are cupped when she approaches, and he realizes that they're full of hazelnuts and what appear to be walnuts. She gives him one of the handfuls before creating a funnel-like shape with her hand and emptying them into her mouth. "Thanks," he says, following suit.

"Don't thank me yet," she says as she brushes the remnants from her palms. "We don't have anything to wash it down with. If we can't find a freshwater spring, we may have to settle for berries. Minimal juice, but at least it's something."

He trails along behind her as they venture deeper into the woods, watching in admiration as she examines various plants. With a shake of her head, she turns away from a number of them until finally settling on one that's dotted in velvet-blue. She plucks a berry from the bush and pops it into her mouth, her face scrunching almost immediately.

"Blueberry?" Braxton asks. "Is it not ripe?"

She shakes her head. "These are huckleberries. And yes, they're ripe, just much tarter than blueberries."

Braxton tries a few, making the exact same face she had just moments ago.

"Told you," she says with a small laugh. Her light-hearted expression suddenly shifts into something much heavier. "Should we talk about what happened back there?"

Braxton pops another berry into his mouth, hoping the tartness will serve as a distraction—but it does little to prolong this inevitable conversation. "I just learned that I'm related to someone who I originally *thought* killed my mother." The moment the words leave his mouth, he realizes just how preposterous the whole thing sounds. He chews on the inside of his lip. "Of all the things I expected my mother and father to hide from me, *that* certainly didn't make the list."

She only watches him, eyes shadowed.

"I don't know what to make of it. I don't know what the right move is. I don't know where to go . . ."

"Back to Trendalath." Her response is decisive, unwavering. "If we don't go back and Darius realizes you're missing—that we're *both* missing—especially after what we pulled at the Cruex dinner . . ." She doesn't have to finish her thought. Braxton gets it.

"I have to find Arden. We need to talk about this, what this means—"

"What *does* it mean?"

A remarkable question. He's only just found this out for himself. Can he really expect Arden to react any differently? What will she do once she finds out she shares blood with the Tymonds—with *him*? The thought in and of itself is enough to make his stomach turn.

"One way or another, we'll find Arden," Lane says, although not as reassuringly as he'd hoped. "But for now, we need to get back." She meets his steady gaze. "Deal?"

He merely nods his head, suddenly wishing that they weren't so far out, in the middle of nowhere. What he wouldn't give for the comforts of his room, the hearth, his bed . . .

Missing Trendalath?

Now *that's* irony if he's ever heard it.

CERYLIA JARETH

Cerylia gazes skyward at the conservatory's glass dome ceiling, the only room in Sardoria castle not entirely composed of marble. The stars glint overhead, winking in the cobalt sky. The sheer number casts a blanket of twinkling lights over the vines that snake up the walls, highlighting their already vibrant shades of green—jade, emerald, sage, viridian—it's as if her surroundings have sprung to life, preferring night over day.

The knob to the vintage ivory door turns to the left. Cerylia patiently waits as Estelle appears. The queen gives her a small nod, but remains in place at the end of the slate-covered walkway. Estelle's boots clink softly with each drop of her foot until she's no more than a few steps away. Even though she bends into a half bow,

Cerylia can tell that her mind is elsewhere—given the furrowed brow and faraway look in her eyes.

"How is she?" Cerylia asks. The paradox of the question is not lost on her. Mere days ago, she was asking Opal the exact same question about Estelle.

But Estelle doesn't seem keen on answering it. "I wasn't aware the castle had a conservatory. It's, well . . . stunning."

Cerylia follows her gaze. "Admittedly, I don't come here as often as I should."

"If I had known this place existed, I would have been here every day with a book and a cup of tea." Her mouth rigs to the side. "At least I know now."

"Perhaps Opal would enjoy the scenery," Cerylia says gently, not wanting to pry but hoping for some answers. "After all, they say that nature is the greatest healer."

"Perhaps," Estelle says. Darkness shrouds her face. "Or perhaps Opal's condition has nothing to do with the world and its natural effects, and everything to do with illusié and magick."

Now they're getting somewhere.

Estelle hangs her head as she steps off the pathway, the golden strands in her midnight hair luminescent in the starlight. "I've only ever seen a condition like Opal's once before." She shudders at a memory she refuses to speak aloud. "With the way she's progressing, and the steady pace at which it's going, I can only come to one conclusion." She stops then, her fingers grazing a curtain of hanging moss.

Cerylia doesn't respond, hoping she'll say more—but Estelle just stands there, brushing the moss back and forth with her hand. "If you would be so kind to indulge me . . ."

Estelle raises her head. "It seems Opal has been accessing veiled memories." Her throat bobs. "And given her current state, it seems she's been doing it for quite some time."

Cerylia knows much of the Veil—how spectacular a creation it is, but not without its perils. Much like Orihia, it's a place where only illusié can travel, but not just *any* illusié. The Keepers, a group of illusié responsible for preserving any and all magickal archives, had worked tirelessly with other mages, such as the Cloakers, to create a place that only *they* could access—a place where they would have absolute control over who entered. Few and far between, enchanted pocket watches became the point of entry. Estelle had had one of those pocket watches—until it'd been stolen by the Caster—but, fortunately, hers isn't the only one.

Arden has one, too. As does Haskell.

Which is exactly why Cerylia had asked Opal to track them down. But Opal has grown weaker. So have her abilities. She's been accessing veiled memories, but why?

A chill snakes down her spine as she recalls the discreet meetings she'd stumbled upon just outside the castle walls between Opal and Xerin—and what of his sudden, and frequent, disappearances? Is it possible that he's been attempting to access the Veil? Had it been he, not the Caster, who had stolen Estelle's watch? Could they be working together? And, in using Opal's abilities, exactly what memories might they be trying to access?

If only she could extract the memories from the speculor she'd found on the tea cart, she's certain many of these questions would be answered. If Opal is bound to Xerin in some way, if she owes him some sort of debt— which seems to be the case, given her unwillingness to disclose *anything* regarding their unusual partnership— it's unlikely Cerylia will get the answers she seeks. As fed up as she is with Opal's antics, she can't just leave the girl to wither away and die . . .

Not in her castle. Not while she is queen.

"You know what this means," Cerylia says softly. "What we have to do. Where we have to go."

Estelle meets the queen's determined gaze. "It's where I've been trying to take us this whole time—so that we might have a fighting chance to reinstate your extracting abilities, as well as heal Opal."

The word feels foreign, yet oddly familiar, as it forms on Cerylia's lips. Estelle gives her a firm nod as they say what the other is thinking. "Midvale."

ARDEN ELIRI

NOT EVERYONE SEEMS to be onboard with Felix's theory about this so-called "Veil" and my pocket watch. Seeing as the majority of the Caldari here are newer to the group, no one's had any experience with either. I know if Estelle were here, she'd back Felix up in a heartbeat. Vira and Avery are convinced that the whole thing is just legend; Rydan appears to be preoccupied with something else entirely; but thankfully, Haskell seems intrigued enough by the idea to at least entertain Felix's point of view.

"I'm telling you, Estelle knows how to use one of these," he says, my pocket watch swaying from his finger.

"Haskell has one, too," I chime in. I raise my brows, hoping he'll get the hint.

Haskell grunts, but instead of reaching into his pocket like I expect, he exchanges a glance with Rydan.

"Oh. Right," Rydan mutters before producing my brother's pocket watch and tossing it to Felix.

The interaction causes several questions to circle my mind, but before I can ask how and, more importantly, *why* Rydan's had his watch this whole time, Felix makes an uncanny sound that draws all eyes to him.

"Fascinating," he whispers, holding them up, side by side. "Did yours used to look like this?"

The question is directed at me. I slowly move my gaze from Rydan to the two pieces of metal dangling from Felix's hands. I nod, knowing exactly what he's going to ask next.

"What happened?"

The only thing I'm compelled to say is, "I wish I knew." On the left is Haskell's watch, in near mint condition—shiny, smooth, hardly any surface scratches. And then, on the right, there's mine—gold turning silver, yet also rusting, with a nondescript image that certainly wasn't there before. The only thing they have in common is the name inscribed on the back plate.

Eliri.

Felix shoots me a sidelong glance before handing my watch back to me and Haskell's back to him.

"When you last left Sardoria, Estelle was there?" Felix nods in response to my question. "Then that's where we need to go."

"It'll take days," Felix replies, although the way his brows furrow tells me he's ruminating over more than just the length of the trip. "And with the Mallum and Darius and the Savant looking for you . . . well, you're lucky we got you out of that tavern before they did."

The moment he mentions the tavern, everything clicks into place—not just for me, but for Haskell and Felix, too. I can see it on their faces.

"I can transport as soon as right now," Haskell says with a determined nod. "Just say the word."

At this, Vira and Avery finally leave their post around the fire and join in on the conversation.

"Someone should go with you," Rydan says as he shoves his hands in his pockets. "We can't risk traveling alone—any of us." The corners of his mouth tug upward as he glances at Vira. "If Vira hadn't trailed me that night in Sardoria, I'm not sure what would have happened."

I notice my chest tighten at the sentiment, feeling a twinge of betrayal. *I'd* been the one who'd discovered Rydan's igniting abilities right alongside him that night in Sardoria—but I hadn't followed him. He'd fled, and it was Vira who had gone with him. I push the thought from my mind, inching closer to Felix. From underneath his cloak, his hand grazes mine, the warmth filling me from the inside.

"I'll go." It must be the surprise on all our faces that has Avery changing his mind shortly thereafter. "Or maybe I should just wait until the next trip . . ."

There's an obvious choice here. Rydan and Vira fled, as did I. Avery's never met Queen Jareth or Estelle. So that leaves Felix.

He gives my hand a light squeeze before breaking our grip. He nods at Haskell before walking over to him, then takes his place at his side. My brother grips Felix's upper arm. "We'll be back before you know it."

My expression must be riddled with anxiety because Felix shoots me a reassuring smile. "Promise," he says.

I can hardly watch as the two people I care for most disappear in a flash of green light.

RYDAN HELSTROM

RYDAN CAN SEE the worry in Arden's eyes the moment her brother and Felix vanish from sight. Now probably isn't the best time to tell her what he's recently learned about the Soames crest and the crescent fire, thanks to Vira—but on second thought, maybe it is. She might appreciate the distraction, at least until Haskell and Felix return.

He turns to his left to talk to Vira, quickly realizing that she's no longer standing next to him, but is walking toward Arden. As discreetly as he can, he observes their conversation from afar when a slap on his shoulder startles him.

"You look like you could use a drink," Avery says, holding up a sloshing bottle of ale with his free hand.

Rydan shakes his head, his gaze still fixed on the two women in front of him. "No thanks," he says, shrugging Avery's hand from his shoulder.

"Suit yourself."

Avery's footsteps trail off as he wanders back toward the fire, leaving Rydan alone with his thoughts. Not wanting to appear nosy, but also wanting to keep an eye on whatever might unfold, he makes for a nearby willow tree and slides down the trunk. He pulls his legs in toward his chest before propping his elbows on his knees. With his hands folded, he continues to watch Arden and Vira, thankful for the hanging leaves that mostly conceal him.

More likely than not, Vira's telling Arden everything she's told him—about the Council, about the crest, about the crescent fire—which is probably for the best, seeing as Rydan would no doubt butcher the retelling anyway. A warmth rises in his chest, crawling all the way up his neck to the whole of his face. The sweat beading along his hairline is distraction enough for him to break his gaze, although only momentarily. He looks down at his hands. There's no mistaking the reddish-orange tint traveling through his fingertips. He steals a glance at Avery, recalling what his friend had said during their first igniting lesson. *Summon heated emotion and you're bound to ignite.*

His mind reels back to his joint mission with Arden in Lonia—the day he'd assassinated the Soames family. The sparks that had shot from Radelle's fingertips—she'd been an Ignitor, too. Regardless of whether they were sparks, shocks, or flames, he'd murdered one of his own. Darius had marked them as heretics, had announced Arden's name for that first mission—a mission she could have easily handled on her own. But Darius had assigned him as her partner at the last moment. *Why?*

Before he can stew over the past any longer, both of his hands burst into flames, catching him completely by surprise. The fire is bright enough to garner Avery's attention, who's now whooping loudly from the other side of the grounds. It'll be mere seconds before it grabs the attention of Vira and Arden as well.

Not wanting to set the tree ablaze like he's accidentally done in the past, Rydan carefully extends his arms in front of him before ducking underneath the willow branches. He makes it out into the clearing, both he and the tree unscathed. Avery's still cheering from afar, but Rydan's focus isn't on him—it's on the changing colors of the flames burning at his fingertips.

What was once orange transforms into a deep mauve bordering on plum. The heat becomes so intense, he questions whether he might pass out, but the sight is so glorious, he can't look away. The fire within him rages so intensely that all logic points to the fact that he *should* be dead right now. No human being can withstand this kind of heat—unless, of course, you have the privilege of being illusié.

Rydan raises his arms in the air so that the flames extend skyward. A miraculous show of reds, oranges, blues, and purples rise higher and higher before cascading in a shower of fading sparks. He intentionally drops his arms to his sides, closing his hands into tight fists. The fire goes out, but the burning sensation lingers.

When he looks up, it's Arden he looks at.

The grin on her face is priceless.

227

DARIUS TYMOND

DARIUS IS JUST securing the door to the Daegrum Chambers when the sensation of cold metal touches the back of his neck. His skin prickles as he slowly releases the handle of the door, raising his arms at his sides in surrender. At first, he imagines it's Clive, returning once more to torture him with another vile illusion—but the nervous breathing behind him indicates otherwise.

"Drop your weapon and face me like a man," Darius says through gritted teeth.

"You're no more a man than I am. Not after what I've seen." Although the Cruex's voice shakes, it's familiar.

"Sir Darby," Darius says, feeling less threatened. He lowers his arms. "What is the meaning of this? You're aware that this sort of behavior will have you locked in the dungeons pending an order for execution?"

While the Cruex's voice may continue to tremble, the blade resting against his neck most certainly does not. "You killed my cousin. You *murdered* Elias."

Darius scoffs, briefly wondering how Hugh happened to come across this information . . . and then it dawns on him. Clive had witnessed everything that day in the Daegrum Chambers with Arden. Had seen Darius snap the kid's neck with no remorse. "Murder is no more a crime than freeing another murderer." When Hugh doesn't respond, he says, "You freed Sir Ridley, which is yet another punishable offense. Quite a tally you're racking up here."

It's then that the blade that's been pressing further into his neck softens. Darius doesn't waste a single second. He whirls around, immediately grabbing Hugh by the throat with his right hand, the other securing the Cruex's left wrist. Darius squeezes so tight that the knife clatters to the ground.

"Pity. I had such high hopes for you. The progress you've shown in your training has not gone unnoticed." He shakes his head mockingly as his hand tightens, the Cruex's eyes bulging amongst a canvas of blue. "But what you *think* you know could pose a greater threat than you might realize. Do you know what I do with those who seek to threaten my reign?"

"Please," Hugh manages to gasp. "I'm not the only one who knows."

At this, Darius loosens his grip. "Tell me."

Hugh takes a few giant gulps of air. "I wasn't alone in the dungeons. He was with me—we did it together, freed your prisoner together." The words are barely audible as they weave in and out of short stints of breath. "I'll tell you, but you have to let me go. I'll leave here. I won't tell a soul. It'll be like I never existed."

A flare of impatience seizes him. "Do not make me ask again. *Who* was with you?"

"Braxton," Hugh says. "Your son."

Darius can't help but resume his ever-tightening grip on the boy's throat, using both hands this time. "You dragged my son into this? Into *treason*?" he bellows as Hugh gasps even more than before. "You don't deserve to waste away in the dungeons. You deserve a fate far, *far* worse."

He lifts the Cruex higher into the air until his feet are just grazing the surface below. Hugh's body begins to tremor at the lack of air as his eyes roll into the back of his head.

"Although his death was swift, I will kill you just as I killed your cousin." A sickening crack follows a sharp turn of his wrists and, just like that, Hugh's body falls to the ground in a lifeless heap of limbs.

Darius wipes his hands against his robes before straightening the crooked ring on his index finger. He smirks at the violet glow that emanates from the stone.

Just like his cousin's, Hugh's soul will be put to good use—and for a purpose far greater than any he could have ever hoped for.

BRAXTON HORNSBY

BRAXTON JOLTS AWAKE, nearly stabbing himself in the eye with a low-hanging tree branch. He swipes it to the side before pushing himself off the base of the tree, surveying his surroundings as he tries to get a grip on exactly where he is. To his right, the Vaekith Mountains. To his left, a vast expanse of seemingly never-ending trees. Ahead, even more trees.

Right, the Roviel Woods.

He glances behind him, realizing that Lane isn't where he last left her. In fact, she's nowhere in sight. Rubbing the sleep from his eyes, he tries to recall the moments just before he'd drifted off. Lane had been right next to him, using every tool in her arsenal to convince him that they needed to head back to Trendalath as soon as possible.

Of course, her logic is sound—but they'd agreed to stay the rest of the night in the woods. Given the Mallum and the potential of the recently freed, lurking Savant, they figured it'd be safer to wait until dawn to travel back.

"Daylight's here but, for some reason, you're not," Braxton mutters to himself as he stomps his way through the thick brush. He searches the perimeter for what feels like hours, and, by his eighth go-around, he's starting to wonder if perhaps she'd changed her mind and left for the castle without him.

An unwelcome memory of Xerin abandoning him in the woods flits across his mind, but he quickly shoves it away. Downtrodden, he walks back to where he'd started. He's about to resume his post at the trunk when something glimmers out of the corner of his eye. He pushes the branches aside to see . . . Lane—or the back of her head, anyway.

Confused, Braxton spins around in a circle, retracing his steps as he walks over to her. Even with her back to him, he can clearly see that she's fidgeting with her pockets. Not wanting to startle her, he clears his throat before saying, "Have you been here this whole time?"

Seems his attempt not to startle her has failed because she whips her head toward him, her hand flying from her pocket to her chest. "Lords, Braxton. You frightened me."

"Where were you?"

She studies him, perplexed. "What do you mean? I've been right here."

Braxton gives an adamant shake of his head. "I looked—right here, where you're standing. We fell asleep underneath that tree." He points to it for emphasis. "We said we'd leave before sunrise." He points to the sky, again for emphasis. "When I awoke, you weren't here. Believe me, I looked. I've *been* looking."

She must sense how shaken up he is because she moves in close enough to place her hands atop his shoulders. She looks him right in the eyes as she says, "I must have trailed off without realizing it. I'm sorry."

Braxton takes a step back, eyeing the pocket she'd been fidgeting with earlier. "Trailed off to *where*?"

Her hands drop to her sides, her mouth pressing into a firm line at his tone. "You ask a lot of questions, you know that?"

He crosses his arms over his chest. "Tell me what's going on."

She hesitates before releasing a long sigh. "Fine. I've been accessing the Veil—or at least trying to, anyway. I've only ever traveled alone, so I wanted to make sure I had it down pat before attempting it with the both of us."

"You think there's something in the Veil that can help us with the speculor?" There's no fumbling over any of the words, and he's pleasantly surprised at how smooth the question rolls off his tongue.

"I think there are a lot of things in the Veil that can help us with a lot of different things. But yes, that's certainly one of them."

"Well, have you got it sorted out?"

She glances down at the watch, running her thumb over the raised front. "I think so. But entering the Veil won't do us any good if we don't have the speculor in our possession."

"Do you think he took it back with him?"

"I doubt he'd leave it behind," Lane says. "If he was desperate enough to steal it from your room, I'm sure he'll have it near him, or on him, at all times."

"If I know my father, he's probably tucked it away, hidden it somewhere. He loves hiding things—both literally and figuratively."

To his surprise, Lane laughs, causing any lingering tension between them to dissipate. "Well then, it seems we have a lot of searching to do." She looks past his shoulder at the forest beyond before adding, "And a whole lot of walking."

❧ ❧ ❧

About halfway into their journey on foot, they're fortunate enough to come across some wild horses, making the second half of the trip whiz by in comparison, as if they hadn't just been trekking for miles upon miles with no end in sight.

Lane's affinity for animals really shines through once they near the edge of the Roviel Woods when the horses slow on her command before halting completely. Braxton follows her lead and dismounts without taking his eyes off the castle. Although they'd left at dawn, the cloudy spring day hasn't done much in the way of sunlight. A dark storm cloud hangs overhead and rolling thunder sounds from nearby.

Braxton breaks his gaze from the kingdom ahead, relishing the feel of raindrops splattering against his face. It's a light drizzle, but if that patch of clouds gets any closer, they're going to be in for a very damp morning—not exactly ideal when you're trying to sneak back inside, unnoticed.

There's the soft padding of hooves against the dirt as the horses trot off, free to roam wherever they so please. Braxton feels a brief stab of envy but shakes it off as he follows Lane to the edge of the woods.

They're just passing the final row of trees when she suddenly sticks her arm out to keep Braxton from going any farther. She grabs the sleeve of his tunic and pulls him behind the nearest trunk. He's about to ask what's going on when she brings a finger to her mouth, eyes wide. He tries to communicate with her, but she just shakes her head before squeezing her eyes completely shut—as if she's just seen something dreadful.

Braxton wriggles free from her grip and, with a deep breath, leans to the left until he can finally see what has her so shaken up. The rain is coming down harder now, but not enough to blur what's playing out at the rear of the castle. Even at this angle, there's no mistaking it.

Cyrus is at one end with Darius at the other—and there's something . . . *draped* between them. It doesn't take long for Braxton to distinguish that they're lugging something of a decent size. It's when his eyes land on the partially covered Cruex boots that his stomach sinks, even further still when he realizes that the body they're carrying . . . must be Hugh's.

CERYLIA JARETH

CERYLIA CAN'T REMEMBER the last time she'd boarded a ship in Miraenia. In all honesty, she can't remember the last time she'd *left* Sardoria. Her queendom—that castle—has been a haven for many, many years. Everything she needs, it provides. But riding Briar for this length of time through the Roviel Woods? She hadn't realized what she's been missing out on all these years. The security awarded a life of safety is mysteriously akin to the liberation of a spontaneously lived life. What a shame she's been focused solely on the former.

Mere hours ago, they'd exchanged heartfelt goodbyes with Delwynn, who'd then turned the carriage around for the long journey back to Sardoria. Alone. Although Opal's condition has worsened, she's still been able to move at a decent pace. Estelle had cloaked them, and they'd waited at the docks for the next ship sailing for Lonia. It'd taken longer than expected, but they'd boarded undetected, and had even been able to uncloak down in the cargo hold.

Having spent most of her time in the isle, Estelle is the perfect person to travel with. She certainly knows the ropes, more than Cerylia ever could have figured out on her own. Estelle had managed to get the queen and Opal inside another carriage, once again undetected, only uncloaking to drop some riyals into the stablemaster's outstretched hand—and then, off they went.

The trip through the Thering Forest is long, but smooth, nonetheless. Cerylia leans out the front window, looking up at Estelle, the reins slack in her hands. She's about to offer to switch for a bit so that Estelle can take a break, but before Cerylia can say anything, Estelle glances down from her post. "I'm good," she says with a nod, as if reading the queen's thoughts.

Cerylia gives her a curt nod before dipping her head back inside the carriage. Her gaze travels to Opal, who's currently sitting sideways against the plush interior, her knees curled into her chest, hood thrown over her head. Cerylia scoots to the left to try and get a view of her face to see whether she's asleep, but there's no telling with the way her entire body is turned, masked by her cloak. With a sigh, the queen leans back and crosses an ankle over her knee before resting her head against the velvet seat.

Her eyelids grow heavy . . .

❧ ❧ ❧

The carriage jolts to a stop. Startled, Cerylia's eyes fly open, immediately noticing a dull ache in the side of her neck. She rolls it back and forth a few times, realizing she must have dozed off. A loud thump sounds from just outside the window, indicating that Estelle's probably just dismounted the mare. The door opens and a cascade of midnight hair appears. "Faulty wheel. This is as far as we go." She looks at Opal—who is somehow still asleep, even after all the commotion—then shifts her focus to the queen.

Cerylia says what they're both thinking. "Do you want to wake her or should I?"

"I'll do it," Estelle says, stretching out a gloved hand.

Cerylia graciously takes it before stepping out of the carriage, thankful for the firmness of the dirt beneath her feet. She looks ahead, knowing full well that while she can't see much of anything now, it shouldn't take long to reach Orihia.

"You're sure there won't be any problem for me to access it?"

Estelle's voice is muffled as she pulls Opal's semi-limp body from the carriage. "You'll be fine."

Cerylia hurries over to help by taking one of Opal's arms and throwing it around her shoulders. Surprisingly, the girl's eyes are open, and she seems to be conscious, but in a sort of daze.

"Even with our weight supporting her, it'll take too long to get there." Estelle considers their limited options, then says, "I may need to unhitch the horse and leave the carriage behind for now."

Cerylia nods, following Estelle's lead as they gently set Opal against the base of a tree. She takes care of one side of the horse, Estelle the other.

"To answer your question," Estelle says, continuing her previous train of thought as she unfastens the harness, "since you still have your extracting abilities, that means you're still illusié, thereby able to access Orihia—even if you're not able to wield said capabilities at the present moment."

Cerylia unhooks the last buckle, handing over her side of the reins to Estelle. The shire horse follows her, their obsidian manes swaying in time, until they reach where Opal is leaning—nearly falling over, at this point.

With brute strength, Estelle hoists Opal onto the horse, using one of the buckles to secure her in place. "That should suffice for now. We can always make adjustments later on, if needed." The Caldari doesn't so much as take a breath before turning to guide the horse forward. "Ready?"

Cerylia nods. "I'll follow your lead."

ARDEN ELIRI

THEY SHOULD BE back by now.

I'm still staring at the exact spot where my brother and Felix had stood before transporting to Sardoria. By my calculations, although rough, they should have arrived at the castle within seconds, knocked on the door and either talked to Delwynn or the guards—*or*, worst case, snuck around the back to the courtyard. Either way, their not having returned is an indication that something may have gone wrong. *Terribly wrong.*

I've tried to keep myself from pacing as I ruminate over the many possibilities, but it's no use. I can sense that my restless nature is making both Avery and Vira uncomfortable, but Rydan doesn't seem nearly as bothered by it. I suppose he's used to my quirks from our Cruex days. *Lords*, the pacing I used to do in my chambers, with him sitting on the trunk at the foot of my bed. I'm surprised he didn't write me off as a total lunatic right then and there.

We haven't spoken since I'd caught him watching Vira and me from afar. When she'd approached me, I'd almost turned on my heel to head for my cabin—but the solemn look on her face had persuaded me to stay put. I knew that whatever she had to tell me was important.

And it was.

How she knows what she knows about the crescent fire is a mystery in and of itself, but the certainty in her tone had been undeniable. Although, she *had* caught me off guard when she'd inquired into Rydan's past—about his parents. That's something that not even I know.

Hell, I'm not sure Rydan *himself* even knows.

Our conversation had been cut short the moment we'd noticed flames in our periphery. Vira had also mentioned Rydan's struggle with wielding his igniting abilities—which had finally answered my question as to why and how Avery had gotten here—so to see his hands burst into flames, seemingly at random, yet with enough control, was more than enough to make me smile. The pride on his face had shone brighter than the sun on its hottest day—and from the way he'd looked at me, looking at him . . . I'd say it'd only added to it.

Afterwards, Vira had been the one to approach him, not me. While I can't justify why, it just hadn't felt right. So, it's here I remain, pacing, watching the two of them near the willow tree. Here's hoping it'll distract me enough from my thoughts until Haskell and Felix return in one piece. I can't help but shudder at the thought of Haskell's last transport to Trendalath—the mess the Cruex had made of him . . .

They didn't go to Trendalath, I remind myself.

My legs begin to feel like they're going to give out on me and take my entire body down with them when a green flash enters my view. A loud sigh of relief follows the moment I see their faces—not marred, no scratches or cuts or bruises. I whisper a silent prayer to the lords that be before running up to hug them both.

As if just remembering why they'd left in the first place, I pull away from the embrace with a frown. There's no one else with them. My heart sinks, hoping that any news they bring errs on the positive . . .

The rest of the group joins us just as Haskell says, "They weren't there. We looked everywhere, even spoke to the Queen's Guard."

"We couldn't find Delwynn either." I meet Felix's gaze, the concern in his eyes a direct reflection of my own. "I'm not sure what to make of it, where they could have gone. Cerylia wouldn't just leave Sardoria on a whim. And Estelle had promised to stay behind, to watch over things. Opal, too."

I can see the confusion etched all over his face, most noticeably in the deepening crease along his forehead. I resist the urge to go to him, knowing that now—in front of everyone—isn't the time or place.

A long silence stretches amongst the group before Felix finally says, "I need to go back. Perhaps check some other areas, like the perimeter, the neighboring towns—"

"We've already covered the majority of that," Haskell interrupts with a shake of his head.

So *that's* what had taken them so long.

Before we can come up with another plan, there's a slight rustling in the bushes at the end of the path Felix and I had walked down earlier. I realize that none of us are armed as both Haskell and Felix step in front of me—well, except for Rydan and Avery, who could have this whole place covered in flames in mere seconds.

Collectively, we hold our breaths as a figure emerges.

"Happy to see you're all together and doing well," a silken voice says.

Recognizing it immediately, I push through the male barricade in front of me and race toward Estelle. She flashes me a toothy grin as I throw my arms around her, squeezing her tight. "Careful now," she says with a small laugh. "I'm not the only one here."

I release my embrace, not seeing anyone behind her at first. That is, until she uncloaks Opal atop a beautiful steed—and guiding that steed, reins in hand . . . is Queen Jareth herself. My breath hitches as her eyes lock on mine. "Well, hello again, Arden."

RYDAN HELSTROM

DISCOMFORT SINKS DEEP into his bones, as if Cerylia were staring directly at him instead of at Arden. The last interaction he'd had with Queen Jareth had been just before he'd fled Sardoria without so much as a farewell.

Her gaze lingers for a moment longer before shifting to Vira, then to him. There's something unexpected in her stare. It isn't so much angry as it is pained. He's about to address her when his eyes catch the crone-like figure slumped against the back of the horse. He narrows his eyes, not believing what he's seeing. Arden takes the words right out of his mouth.

"Is that *Opal?*"

At the sound of the familiar name, Avery perks up from his semi-inebriated state. "Ah, the infamous Opal. I wondered when I'd finally—" His jaw goes slack as he watches Felix and Estelle help her down from the mare.

Once she's settled on the ground, she slowly lifts her head, the hood doing little to hide the fine wrinkles and lines on her face. Although Rydan hasn't known her for long, it's obvious her aging is occurring at an abnormally rapid rate. Her hair has always been tinted silver, but, before, it'd had a radiant, platinum sheen to it. Now, like the rest of her, it's dry and brittle—lackluster is an understatement.

Waving away Estelle's help, Opal takes a deliberate step toward Arden. Arden fidgets under her stare, and Rydan can't help but wonder why. Opal isn't exactly a force to be reckoned with—unless he'd missed something before he'd left? Fortunately, he's standing within range to hear most of their conversation.

"Opal," Arden whispers, reaching for her arm.

Opal shakes her away, her tone harsh as she says, "Take a good long look, Arden." She sweeps a weathered hand along the side of her body. "This is because of *you.*"

From the side, he can see Arden's mouth drop, eyes brimming with tears. "How? I—I don't understand."

"You fled. I've been searching. Tirelessly searching."

"I didn't know—"

"You didn't *care,*" Opal interrupts. "You never did. Not about Queen Jareth. Not about Sardoria. Certainly not about the Caldari."

Arden's eyes flick to the queen, but neither one refute the statement.

"Honestly, I wondered why we were coming here at all. But, it seems that, once again, the Eliris take priority over all else."

Haskell steps forward so that he's standing directly in line with his sister. "What exactly are you implying?"

Opal ignores him, but there's a dark glint in her eyes as she observes the proximity between Arden and Felix. "I expected more from you," she says to him, as if this were suddenly a conversation between just the two of them. She narrows her eyes before addressing the group without a hint of remorse in her voice. "I'll be inside, resting. Estelle will give you the details, I'm sure."

Arden steps to the side, but not before Opal brushes past her with surprising force. Slow, but determined, she disappears behind the door to Felix's cabin.

"I should probably follow her." Felix bows his head, intentionally avoiding eye contact with Arden, then trudges after Opal.

Before Estelle has a chance to speak, Queen Jareth strides forward to greet Haskell. Without saying a word, she smiles and places both hands on his cheeks. His expression is one of surprise, as is his sister's. She then removes her left hand and places it gently on Arden's shoulder. "It's so good to see you two together again."

Although Rydan senses that this is about to become a private conversation, he can't seem to leave. His attention is fixed on Arden and on the dawning realization that yet *another* person in her circle had known about her brother before she had. The pained expression on her face says it all.

"Why didn't you tell me?"

Cerylia's expression is gentle—almost apologetic. Her hands fall gracefully back to her sides. "I wasn't sure if your brother was still alive. I didn't want to give you false hope."

"How did you know about him in the first place? How do you know about our family?"

The queen looks at Rydan then. She scans the rest of the group before settling back on the pair standing before her. She lowers her voice before responding, and Rydan nearly asks her to repeat herself purely out of shock.

"Because . . . I'm your aunt."

CERYLIA JARETH

THE WAVE OF surprise that washes over the group is palpable. In her periphery, she can see that Rydan, Vira, and Avery look just as stunned as her niece and nephew—as if the news were meant for *them* and not for Arden and Haskell. In the long silence that follows, she begins to question whether it's the right time.

They were bound to find out anyway.

Arden's the first to speak. "You knew our parents?"

Cerylia nods. "Let's sit, shall we?" The group follows her like small ducklings around the waning campfire. It hisses in response, crackling and popping. Haskell and Arden take the seats directly across from Cerylia. Her gaze shifts between them as she gathers her thoughts. "I can't say I knew your mother well, but I did know your father. My late husband, Dane, and your father, Stanton, were brothers."

Haskell's gaze is unwavering as he says, "Do you know what happened to our father? If he's alive?"

"It's possible, but unlikely." She sighs. "You must understand, there was terrible unrest in Trendalath, even before the Tymonds"—her throat catches—"well, before the Tymonds took over. From the moment you were born, I promised to look after you. Then, when Dane died, my world fell apart. Tymond got ahold of you." Her gaze flicks to Arden before moving to Haskell. "And you, dear boy, disappeared—in a flash of green light, no less."

Something she's just said seems to snag in Arden's mind. "Wait, you're *here*, in Orihia." She looks around at the group, waiting for everyone to catch on. "Which means you're illusié." She begins to backtrack, caught up in her own thoughts. "Unless you're like me and you aren't anymore, but somehow managed to get in here."

"Indeed, I am illusié. That's actually the reason we came here. You see, I'm what you call an Extractor. I still have my abilities, but they're not what they used to be." She glances briefly at Estelle from across the fire, catching Rydan's stare in the process. "We're here because there's only one place we can go to reclaim the full extent of our abilities. And we need that," she points at Arden's pocket, "to get there."

She digs the watch out of the fabric lining, Haskell following suit. He asks carefully, "You mean, *in* the Veil?"

"Mid*vale*," Arden whispers, putting two and two together.

Cerylia nods in confirmation. "And Estelle here can show us exactly how to get there."

FELIX BARLOW

Opal doesn't so much as glance over her shoulder from the chair she's planted herself in as she sneers, "So you've already said."

Felix shuts the door to his cabin behind him and turns the lock. "Wasn't sure you heard me the first time around," he says, pulling on the curtains for privacy.

"Keep them open," Opal barks. "My eyes are only getting worse and making it even darker in here isn't going to help."

Felix grunts, leaving only the curtains on the side of the cabin drawn before joining Opal in an adjacent chair.

"Go ahead," she sighs. "I know you've been dying to interrogate me." She leans back into her seat and crosses her arms. "Have at it, Captain."

"I really wish you'd all stop calling me that."

Opal angles her head with a smirk. "*All?* Who's all?"

He's about to say *Arden* when he realizes that she's actually the only one—but Opal seems to already have that figured out.

"Let me guess . . . she hasn't seen through your bullshit yet?"

His temper flares. "She hasn't seen through yours either, so I suppose we're even."

"Except I'm not the one bedding her."

Fear lodges in his chest, the weight of it dropping straight to his stomach. "That's none of your business."

"It will be soon enough, once Xerin finds out."

"He already knows," Felix retorts, running a hand through his hair.

Opal looks genuinely surprised at the admission. "Is this something you offered up willingly, or did he force it out of you?"

"What does that matter?"

Opal shrugs, uncrossing her arms before resting them in her lap. "I'd just like to know where his head is at these days. Our last few conversations have been cut short, especially with Queen Jareth breathing down our necks."

Now it's Felix's turn to smirk. "She caught you, eh?"

"Only once, to my knowledge. But you know what they say, once is all it takes to sever the tie completely."

He's lucky he hasn't had such a moment with Arden, but that doesn't mean it isn't looming. He leans forward, propping his chin in his hands as he asks, "Is that the reason for your current . . . *condition*?"

She scowls at his derogatory tone. "Not exactly. I've been working on some things on my own—things I'm not willing to disclose, so don't even bother asking."

"There's really no need to ask when I already know," he counters. "So, pray tell, Opal, what are you doing poking around veiled memories?"

She raises a brow, impressed, but doesn't budge.

"If it wasn't clear before how dangerous it is, it should be now," he urges, gesturing to her deteriorating state. "Whatever you're looking for can't be worth dying over—"

A whisper. "And what if it is?"

Felix snaps his head up, meeting her glassy gaze. It's the first time he's seen her on the verge of shattering, and the sight alone is enough to wrench his heart from his chest. "What do you mean?"

She shakes her head despondently. "Timelines."

It's all she says. It's all she needs to say. Felix begrudgingly nods his head in understanding. "When the time is right . . . will you tell me then?"

She inches toward the edge of her chair, leaning far enough over to place her frail hands on top of his, a sad smile pulling at her wrinkled face. "I'll do my best."

BRAXTON HORNSBY

LANE'S FACE HAS fallen just as white as his own. "We can't," she says, her voice shaking.

"We have to," Braxton urges as she leans around the tree once more. While Darius and Cyrus *are* walking rather slowly, if they don't get moving soon, they're bound to lose their trail. Braxton refuses to let that happen.

"I have to see who it is," he says, kneeling in front of her. "Just by the boots alone, I know it's a Cruex, one of *us*. I have a sinking feeling it's Hugh, and if it is . . . well, we deserve to know. *He* deserves for us to know."

"What, that your father is a monster?"

Braxton doesn't disagree with this, but something in him makes him say, "Darius isn't the only perpetrator. Cyrus is with him." As he says the name, a sharp pang hits him right in the chest.

Has Cyrus been this way all along? Or has he just been another one of his father's pawns?

Braxton shakes the thought. He brings his attention back to Lane, taking both of her hands in his. With a light but determined squeeze, he says, "We need to follow them."

Her breath is steadier now, but the expression on her face hasn't changed in the slightest. "I have a feeling we're not going to like what we find."

Braxton hangs his head. "Do we ever?"

ॐ ॐ ॐ

They'd been clever enough to use Lane's affinity to round up another couple of wild horses to hide behind in their pursuit of the king and his advisor. They've just made it to the far east side of the castle grounds when the men set the body on the ground before opening a grate that looks like it leads to the sewers.

"They can't seriously be dumping a body *in there*?" Lane whispers incredulously.

Braxton is just as disgusted as she is in his reply. "Unfortunately, it would appear so."

Suddenly, Cyrus looks up in their direction. Luckily, Lane's already stopped the horses, which are now grazing near the edge of the forest, while Braxton and Lane crouch behind yet another tree.

"Do you think he can see us?"

Braxton shakes his head. "Not from where he's standing."

His assumption stands correct as Darius snaps to get his advisor's attention. Braxton can't hear the conversation, but from the looks of it, they most certainly are heading underground.

Lane's no longer observing the scene that's unfolding before them but is instead leaning her head against the base of the trunk with her eyes closed. Honestly, he doesn't blame her—not after they've just watched, in horror, the draped body being tossed into the depths below. He can't help but cringe at the sound he can't hear but knows it made. Darius is the first to make his way down what he assumes is a ladder before Cyrus follows. He pulls on the grate to bring it closed but leaves it partially open.

"Come on," Braxton utters to Lane as he pulls her to her feet. "We don't have much time."

They walk past the horses, Lane patting them on the neck to thank them. They neigh in what seems to be understanding before galloping off into the woods. "We're not following them *down there* . . . are we?"

Braxton drops to his stomach and peers into the darkness below. "How else are we supposed to find out?"

Lane glances around nervously. "This isn't a good idea, Braxton."

"Don't you want to know whose body it is? And where they're taking it?"

"All I know is that if it's *below* the surface, it can't be good."

"He's my father, Lane. He's not going to hurt me."

"You're not the one I'm worried about."

He glances up at her then, the color returning to her face. Her cheeks are rose-tinted as she says, "That came out wrong. I'm sorry. It's just that if it *is* Hugh, there's no telling what he'll do to me if he catches us down there. To him, I'm just as disposable as the rest of them."

"I won't let anything happen to you." While the sentiment is pure, the truth behind those words is anything but. Perhaps if he were still able to deviate, he'd feel more confident in protecting her—and himself.

Lane cracks a smile. "Don't you find it somewhat ironic that after just following your father into Volkharn, we're now following him into the sewers?"

"Ironic is an understatement," he says as he slides the grate off the rest of the way. "I've learned more about him in the past twenty-four hours than my entire childhood spent in that castle."

"Maybe that's a good thing."

She falls silent, as does he. Perhaps she's right. He's wanted answers for so long—who's to say this isn't leading him to the truth? And straight from the source, no less. Braxton leans over the edge, the darkness looming below. "Do you want to go first or should I?"

DARIUS TYMOND

"NOT MUCH FARTHER," Darius says as they trek deeper into the tunnels. Hugh's body seems to grow heavier with each step but, fortunately, Cyrus is carrying most of the weight. Darius has been down here so many times, he hardly needs the sconces on the walls to light the way.

"Tell me again, Your Majesty, what was his crime?"

Darius stops walking. He drops his end of the body, causing Cyrus to lurch forward. "Attempted murder."

"Any witnesses?"

"Why would a king need them?"

Even in the dim light, the disdain on Cyrus's face is clear. "This will raise suspicion. First Elias, then his cousin, Hugh? It's only a matter of time before the rest of the Cruex start asking questions. And what about Braxton? You assigned him to train with Hugh."

"Yes," Darius sneers, "what about Braxton? Perhaps we should discuss how you failed to bring his betrayal to my attention?"

Cyrus pales. He gently sets the upper half of Hugh's body on the ground between them. "I told you, as soon as I found out Clive was missing, I went searching for him—"

"Without so much as bothering to inform me."

"I admit, that was careless on my part," he says, the words coming out faster than he can seem to think them, "but I wanted to return with Clive apprehended. I was trying to solve a problem before you even knew there was one."

There it is. There's the Cyrus he knows.

"For future reference, I prefer information first, *then* action," Darius says as he picks Hugh up by the boots.

"Duly noted, Your Majesty," Cyrus says with a grunt, his arms looping underneath the boy's shoulders.

They resume carrying the body all the way down the dank tunnels, making two rights and a left, before the putrid smell of decay and rotting human flesh fills the air. Once the corpse is tossed on top of the others, Darius clasps his hands together before turning to look at the vile display. "This should be more than enough," he mutters, just low enough so that Cyrus can't hear him.

"I hate to leave you here, Your Majesty, but the smell," he waves a hand in the air, "well, to put it plainly, it's a bit too pungent for my stomach to handle."

Darius is about to respond when a clatter echoes behind them. Cyrus shoots him a concerned glance before scurrying off to grab a torch from one of the sconces.

Distant whispering follows.

Wondering who he'll be adding to the wretched pile next, Darius flings his robes behind him and marches toward the tunnel's opening. It gets brighter as Cyrus raises the torch just above his shoulder. Slowly, a figure begins to come into view, as does another. His stomach drops at the sound of his son's voice.

"Don't waste your breath, *father*. I heard everything."

ARDEN ELIRI

I KNOW THE look on Estelle's face better than anybody. We're in my cabin, just the two of us, as she examines the pocket watches side by side. "Did you know? About Cerylia being my aunt?"

Estelle stops what she's doing to look at me. "No. I can't say that I did. It's not surprising, though. She was so concerned when you fled Sardoria—for two strangers who had just met, I couldn't help but find that odd."

"You never thought to ask her?"

"Did you?"

My cheeks warm at the remark. "If I had known, I wouldn't have left."

"One way or another, the truth always comes out— seems this one just took a little longer." She turns my brother's nearly flawless watch over before picking mine up by its chain. The subject changes entirely as she asks, "Did this start after your encounters with the Mallum?" She angles her head to indicate the rusting.

I look at her, surprised that she knows there was more than one encounter, but she answers my question before I can get the words out.

"Felix told me." Her eyes suddenly turn dark. "This kind of tarnishing certainly isn't from natural elements—*especially* on gold." She lifts the object, bringing it mere inches from her face. "And this?" She points to the mark that seems to have embedded itself even deeper into the metal.

"Also after the Mallum," I say, trying as best I can to keep my voice steady. "Do you know what it is?"

"Hard to be sure, but there's no mistaking the fact that your watch is tainted." She narrows her eyes, deep in thought as she trails her index finger along the unusual insignia. "Tell me again how you came across Midvale?"

I think back to the conversation I just had with Cerylia—*with the entire group listening*—before Estelle had pulled me aside to talk. "Rydan wanted to show me a cave he'd found just north of here, but when we went looking for it, we couldn't find it. I had my pocket watch with me and when I looked at it, the hands had stopped. I just figured it'd stopped working. But then, out of nowhere, there was an *opening* where a solid wall had been just moments prior—"

"My watch," she murmurs, her jaw clenching. "He entered the Veil using my damn watch. You and Rydan must have timed it perfectly without even knowing it. The gateway hadn't been closed yet and, because you had your watch on you, you managed to slip right through."

Even though I've heard everything she's just said, I can only seem to focus on the first part. "*He*? Who's he?"

"Just one of the Savant." She waves her hand in the air. "Anyway, it doesn't matter—"

My hand meets her wrist. "It *does* matter. This Savant . . . did he have red hair? Green eyes?"

Her eyes widen. "Yes. And he cast the most dreadful illusion around me—"

"He's Tymond's Caster," I say, thankful to have someone to talk to about this. "He was there in the woods when I saw my father, and again in the healing ward, in the Daegrum Chambers . . . ." An unwelcome realization begins to dawn on me. "And in the tavern, in Chialka."

Estelle sets my watch down before releasing a heavy sigh. "It seems he needed to find a watch so that he could enter the Veil, and when he couldn't get yours, he went after mine."

I nod in understanding, even though I believe there's much more to the story. "And what about Rydan, the first time he unknowingly entered the Veil?"

Estelle shrugs. "Your guess is as good as mine."

A long silence stretches between us. "The Caster . . . he knew my father," I whisper, recalling our encounter in the Roviel Woods. "At least, I *think* he did. For all I know, that could have been an illusion as well, just one of his castings. But it felt so real."

"They always do." Estelle pushes her chair back from the table, running both hands through her soft ebony waves. "He's a highly experienced Caster, Arden. He can make you see whatever he wants you to see—which certainly makes his job a hell of a lot easier."

I reach across the table before pulling both pocket watches toward me. "So, what do we do?"

"Seeing as Haskell's watch is in near mint condition, we can travel to Midvale using his. Once we're there, I can do some research and ask around about yours. Perhaps I can find someone who will be able to enlighten us on the cause of the tarnishing—maybe even find a way to cleanse it. Honestly, I'm surprised you were able to enter the Veil at all, given its condition. I'd suggest securing it somewhere safe until we know more." She swipes Haskell's watch from the table. "Now to take this one for a test run."

I grab my own watch as she makes for the door, offering a small smile and a wave as she closes it behind her. I trace my thumb across the mark, over and over again, before setting it on the nightstand and pulling my knapsack out from underneath the bed.

A wave of sadness crashes over me as I open one of the inner pockets. Ever since I can remember, I've had this watch on me. It's been with me ever since my Cruex days, on all of my missions, when I first met the Caldari, up until now. It's the only piece of my father I have and tucking it away, even with the intention of safekeeping, would feel like tucking his memory away . . .

Like hiding my own past from myself.

But, like Estelle said, it's tainted. And I've already unknowingly used it once. Even though I'll never know my parents, the Caldari have managed to fill the gaping hole I always assumed would remain empty. They *are* my family—I can't possibly risk putting them in harm's way, yet again. Lords know I've already done that more times than I can count.

Tears threaten to fall as I unroll a small scrap of linen and delicately place my watch in its center. I look at it one last time before bringing it to my lips, the metal cool against my skin. I shudder, then squeeze my eyes shut and quickly pull it away.

Once it's all wrapped up, I place it in the knapsack before sliding it back underneath my bed. With a deep sigh, I push up from the floor and head outside to join the family that's waiting for me.

RYDAN HELSTROM

THE QUEEN'S BEEN eyeing him ever since she arrived in Orihia. It's been unsettling, to say the least, and Rydan's done everything he can to keep his circle of friends nearby in the hopes that it'll deter her from grabbing him to speak one on one—although, there *is* a chance she might know something about the crescent fire, seeing as she's illusié. A little-known fact to everyone here, up until a few hours ago.

He's so lost in thought that he hardly even notices when both Avery and Vira leave their posts around the fire to join Haskell and Cerylia in what appears to be a less-than-riveting conversation. From over his shoulder, he can see Felix and Estelle leaning against a tree near Arden's cabin. Seconds later, the door swings open and Arden herself comes bounding down the steps. She brushes past them, but Felix manages to stop her, pulling her in close. Rydan's wondering what has her so upset when the clearing of a throat startles him. He whirls back around to see Opal, surprisingly enough, standing directly in front of him. She gestures to the adjacent seat. "Do you mind?"

Flushed and fumbling for words, he obliges her, but not before noticing Cerylia's brief glance in their direction. He turns to the side to face Opal, hoping to block the queen's view (or at least *his* view of her), but all logic escapes him when he takes in Opal's appearance, which is only continuing to severely deteriorate.

"Go ahead, say what you will," Opal quips, although Rydan *does* detect a layer of sarcasm in her tone. "I've been avoiding mirrors for what feels like decades."

"It's not so bad," Rydan says, the lie hot on his tongue. "You just look . . . *wiser* is all."

She cracks a smile, her wrinkles deepening. "How I wish that were true. Regrettably, there isn't much wisdom to be had from a life yet to be lived."

His heart sinks at her fading smile. It wasn't his intention to make her feel even worse. "But you've seen a lot, I'm sure," he says, trying to recover a semblance of light-heartedness from before.

"I suppose you could say that." She sighs. "Nothing worth *this* though. Nothing worth losing my youth over. I can't remember the last time I woke up feeling vibrant, excited—with a sense of purpose." There's a flicker of remorse in her eyes. "It's all just a jumbled mess now."

"I'm sure we can find a way to reverse this. To get you back to the way you were. That's why we're going to Midvale, isn't it? To strengthen Queen Jareth's abilities, to find out what's happened with Arden's, to help you overcome this strange condition . . ."

The sadness in her expression gleams like fresh morning dew. "I'm afraid you are mistaken, Rydan. There is no 'going back' for me. I've seen far too much."

He's tempted to ask her what she means, if it has anything to do with the crescent fire—if she might know something useful—when she drifts back into the chair, her eyes shutting. "Give me a moment, would you?"

Rydan's not sure whether she means for him to get up and leave, or to stay and remain quiet. He glances around, preferring not to join the conversations taking place in either group. Oddly enough, being here with Opal is the most comfortable he's felt in a while.

Less than a minute passes when Opal suddenly jerks in her chair. Alarmed, Rydan moves closer, leaning over her to make sure she's still breathing. "Opal?" he says, as he lays a hand over hers. "Are you—?"

Before he can finish asking the question, her eyes shoot open. The word leaves her mouth without a sound, but Rydan understands all the same. *Don't.*

A second is all it takes to pull him in with her.

≼ ≼ ≼

Immersed in complete and utter darkness, Rydan blinks once, twice, hoping to see *something* familiar come into view—a hue, a shape . . . anything. He takes a step forward, not knowing whether to expect a flat surface, a steep incline, a sharp decline—but the movement doesn't feel like *anything*. As if he hadn't even made one at all.

"Hello?" His voice echoes in the vast chamber. "Opal, are you there?" He reaches out in front of him, grasping at a phantom wind. A dreadful feeling washes over him as he tries to move again, desperate for sensory recognition.

Minutes pass, although it feels *much* longer, until finally, there's a sound. A voice. Opal's.

We're too far in now. A pause. *I tried.*

"Opal?" he says again, wondering why he can hear her, but she can't seem to hear him. The conversation carries on without him, like she's talking to someone else entirely. A chill lodges in his chest as a phrase that seems directed straight at him seeps into every pore of his being.

Let go. Let go. Let go.

Even though he can't physically see anything, he still glances down at his hands. He hears a low grunt of frustration that doesn't come from him—nor Opal. It's convincing enough for him to believe that there must be another person—another presence—here with them.

I'm sorry. I can't hold him off much longer . . .

The invisible tether snaps, and whatever it was he'd been bound to severs along with it. Even without his sight, he can sense he's falling backwards, catapulting into what he hopes is Orihia—and it *is*, but there's something not quite right about it.

It isn't present day.

Knowing that Opal is an Inverter, he quickly realizes that he's been taken back to the night when Xerin had suddenly appeared in his and Vira's cabin, his skin shredded and stained crimson—the same night the fabric with the Soames crest had disappeared. Except the person writhing on the blood-soaked floor isn't Xerin.

It's someone he's never seen before.

As Rydan observes his surroundings, he notices something else about the memory—something *off.* Everything around him appears dull and fuzzy, as if whatever had taken place had somehow occurred in the past. Or in another time, another dimension.

Is it possible the memory had been tampered with?

To hide Xerin's tracks?

An outsider to the scene playing out before him, Rydan watches as he and Vira try to staunch the flow of blood and dress the stranger's wounds. Time seems to speed up then, and he almost loses his footing as he's hurtled into the memory from later that evening, with him fast asleep and Vira in the bed beside him. Just how he'd thought Xerin had taken the crest, the man with dark features, save for his eyes, sneaks in and takes it for himself.

And then Rydan's falling again—down, down, down, spinning left and right and every direction—until he lands right-side up on a long, winding pathway made of slate. Although slightly lighter in color, the sky is also gray, and so are the trees and the grass . . . all still as stone.

A world devoid of color. Of motion. Of *life.*

He presses his boot, which is also tinted gray, onto the pathway to test its validity before taking a step forward. Alarm surges through him as the realization that his pants, his tunic, his hands, his *skin* . . . are all gray. He races forward, shaking his arms in a futile attempt to bring the color back, to wake himself up, to get the hell out of here, wherever *here* is—but it's no use.

Just when he's about to give in and let this desolate world swallow him whole, something catches his eye. The faintest of glimmers. He maneuvers left, straining to see.

It can't be.

He nearly falls to his knees at the sight of it, in all its metallic glory. *The Soames crest.*

CERYLIA JARETH

CERYLIA KNOWS EXACTLY what's going on with just a single glance in Rydan's direction. Without a word, she breaks away from the group and rushes over to the campfire, worry creasing her brow as she kneels next to Opal. Rydan's hand is set gently atop hers, an indication of the unmistakeable gateway into Opal's abilities.

Where have you gone?

Cerylia shakes her head, hardly taking notice when the others gather around the fire as well. It crosses her mind to remove Rydan's hand—to break the bond between them—but the danger in doing so could result in irreparable damage to both Rydan *and* Opal. And given Opal's current condition, it's far too risky.

Cerylia's deep in thought, weighing every possible scenario, when a hand lands gently on her shoulder. She angles her head to see Estelle crouching next to her—and behind her, Arden and Felix. Estelle confirms exactly what she's thinking. "We have to let it run its course." She looks between Rydan and Opal to assess the situation further. "If we remove his hand from hers, we'll break the connection. And depending on where they are, I'm not sure they'll be able to come back—"

"You mean you're not sure *she'll* come back." The words come out much harsher than intended, but Cerylia means them all the same.

A long stretch of silence falls over the group before Arden whispers, "What does that mean? Where could they have possibly gone that they can't return from?"

Cerylia shoots Felix a sidelong glance, hoping he'll take the hint. Although she'll never admit it, Arden's too close to the situation—*to Rydan*—to be able to discern any information she might be given. Cerylia waits patiently as the fear in her niece's eyes shifts to concern as Felix helps her to her feet and walks them both away from the fire.

"Where do you think they've gone?" Estelle whispers.

"I was hoping you'd be able to tell me."

Estelle gives a dismal shake of her head before releasing an overdue sigh. "Wherever it is, it isn't good." She points to the draining color of Rydan's already pale face. "If they don't return soon, I'll have no choice but to intervene."

Cerylia chews on her lower lip, the remaining flicker of hope nearly distinguished.

"Although," Estelle murmurs, reaching for Haskell's pocket watch, "perhaps I can reach them through this."

At first, Cerylia doesn't seem to follow. "I doubt they're in a memory in the Veil . . ." As her thought trails off and she looks once more at Rydan's pallid face, it dawns on her.

"There's only one other place they could be," Estelle says, her tone solemn. "And if we're as smart as I think we are, it's best if we stay as far away from it as possible."

DARIUS TYMOND

THE REALIZATION HITS him right between the eyes. *He knows. Braxton knows.*

His eyes flick from his son to the feminine figure behind him. Lane Devall. He should have known she'd end up being trouble. Seems the Cruex have no qualms around causing him more headaches than they're worth.

Darius can sense the question Cyrus wants to ask, but raises his hand in the air before he can do so. "How did you get down here?"

"We followed you." Even in the dim light, there's no mistaking the tenacity in Braxton's expression.

The words snag on something in Darius's mind, causing his heart rate to climb. *How long have they been following him? Had they followed him to the jaded spring?*

Is it possible he'd misinterpreted the sounds in the woods? And what about where he'd hidden Aldreda's speculor?

Cyrus steps forward, his statement directed at no one in particular. "Perhaps we should take this discussion to the Great Room." A chill sweeps through the already dank chambers, causing them all to visibly shiver, Darius included.

The king ignores his advisor before narrowing his eyes at his son. "It would seem you've given me no choice then." He brings his hands together, tapping his finger over the amethyst ring. Yes, the Mallum has already absorbed Braxton's abilities—a mistake, of course—but perhaps it's been for the best. In light of what he now knows, he sees no other option than to get rid of them both. As much as it pains him to think of taking his only son's life, there's reassurance that his soul will be put to good use.

Just like his friend's.

Just like his mother's.

They're already in the place to do it, a graveyard of corpses.

With his palms facing up, Darius closes his eyes and sweeps his hands out beside him. The ring begins to pulse against his skin, an indication that the Mallum has successfully been summoned. When he opens his eyes, the violet hue that paints the walls of the tunnel further illuminates the horrified faces of Braxton and Lane. But there's a hint of something else on his son's face that appears to be a sort of . . . *recognition?*

Braxton protectively grabs Lane's arm and moves her behind him. Although Darius's view of her is now mostly blocked, he can tell she's frantically fumbling in her pockets. Her sense of urgency heightens as a black mist seeps into the tunnels, and even more so as a red cloak begins to take shape.

He can hear Cyrus in his ear, pleading with him to stop, to find another way—but Darius doesn't listen. He continues with his silent commands of the Mallum's next movements. *Lethal movements.*

Darius only breaks his concentration to get one final look at his son, but it's just enough time for the unexpected to occur. Through the sheer-robed figure, he watches, enraged, as both Braxton and Lane vanish from view.

BRAXTON HORNSBY

WHICH WAY IS up and which way is down, he couldn't possibly know. Time both expands and contracts, a myriad of endless loops desperate to invite him in. In a free fall, the tether that binds him to Lane both stretches and releases the closer he gets, the farther he gets . . . until he feels like he's floating, completely alone, and yet still surrounded by all that's unfamiliar.

Where the hell am I?

Braxton looks ahead of him, for a sign of Lane, but he can only see so far. Darkness encroaches, threatening to take away what little familiarity is left. He opens his mouth to speak, to call out her name, but a mere wisp of breath is all that manages to come out.

Still falling, he notices he's unintentionally heading toward a vivid tunnel—a kaleidoscope of magnificent colors. When he glances to his left, he finally locates Lane. But there's something off-putting etched in her expression—a warning. *Danger.* And then, as if the tether itself has transmuted into pure emotion, he feels it.

Everything she's feeling.

The dread.

The fear.

The immensity of all things unknown.

He reaches for her—for that inextricable link—when he feels something else. *Release.* Like a cord being cut. A bridge being burned. A rope fraying at the edges. A grip loosening. A hand finally letting go.

He tries to grip it tighter, this invisible force, as the words he so desperately needs to express roil within his chest. He forces them up, resisting their pulling and pushing against one another, until they have no choice but to finally escape the confines of his lungs.

"I'm . . . losing . . . you!"

The feeling of falling is momentarily suspended as Lane comes back into view. Her hazel eyes close. Her body softens, the tension releasing with it. Her ebony ringlets float ever so gently around her face, forming a delicate frame. The expression she wears is serene, tranquil—a stark contrast to the one she'd worn just moments prior.

He watches in vain as she's suddenly dragged, with sheer force, in the direction opposite him. Panicked, he screams her name, but within the blink of an eye, she's disappeared into a phantasmagoria of ever-shifting hues.

Before he can figure out how to go after her, how to reconnect their dismantled tether, he's falling again, faster this time. Past the morphing web of indigo, violet, and gold; past the mirage of phantom dreams; past anything that holds any realistic context of waking life— until he's in a place so dense, so *unrecognizable*, it's impossible to see even two steps ahead of him. It's then he realizes that he's upright. Standing. No longer in a free fall. Albeit slight, a sense of normalcy returns.

Darkness invades as he rushes forward into the unknown, unstable on his feet. The more his legs shake, the more he worries that it isn't a state of impermanence. Whatever they've fallen into—whatever *he's* fallen into—is a place no soul should roam. A disturbing thought enters his mind as he continues to venture deeper into obscurity, his destination unknown.

Has the Mallum reigned victorious?

Has he unknowingly submitted to a far worse fate?

Is it possible *his soul* has been absorbed this time?

The vast hollowness within causes him to stop in his tracks. His bottom lip quivers with each solitary blink, each failed attempt to see. He falls to his knees, although he can't be sure what he's landed on, but at least it seems solid. Dirt, grass, stone? It doesn't matter.

There's no other feeling besides despair.

A forgotten plea, Lane's name sits idly in his throat. He squeezes his eyes shut, the desperation to return to the Trendalath tunnels waging war within. At least there, he hadn't been alone. At least there, he'd had context.

But now he's here. Alone, confused—and blind.

And Lane is somewhere else—alone, confused, and possibly suffering the unfathomable . . .

With his eyes still closed, he manages to fill his lungs with a few deep breaths. As he does, he notices a lightness from behind his eyelids that certainly wasn't there before. His eyes shoot open to reveal a world devoid of color, but at least it's no longer dark. He can see!

His surroundings begin to take shape and, from what he can gather, he appears to be in the middle of a forest. It's paper-thin, reminiscent of those moments just before something is reduced to ashes by the unrelenting forces of nature.

Mystified, he spins around in a circle. The fluidity of his thoughts comes to a grinding halt as his eyes settle on the *last* thing he'd expected to see.

Fellow Caldari, Rydan Helstrom.

What is he doing here?

Relief follows as Braxton runs toward this semblance of familiarity, waving his arms and shouting Rydan's name, but he may as well be invisible. From his vantage point, Rydan appears to be oblivious to his surroundings, except for whatever it is he's so intently focused on. And then, as if ripe for the picking by nature herself . . .

Rydan disappears.

ARDEN ELIRI

I REFUSE TO tear my gaze from the scene Felix is escorting me away from. I've never seen Rydan look so lifeless. I'm immediately brought back to when I'd helped him escape from the Trendalath dungeons. He'd been in bad shape then, but at least he'd been conscious, coherent. Whatever Opal's dragged him into appears to be worse—*far* worse.

Overcome by contemplation, I don't realize that we've stopped walking. I look around to get my bearings. We're facing my cabin, the back side of it anyway. The grave expression Felix is wearing doesn't do much in the way of comfort. I start to reach for his hand but think better of it. I'm sure he can already sense my distress. No need to risk amplifying it—for both our sakes.

Felix doesn't say anything at first, which I'm actually grateful for because it allows me to gather my thoughts. I meet his gaze, trying to decide which question I should ask first. I'd been so keen on talking more with Cerylia about my family history that I hadn't expected yet another troubling incident to arise. I'm just thankful I have nothing to do with this one—at least I don't *think* I do.

Felix pulls me back to the present as he says, "You want to know if he'll be okay." Disappointment flickers in his eyes as I realize he means Rydan.

I give an adamant shake of my head, realizing just how selfish it sounds. "If *they'll* be okay."

"Normally, I'd be inclined to say yes. But given Opal's condition and the lack of her usual strength . . ."

The way his words trail off only deepens the gaping pit that's already formed in my stomach. "Where are they? They can't be in the Veil. I've been there. Rydan and I both have." I chew on my lower lip. "This seems . . . different somehow."

A shadow falls over his face, making his russet eyes appear even darker and more ominous than usual. "Just like in this world, there's a way to get lost in others. While it doesn't have a proper name, it's been called something along the lines of . . . a *void*."

My throat tightens. "Why would Opal want to go there?"

Felix lowers his gaze. "It's not exactly somewhere you *try* to go—it's more like you're *pulled* there against your will. Especially if your illusié abilities have weakened, as Opal's have."

"All can't be lost—I mean, Rydan isn't weak." I flash back to the magnificent igniting display he'd put on earlier. "If anything, he's gotten stronger. Much stronger."

"Be that as it may, Opal's the one in charge. Which means Rydan's merely along for the ride."

Floating. Helpless. Desperate. The words rise within me like an erupting volcano. Before my imagination can drag me even further into its dark clutches, I push the thought from my mind.

"All we can do is wait and hope that when Opal comes back to, Rydan's right there alongside her."

Leaving Rydan's fate in Opal's hands certainly doesn't make me feel any more confident, but if Felix says it's the only choice we've got, well . . . I believe him.

I have to.

A long silence stretches between us before I force myself to ask him the one question I hope he has an answer to. "What could be *so* important for Opal to find that she's risking her illusié powers by traversing the Veil?"

Felix stiffens, his jaw tense. "I'm afraid only she has the answer to that."

His gaze lingers on mine until we're both yanked away by a startling sound. Even from where I stand, I can hear coughing and wheezing. Heavy breathing. With all the time spent in the Cruex healing ward, I'd know those sounds anywhere.

Rydan's awake.

RYDAN HELSTROM

THE RINGING IN his ears is unlike anything he's ever felt before. Rydan squints, the world around him suddenly blinding and unclear. The ringing magnifies, making it even more difficult to distinguish where he is. His hands feel heavy as he brings his palms to his ears, but, fortunately, that's all it takes for the torment reverberating within his skull to stop; for the sky and the trees of Orihia to come into view.

Cerylia's concerned face appears first, followed by Estelle's. Their mouths are moving, but he can't hear what they're saying. His head lolls to the side, his gaze landing on Opal. It starts to come back to him.

Don't, she'd said.

The moment his hand had met hers, he'd left this realm and gone to another—but, strangely enough, she hadn't been with him. He'd been completely and utterly alone. But there *had* been something. The Soames crest. Not the fabric, but the *real* metal crest. And the stranger, the one who'd taken the fabric to begin with . . .

Opal's eyelids flutter, but they don't open. Her chest is moving, albeit slightly—the only indication that she's still alive and breathing. His focus begins to sharpen but even so, he can't find the strength to pick himself up off the chair. It's as if paralysis has taken over his body.

Mentally sound. Physically bound.

The voices are growing louder now, clearer. He can tell by the tone of the conversation alone that whatever just happened *shouldn't* have. For once, he's inclined to agree.

"And Opal?" Cerylia furrows her brows.

Rydan's eyes flick from the queen to Estelle, who's now tending to Opal. Her midnight hair sways back and forth as she attempts to wake her friend.

"Well?" Cerylia presses.

"It seems she's still unconscious, but I don't believe she's in the Veil." Her gaze is lethal as it lands on Rydan. "If he was able to be pulled out, she must be, too."

"Then why isn't she awake like him?"

Defeated, Estelle slides away from Opal and moves back toward the queen. Only when she's close enough to whisper does she say, "It's worth noting that *her* condition pales in comparison to Rydan's."

It's taken her this long, but Cerylia looks to him, finally noticing that he's come back to. "Where did you ask her to take you?" Although her tone is stiff, much like the rest of her body, there's also a hint of desperation lining her voice.

"I believe you're mistaken. *She* took *me*. Not the other way around."

"Where did you go?" Cerylia presses again.

"I don't know," Rydan says, slowly lifting both his head and back from the chair, "but wherever it was . . . it was nowhere like here."

"How do you mean?"

"We were falling," Rydan recalls, his mind racing with the memory. "Endlessly falling, until we reached a tunnel. It was so vivid—I've never seen anything quite like it. I could feel that I was connected to Opal, bound by some invisible force, but as soon as we reached the tunnel, it snapped." He fists his hands at his sides. "She was pulled one way and I was pulled another."

Estelle glances at Cerylia. "There you have it—all tell-tale signs of traversing the Veil."

The queen gives a solemn nod in confirmation.

Estelle remains quiet for a moment, briefly hanging her head before locking eyes with him. "So, if Opal was in the Veil, where were you?"

By now, the rest of the group has joined, circling around the waning fire. Even though he can only see the top of her head from behind Felix's shoulder, Arden's presence is unmistakeable.

"I was somewhere I never hope to return to." Rydan tries to find the words to describe what he'd seen, what he'd felt, but the only one that comes to mind is . . . *empty*. "It was devoid of everything—of color, of people, of sound, of feeling." His voice catches. "There was no sense of direction, of time—and yet it stretched on and on, mocking an endpoint that never even existed to begin with. It was like an infinite, eternal expanse of absolutely nothing." Surprised at his own eloquence, he sits back in the chair, watching their changing expressions as what he's just said sinks in.

Felix is the first to speak. "He was in the Void."

Estelle turns, shaking her head. "Impossible. If he'd been in the Void, he'd still be there." And then, as if she's realized something for the very first time, she whispers, "Unless Opal went back for him—in which case, she won't be able to find her way back out."

"Just to be clear, she's only traversed *memories* that took place inside the Veil, not the Veil itself," Felix says, leaving Arden's side to kneel next to Estelle. "And so whatever Rydan fell into must have been a memory of hers—"

"A memory of *the Void*?" Cerylia asks, stunned. "Why would Opal have a memory there? Furthermore, how could she have survived it? Souls are known to get lost there, trapped for all eternity."

A muscle twitches in Felix's jaw as his gaze settles on Rydan. "That I wouldn't know."

"How do we get her out?" Arden's voice is determined as she lays a protective hand on Felix's shoulder.

Felix turns to look at Haskell. He shakes his head.

"In the past, some Transporters have been able to bring lost souls back from the Void. But seeing as Opal is likely in a *memory* of the Void and not the Void itself, the chances of that working are slim."

"Not to mention dangerous," Haskell scoffs. "I don't know Opal well enough, nor have I ever traversed with her. Our connection would be faulty at best. I'd be shooting in the dark, just like the rest of you."

Rydan's so focused on Arden's bewildered expression that he doesn't even notice Felix's searing stare. "There's another option," he says through clenched teeth. "I can amplify."

"Would that work?" the queen asks.

"Opal and I are very close." Rydan can't help but notice how quickly Arden's hand leaves his shoulder at the mention of it. "When she senses the amplification, all she has to do is think about Orihia. As those feelings are amplified, she'll be able to follow them out of the memory—out of the Void—and back here. To us."

Arden's tone is curt. "Sounds like you've done this before."

His shoulders tense, but he neither confirms nor denies it. He looks to Estelle. "What do you think?"

Estelle sighs. "We can't possibly travel to the Veil, to *Midvale*, in her current condition. She must be conscious to make the trip, or we'll risk losing her entirely."

Although it isn't really his place, Rydan feels bold enough to speak up before they talk themselves into a circle. "It's settled, then. Felix will amplify and lead Opal out of her memory and back to Orihia."

"And if that doesn't work?"

Although Vira's the one who's asked the question, Felix hasn't so much as blinked past Rydan. "If it doesn't work, then I guess we know who's to blame."

CERYLIA JARETH

EVEN THOUGH THEY'VE all dispersed, Cerylia can feel the mounting tension between the Caldari on the rise. She's sitting on the front deck of Opal's cabin, watching from a distance as Estelle hovers over Felix and his subject. They've been at it for hours now—amplifying, that is—with no luck of aiding Opal in her return.

Cerylia had decided to give them room to work, suggesting that the others do the same. To her left, she can see both Rydan and Vira standing at their front window, their gazes fixed on the scene before them; Avery and Haskell are just off the beaten path, no longer within earshot; and Arden is . . . walking toward her. In her hands she holds a wooden tray, and the glass sitting atop it clinks as she climbs the steps. "I thought you might like some tea."

Cerylia smiles and gestures to the open seat next to her. "How very thoughtful of you. Then again, I wouldn't expect anything less." She watches as Arden arranges the cups and saucers, her hands shaking as she lifts the kettle. Knowing exactly how she must be feeling, Cerylia leans forward, winks, and gently takes it from her. Arden gives her a sincere look of appreciation before occupying the seat across from her.

Cerylia begins to pour into each of the cups, the steam of the warm golden liquid rising to greet her. A drip of honey here, a dash of sugar there, and their calendula tea is ripe for sipping.

Arden leans back in her seat, the cup resting just above her bosom. She lowers her gaze before saying, "I'm sorry I left Sardoria without saying anything."

Cerylia knew this conversation was bound to happen sooner or later. Quite frankly, she's glad it's happening now. "Why did you? Leave, that is?"

Arden squeezes her eyes shut. "I couldn't possibly stay knowing my capacity to inflict pain was only growing stronger with each passing day. First Felix, then Braxton, then Delwynn—"

"You healed Delwynn," Cerylia interrupts.

Arden slowly opens one eye, then the other. "I didn't. I couldn't have. He was writhing on the floor, in so much pain—pain that *I* caused."

"He's perfectly healthy, even walking without his staff, I might add." She winks. "Best shape I've ever seen him in."

Arden's spirits seem to lift. "And what of Braxton?"

"I wouldn't know. He fled not long after you did." She shakes her head at the memory. "After his encounter with the Mallum, I suppose I can't blame him."

"What encounter?"

"You'd already left, but the Mallum infiltrated the castle, taking Braxton's abilities along with it." She takes a long sip of her tea. "You two never crossed paths?"

"I haven't seen Braxton since Sardoria."

Cerylia can sense the hurt in her voice, so she decides not to press any further. "But what about you? Is there anything you'd like to talk about? Any questions you need answers to?"

Arden lets out a guttural laugh, throwing her head back in response. "Where do I even begin?" Almost instantly, her tone turns serious. "I've had a number of encounters with the Mallum, each strangely more enticing than the last."

Cerylia tilts her head, curious as to the choice of words. "Enticing? How so?"

"Well, I'm here in Orihia as non-illusié, without the ability to heal, which I've been told is impossible. I haven't seen the Mallum since I've been here, but my most recent encounter is one I can't seem to shake." Her brows furrow as she recounts the experience. "I was somehow taken to a memory that I believe happened right before I was born, with my mother and my brother. My father was nowhere in sight. It got me thinking about Haskell's discovery in Braxton's room—of a photograph that had my birth date on it. Aldreda and Braxton were in it, along with my brother and my mother. She was . . . cradling me in her arms."

There are tears streaming down her face now, and as much as Cerylia wants to comfort her, she knows Arden needs to get it *all* out.

"Haskell and I concluded that we *must* share blood with the Tymonds because there is no logical explanation for that photo. How did my mother even know the Tymonds? And beyond that, how could she trust them? Especially after the Savant—*Tymond's Savant*—allegedly murdered her?"

The tears are in full force now, and Cerylia rises from her chair to console her distraught niece. It's just as she'd feared. Arden's discovered far more than she'd expected—and Darius has been tormenting her *through* the Mallum with the ghosts of memories past.

Cerylia wraps her arms around her niece, pulling her in close, before rocking her back and forth. "I should have told you when you first arrived on my doorstep."

"So, it's true?" Arden looks up at her, blinking back tears. "My brother and I share blood with the Tymonds?"

Cerylia gives her shoulders a light squeeze. "I'm afraid so."

Arden exhales a shaky breath. "How?"

Cerylia bites the inside of her cheek. The urge to keep her niece safe all these years has clearly done more harm than good. She never wanted it to come to this. She'd made a promise—a promise to keep them sheltered from it all, from the *truth*. She knows that once it's spoken it can't be undone, but perhaps it's time.

Cerylia lowers her voice, refusing to be afraid of the words themselves. "I may not have told you then, but I can tell you now. Your mother and Aldreda," she says with as much courage as she can muster, "were sisters."

ARDEN ELIRI

AT FIRST, I'M certain I haven't heard her correctly. *Sisters? My mother and Aldreda?*

And then another thought terrorizes me.

I killed my aunt. My . . . other aunt.

I cannot catch a fucking break.

I bring my palms to my forehead, pressing in and out, as I try to make sense of this. If my mother and Aldreda were sisters, then that means . . .

"Braxton is my *cousin*?" The words fly out of my mouth before I can stop them. I can feel Cerylia's arms around me still, but they're doing very little in the way of consolation. Not meaning to be brash, I pull away from her, suddenly feeling like I can't breathe—like all the air has been squashed from my lungs.

"Arden, you are *not* a Tymond. You are an Eliri, through and through."

I can hear the words, but I'm more focused on the uncontrollable rage that's swirling in my chest. "So, let me get this straight. *Darius's* Savant killed my mother? Killed *his wife's* sister?"

Cousin Braxton. Aunt Aldreda. *Uncle Darius.*

Bile rises in my throat, threatening to force its way up and out. There's no way. No way. *No. Way.*

My rage turns to disgust, which eventually shifts to complete and utter despair. I don't know when I went from sitting to standing, but my arms are now crossed over my chest and I'm gripping my shoulders so tightly that I swear if I let go, I'll never escape this nightmarish moment of reality. My voice breaks as I ask, "Does Haskell know?"

Cerylia lets out a defeated sigh. "He knows only what you've known—up until this point."

"Why didn't you tell me before?"

She gives me a pained expression. "I wanted to, but we'd only just met. I was hoping I could protect you from it . . . shield you from it somehow."

I turn away from her, looking off in the distance at my brother. After all these years, we'd finally found each other. After all these years, I'd finally clawed my way out from underneath Tymond's clutches. It's all beginning to make sense now.

The way I'd been treated growing up.

Why I'd been the only female member of the Cruex.

Why I could never seem to do *anything* right.

Because I was the estranged niece.

The overwhelming burden no one wanted.

"You didn't come for me." I barely manage to choke out the words. "Why not?"

"You were always being watched over, Arden. Even when it didn't feel like it."

The glimmer in her eyes reminds me of someone . . .

Cyrus.

"Cyrus was a good friend of your father's," Cerylia continues, reading my mind. "Until we could be sure of Darius's motives, we didn't want to put you—or any of us, for that matter—even further at risk."

"His motives?" I scoff, my anger rising again. "Cyrus is the one who took me as *prisoner* to Trendalath! He's the reason I got into that whole mess to begin with."

"I'll admit, it was foolish of him. But I assure you, his intentions were pure. They always have been. Darius's, on the other hand, are not." She raises her own hand, wiggling her fingers to emphasize her point.

"The ring," I murmur in understanding. "The Mallum, then?"

"Whoever wears that ring controls the actions of the Mallum." A shadow flickers in her eyes and, as if she's said too much, she quickly adds, "Or so it's said."

I flash back to all my previous encounters—every last one. I clearly recall Darius hovering over me during those final moments in my attempt to heal Aldreda. He had been there. The Mallum had been there. And he'd been wearing that damn ring.

But in the tavern, in Chialka . . . the Mallum had told me it had been *Darius* who had killed Aldreda—not me. Why would he want to kill his wife? Why *did* he kill his wife? And why would Darius send the Mallum to reveal the truth? Why take me back to past memories of my mother, my brother? It's almost as if the Mallum has a mind of its own, but that's impossible . . . *isn't it?*

Even though I haven't spoken them aloud, the questions hang in the air. Lingering. Waiting for answers that can't be given here.

I bring my attention back to Cerylia, who's been watching me like a hawk. I'm hoping that, while deep in thought, my expression hasn't given too much away. As much as I want to confide in her, I want to talk to Haskell first. And Felix.

As always, with her uncanny sense of knowing, she says, "You know you can talk to me about anything. I promised your father I would protect you and your brother at all costs. I'm sorry it's taken this long for the truth to come out, for us to be together again. I hope you can forgive me. Furthermore, I hope you can trust me."

Something in her words touches my heart in a way that only an aunt's can. I rise from my seat and walk over to her. The embrace is longer this time, and when I finally let go, there are tears brimming in her eyes. "I can't even begin to tell you what this means to me." She seems to want to say more, but merely smiles as she dabs at her eyes. "Why don't I go get Haskell? We can finish up our tea, together. As a family."

I give her a comforting grin. "I'd like that very much."

DARIUS TYMOND

DARIUS FISTS HIS hands at his sides, not bothering to coax the Mallum back into submission. He whirls around to face Cyrus. "You had a part in this," he says through gritted teeth.

Cyrus's face falls and confusion takes over. "I most certainly did not, Your Majesty."

"You led them here."

Cyrus shakes his head, his panic spreading like a virus. He opens his mouth to speak, but Darius cuts him off. "How long have they been following me? How long have *you* been guiding them?"

"I have done nothing of the sort." Cyrus's eyes flick to the hovering cloak behind the king. "There is no one to blame here. The boy is smart. He's your *son*." He takes a bold step forward. "Can't you see? How out of hand this has all gotten? You almost killed your only son—and over what?"

"He's no son of mine," he sneers. "Not any longer."

"Surely you don't mean that."

Darius gestures behind him. "He's chosen his side."

"Aldreda would—"

"Don't you dare," he growls, "mention that vile woman's name to me ever again." The ring pulses deeper, the Mallum growing stronger with each angry breath he takes. "She's the reason I have to do all of this in the first place!"

"I implore you to find another way," Cyrus pleads. "Hear me, Your Majesty. Please. There *has* to be another way."

Darius senses the cloaked figure inching forward but extends his arm in a silent command for it to stay where it is. "If there *was* another way, don't you think I would have found it? Don't you think I would have *tried* anything other than this?"

"The man I once knew would have. But this"—he angles his head at the crimson and black mist—"is beyond any of our control."

"You shouldn't speak of what you don't know."

"Then *tell* me," Cyrus says firmly. "You can only keep me in the dark for so long."

"Perhaps I prefer it that way." Darius sighs, closing his eyes as he clasps his hands together. The pulse of the ring slows until it fades entirely. The mist dissipates along with it.

"Find out where they went," he barks as he brushes past Cyrus. "And don't bother coming to find me until you know."

BRAXTON HORNSBY

BRAXTON RUSHES OVER to where Rydan had just stood, wondering why the ex-Cruex hadn't been able to see him. It's not like there was anything blocking his view—unless, of course, he'd somehow blended in so much with his surroundings that Rydan couldn't tell the difference either way; but from where he's standing, that theory is unlikely.

Braxton tilts his head skyward, hoping that whatever had pulled Rydan out of this place will return and take him, too—but as the minutes tick by, he knows better than to build false hope more than he already has.

It's then he recalls what Rydan had been doing in this spot in the first place. He'd *seen* something. Braxton lowers his gaze, noticing, much like everything else around him, a gray stone. But when he bends to pick it up, he's more than surprised at the feel of cool metal against his skin. He brushes the dirt from the circular object before turning it every which way to examine its unique embeddings. No larger than his palm, it's much heavier than it looks. He traces the flame-like symbols with his index finger, trailing them to the very top until he's formed a backwards C. It makes him wonder . . .

Of all the nothingness that's here, why this?

And why had Rydan been here? *How?*

Was this what he'd been looking for?

Could this possibly be his ticket out of here?

Knowing better than to leave it behind, Braxton secures the object in his pocket. If Rydan had come here specifically looking for it, perhaps there's a chance he'll come back—and if not . . . well, he refuses to think about what that might mean for life as he knows it.

RYDAN HELSTROM

STARING BLANKLY OUT the window, Rydan's trying his best to piece it all together. Felix has been out there for hours with Estelle at his side, Opal still unconscious—just as lifeless as she'd been before he'd awoken.

The delicate brush of an arm against his pulls him from his thoughts, but only momentarily. Vira gently sets a half-empty bottle of tonic on the ledge before giving him her undivided attention. "Any signs of improvement?"

He shoots her a sidelong glance, then angles his head at the scene outside. "Doesn't look like it."

"They'll find her. I'm certain of it."

"How can you be so sure?"

She trails her hand along his arm in a comforting way, although it feels anything but. "It's just like Felix said. He has a strong relationship with Opal. They've known each other for quite some time. If anyone's going to find her, it's him."

Oddly enough, Rydan feels a pang of envy on Arden's behalf. For once, he's happy she's nowhere near them—or this conversation, truth be told.

Vira's hand suddenly stops. She brings it to her wrist, her grip tightening, almost as if bracing herself for what she's about to say next. Her voice is merely a whisper when she asks, "What was it like?"

At first, he has no idea to what she's referring, but when he takes in the darkness that's suddenly shrouding her expression, he knows her question can only be about one thing. *The Void.* "Well, for starters, it's certainly a place I never wish to return to." He shudders. "Devoid of color, of meaning, of *life*. If an underworld exists, I imagine its gateway would look something like the Void." He turns to face her. "Why do you ask?"

It isn't the first time she seems reluctant to speak, her voice cracking when she finally says, "Sometimes I can't help but wonder if that's where my mother ended up."

Shit. The guilt he feels right now is insurmountable. He backpedals in his mind, searching for *something* to say that'll right this wrong, that'll make Vira feel better— but he comes up empty. That is, until he remembers what he saw . . . and *who* he didn't see.

Vira sighs, seemingly ready to dismiss herself from their conversation when Rydan smoothly changes the subject. "I did see something rather unusual in the

Void—something I believe only you can help me figure out."

Her downtrodden expression lightens. "Oh?"

"That night, when your brother appeared in Orihia, here in this very cabin, wounded—"

Vira waves a hand in the air. "No need to recount what I so vividly remember."

His cheeks warm. Despite feeling flustered, he continues, "Well, in the Void, it wasn't Xerin who showed up. It was someone else—a man I've never seen before."

"But I was there," Vira says, her brows furrowing. "I clearly remember dressing *my brother's* wounds. Are you saying I wouldn't know my own brother, even when he's literally bleeding to death right in front of me?"

Rydan backs off a little, softening his tone. "I'm not saying that at all. I'm just telling you what I saw."

"Tell me, then, what did this stranger look like?"

"He had dark features."

She waits a moment before pursing her lips. "That's it? That's all you're going to give me?"

"That's all I remember."

He can tell by the way she turns to leave that she no longer cares to continue their discussion. Before she can get too far out of earshot, he says, "There's something else."

Exasperated, she throws her head back. "What?"

"It was there," Rydan says. "And not the fabric, but the real thing. I saw it with my own eyes."

At first, what he's said doesn't seem to register, but then recognition floods her face. "You mean—?"

Rydan nods. "The crescent fire."

ARDEN ELIRI

HASKELL HAS JUST as many questions for Cerylia as I did, but I'm only half-listening as she repeats everything she's just told me. My focus is somewhere else entirely—across the grounds, to be exact.

Namely on Felix, Estelle, and Opal.

Felix hangs his head as he pulls away from Opal, which must mean another failed attempt in the way of amplifying to bring her back to this plane. Estelle reaches for him, but he recoils at her touch. He's frustrated.

We all are.

Out of the corner of my eye, I watch as he walks to the edge of the forest, fuming. I know that now isn't the best time to talk to him about everything I've just learned, but perhaps it'll serve as a welcome distraction.

I silently excuse myself from the conversation that Haskell and Cerylia are so engrossed in before walking down the steps in Felix's direction. He seems to sense my presence because my feet have hardly hit the pavement when he locks eyes with me. Even from a distance, I can see the defeat written all over his face—but as I draw closer, there's something else there. Barely discernible, but I'd recognize it anywhere. *He's hiding something.*

Knowing that our inextricable link makes it all too easy for him to read that thought, I quickly dismiss it and greet him with a warm smile. He has enough to worry about—no need to add my suspicions to the list.

"How's it going over there?" I ask.

"How does it look like it's going?"

His terse response causes me to stop in my tracks, heat rising to my cheeks. "You've been at it for hours. You must be getting close," I offer wistfully.

He studies me, his face softening as he realizes how curt he's just been. He takes my hands in his before pulling me close and pressing his lips to my forehead. "I didn't mean that the way it sounded. Forgive me."

I remain in his embrace, nodding. "I know. Tensions are high right now, as expected."

He pulls away from me then, concern alight in his eyes. "Something's . . . different."

I sigh. "Cerylia just gave me an entire history lesson."

He raises a brow. "About your family?"

Without meaning to, I grimace. "Seems I'm a blood relative of the Tymonds, if that answers your question."

Much to my surprise, he doesn't seem even the slightest bit shocked by the news. It's then he says something that catches me completely off guard. "There are worse fates than that, you know."

"Maybe for you," I scoff, "but for me, sharing a lineage with one of the most despicable families to ever reign over Trendalath is pretty high up there."

"Despicable? Is that how you'd categorize Braxton?"

I wave a hand in the air, my annoyance mounting at the miscommunication. "No, that's not what I meant, and you know it."

"Might I remind you that, by blood, Braxton *is* a Tymond."

I narrow my eyes at him. This certainly isn't the way I thought this conversation would go. "Braxton has been so far removed from Trendalath Kingdom—by *choice*, I might add—that he may as well belong to a different family entirely."

"Are those who raised him *not* his family?'

"Not when there's murder in cold blood at play."

Something unsettling flickers in his expression. And just like that, it's gone. He opens his mouth to respond, then closes it, shaking his head instead.

"Darius killed Aldreda." It comes out as a whisper, but I know he's heard me.

"*The Mallum* killed Aldreda."

"And who controls the Mallum?" I counter, my temper flaring.

He doesn't argue or disagree with me, but I can tell I've rattled something loose inside of him. What it is, though, I don't know.

After an extremely uncomfortable silence, he looks at me with an icy glare. "How well can you *really* know your family, Arden? Even after what Cerylia's just told you . . . how can you judge one family without ever truly knowing your own?"

His words slice right through me, not necessarily because they're harsh, but because they're *true.* I take a step back, my heart walling up like it has so many times before. Just when I think he's on my side, just when I think he cares for me and has my back, regardless . . .

I can see my own hurt reflected in his eyes.

From a distance, Estelle begins shouting.

"I suppose I should let you get back." I glance over my shoulder before glaring at him. "I mean, they're *your* family, right? You know them better than anyone."

"Arden . . ."

I stalk away from him, not bothering to hear yet another excuse. It'd just be one more thing to add to the growing list of insincere apologies.

CERYLIA JARETH

CERYLIA'S JUST FINISHING up her conversation with Haskell when the sight of Estelle, who's wildly flailing her arms, grabs her attention.

Haskell turns over his shoulder, no doubt noticing the commotion. "We should probably head over there."

Cerylia nods. "I'm right behind you."

They bound down the steps of the cabin, rushing toward the waning campfire. To her right, she spots Arden and Felix, who are both heading in the same direction they are. From her vantage point, there's no noticeable movement in Rydan and Vira's cabin, which means they might be asleep—probably for the best, anyway, because when Opal comes back to, the last person she needs to see is Rydan.

Cerylia arrives at the scene just behind Haskell, and is followed by Arden and Felix shortly after.

"What happened?" she asks, feeling more breathless than usual.

Felix pushes his way through before kneeling next to Opal. There's no mistaking the flare of irritation that blazes in Arden's eyes. Cerylia shifts her attention to Estelle, who appears to be frantically searching for an answer.

"She stirred," Estelle finally manages to say. "Her eyelids fluttered and she was mumbling incoherently—something I couldn't quite understand."

"For how long?"

"Just seconds, but it's more movement than we've gotten from her in *hours*." She turns a hopeful gaze toward Felix. "I think if you amplify now, she'll be able to find her way. She can make it back to us."

Felix doesn't waste a single second. He inhales deeply to center himself, then casts an unwavering stare at his subject—Opal. Cerylia's about to ask if there's anything she can do to assist when Felix suddenly grunts, "Arden. Put your hand on my shoulder. Now."

Cerylia looks to Arden. Her stunned expression says it all. "Well, don't just stand there," she says, ushering her niece forward. "Do as he says."

Haskell steps beside his sister, and Cerylia catches the whisper of a reassuring sentiment. Within seconds of witnessing the expression on Felix's face, the look on Arden's tells her that there's something more going on between them than just support. Their connection is so obvious that, as it grows, Haskell is forced to step back. A display of magnificent violet sparks erupts all around them. Enclosed in an electric field of their own making, Cerylia's mouth drops as a memory comes flooding back to her. She's only seen this one other time in the past—and it hadn't ended well.

Now concerned for her niece's well-being, Cerylia racks her brain for what to do, how to come out of this unscathed. In such an uncontrolled state, power this immense could blast Arden into oblivion . . .

Could blast them *all* into oblivion.

She's considering the worst when, suddenly, Arden lifts her hand, the sparks fizzling out. Much to her surprise, the energy field dissipates, leaving only brightly colored ashes in its wake.

Cerylia presses her hand against her chest, her stomach. *Still here. Still in one piece.* She looks to the group, but their attention is on something even more mesmerizing. Opal's eyes are wide open, but that's not what they're all staring at . . .

The voluptuous silver hair.

The smooth porcelain skin.

Not only has Opal *returned*—somehow, she's wound the clock back to her original age.

BRAXTON HORNSBY

THE SHAPE-SHIFTING nature of his mind in this place is unsettling, to say the least. Braxton has no idea how long he's been stuck in this gray realm, but he imagines it's been at least a day or two, although it feels far longer. He's also noticed that no matter where he wanders off to, there's never an endpoint. Oftentimes, it feels like he's walking in circles—ending up right back where he'd started.

After briefly seeing Rydan in this lords-forgotten place, he's made it a point to return to that same spot, over and over again, to no avail. Rydan had been plucked from the ethers, a fortunate turn of events for his fellow Caldari—not so fortunate for him, though. Even so, he's been carrying around the strange metal crest he'd found Rydan staring at, hoping that it holds enough significance for him to return . . . but as the gray vanquishes all feasibility of the world he once belonged to, so his hope diminishes.

Who had helped him escape?

Who had known he was even here?

And how?

Braxton kicks at the dirt beneath him, not the least bit surprised when no dust forms. Not only is this place devoid of color, sound, and smell, it's also devoid of action. He can touch the dirt, but if he were to pick it up, it wouldn't slide through his fingers. In fact, the only thing he's been successful in *holding* is the crest itself— which is how he knows it must not have originated here.

He can't help but wonder . . .

If it came from his world, from *Aeridon*, how did it get here? Had someone lost it? Misplaced it? Hidden it?

Even though he knows, for certain, that the crest is secure in his arms, he glances down at it one more time. He's considering examining it, yet again (because really, what else is there for him to do?), when something unusual catches his eye.

In the distance, a shimmer with a dark green and gold hue comes into view. Flummoxed, Braxton stumbles toward it, having momentarily forgotten what it's like to see color, to see movement. It grows more distinct the closer he gets, in both color and in size, until it begins to spin, slowly, in a counterclockwise direction.

Entranced, he gapes at the simplicity, the *beauty,* of it. He's so taken by the sight that only when he looks at the center of the shimmering vortex does he recognize the person inside of it. *Opal Marston.*

But that's not even the most surprising part. Just above the center, where Opal stands, are two figures Braxton would know anywhere. Felix. And Arden.

They've found him!

They've found him and they've come for him!

His hope restored, he draws closer, waving his arms to catch their attention—but he's dismayed to find that with each step, the vortex drops even further out of reach. Not daring to lose sight of his only saving grace, he tilts his chin skyward and opens his mouth to shout into the swirling ethers; but his voice doesn't penetrate the orb and is merely echoed back to him.

His frustration climbs along with the shimmering gateway, higher and higher. Braxton falls to his knees, watching in agony as Opal looks around, over and over again, unable to see that Felix and Arden are *right there.*

Unable to see that *he's* right here.

With Arden's name sitting idly at the back of his throat, he thrusts a hand upward, but it's no use. They can't see him. He's invisible to them, just as he'd been invisible to Rydan.

The last thing he sees is the smile on Opal's face as she bears witness to a place he's all too familiar with.

Orihia.

Within moments, Opal fades from view. The shimmering orb closes in on itself. And what flimsy thread remains of Braxton's hope is ripped to shreds all over again.

DARIUS TYMOND

LIKE A PHANTOM, the sickening crack of Hugh's neck lingers in the hallway that leads to the Daegrum Chambers. Darius doesn't so much as take his eyes off the door as he approaches it. Ensuring that it closes and locks behind him, he turns to the cabinet where he'd hidden the speculor Braxton had somehow uncovered in Aldreda's chambers.

While Cyrus is off searching for Braxton and his co-conspirator, Darius had decided to retrace his steps. There's no telling how long he'd been followed—*where* he'd been followed—and, given that the item most at risk is hidden within these very walls . . . well, there's a lot at stake. He's pleased to find that the speculor is exactly where he'd left it, undisturbed.

Knowing the lockbox is secured in its rightful place, he smiles to himself. Braxton may have overheard everything he'd said in the tunnels, but he's far from having all the pieces to this gloriously deceptive puzzle.

He flicks the amethyst ring with his thumb until the gem is facing him. As he always does when he gives himself a spare moment, he admires its flawless cut, its intricate welding. Knowing the power it contains makes it all the more desirable . . . and it's all his.

It will *always* be his, until his final parting breath.

Darius closes his hand into a fist, feeling the sudden urge to visit the jaded spring. It does happen to be next on his list, but just as he's considering rounding up Cyrus, he remembers what he's tasked his advisor with.

Suppose he'll have to go it alone . . . again.

He walks to the other side of the room, sliding open the drawer where he tends to keep his staff. While the indentation is there, the staff isn't. Not wanting to jump to conclusions, he assures himself that there are a few other places it could be.

But it isn't in the armory.

Nor in the Great Room.

Nor in his chambers.

Dread curls in his stomach. Only two other people know about that staff, know of the jaded spring—and those two people had sworn their fealty years ago.

Perhaps he's wrong. Perhaps there *is* an item more at risk than the speculor . . . one that seems to no longer be in his possession.

RYDAN HELSTROM

EVEN THOUGH HIS experience with Opal was quite recent, Rydan's finding it difficult to sketch the man he'd seen in the memory.

Dark features. That's what he'd told Vira. In all honesty, that's all he can remember. A complete stranger with dark features—which really isn't much to go on.

He drops the quill onto the half-sketched page in his leather-bound journal before running a hand through his already disheveled hair. Vira stirs from across the room, causing him to turn around in his seat. Sometimes he forgets that she's a light sleeper, but the steady rise and fall of her chest indicates she's still sound asleep.

When he turns back around, he can't help but notice the gathering that's taking place around the campfire. He rises from his chair, pressing his hands against the glass.

The view before him looks exactly the same as it has for the past couple hours—with one exception, of course.

That being Opal, who's now sitting upright.

She's awake.

The realization snags on another as his eyes drift to the open journal beneath him. He stares at the half-face of the man he's drawn, once again attempting to recall whatever details he can. While he falls short there, he *does* distinctly remember the group saying something right after he'd returned from the mind-bending journey. Huddled all around him, they'd mentioned something about it being a memory . . .

Opal's memory.

"It wasn't the Void itself, but *her memory of it*," he murmurs, suddenly feeling a knot in his chest.

Why Opal would have a memory of that night doesn't make any sense. Even more disturbing is the fact that her memory shows a complete stranger and *not* Xerin. Given the fact that he and Vira so vividly remember seeing her brother and no one else, how is that even possible?

It shouldn't be.

Silent warning bells rattle his sense of calm as he looks out the window again. His gaze lands directly on Arden, who's standing just inches away from Opal. Suddenly fearing for her safety—*all* their safety—he closes the journal and tucks it underneath his arm. He pulls the door open as quietly as he can so as to not disturb Vira, but once he's outside, well, he's never walked with more purpose in his life.

With tense shoulders and a clenched jaw, he finally approaches the group, loosening up just enough to force a smile before stepping next to Arden. Fortunately for him, everyone else seems preoccupied with Opal, so he manages to give Arden a small nudge and simultaneously whisper to her without anyone noticing. "Can we talk?"

Arden angles her head at him, her long braid draped over her shoulder, emerald eyes bright with newfound hope. She seems complacent enough—that is, until her gaze meets his. That's when her face falls to produce an exact replica of the expression he's currently wearing. "Is everything okay?"

He hates to be the one to do this, to rain on her parade, yet again. No matter how far forward they get, they always seem to fall back into the throes of familiarity—and what's been *familiar* for them is something he wouldn't wish on his worst enemy.

Not even King Tymond.

He shakes his head as if to say *not here*, then signals for her to follow him. With a weary look, she eyes the journal tucked underneath his arm. Just as they're about to enter the forest and hide somewhere completely out of sight, Cerylia manages to thwart his plans. She grabs his arm, pulling him away from the group, sans Arden. "I thought you'd be asleep, what with your grand escapade and all."

Rydan doesn't so much as flinch at her domineering tone. "Vira's asleep. I saw the commotion from my window and thought I'd—"

"Come out here and make things worse?" She purses her lips. "You're the last person she needs to see."

Rydan clamps down on his tongue before he can utter a response. Only when he glances over at the group again does he notice something different about Opal. She's *young.* He'd been so focused on speaking with Arden that he hadn't noticed the major alteration in her appearance. He's about to ask Cerylia how something like that is even possible, but the look on her face indicates that she knows just as little as he does.

Only when they're standing at the steps of his cabin does Rydan realize Cerylia's been guiding him here the whole time. "Perhaps it would be in our best interest if we let everyone rest and get a good night's sleep. We've dealt with enough for one day, wouldn't you agree?"

Rydan shifts his gaze, watching as Estelle and Haskell escort Opal to her cabin. Shortly after, Felix follows Arden to what ultimately ends up being a closed door, shut right in his face. As Felix marches over to his cabin, *alone,* Rydan brings his attention back to Cerylia, but it seems she, too, is focused on something else.

Something behind him.

"Opal's awake?" a sleep-deprived voice says.

Rydan turns to see Vira standing at the top of the steps, rubbing the sleep from her eyes. "Yes," he says as he climbs to meet her. "Queen Jareth here was just escorting me back to the cabin."

A hint of a smile touches Vira's lips as she tilts her head and dips into a small curtsy. "How very kind of you, Your Greatness."

Cerylia waves a hand in the air as if it was nothing, then turns to leave. "You two sleep well, now. I'll see you at dawn."

"Goodnight," Vira says before tugging on Rydan's arm to lead him inside. It's a good thing his journal blends in with his tunic—he's not sure he could handle explaining to Vira why he felt the need to tell Arden about it first . . . especially since Vira's been the one there with him, amidst all the chaos.

Rydan manages one last glance at Arden's cabin just as the lights flick off. *Tomorrow*, he tells himself. *We'll get to the bottom of all this tomorrow.*

ARDEN ELIRI

I'VE NEVER FELT such a mix of emotions before. On the one hand, I'm happy that Opal has returned, both literally and figuratively—in presence and in appearance. On the other, I'm frustrated, and a little hurt, by my latest interaction with Felix. And, to add to that, I'm also confused by the energy I was somehow able to tap into to help bring Opal back.

The last time I felt that way was, no surprise here, when I was with Felix—when I felt as though *I* was somehow amplifying. The feelings were nearly identical.

I coddle Juniper as I kick my boots the rest of the way off and meander over to the bed. She jumps out of my arms and curls up right beside me. I lean back into the pillows, pulling the plush blanket as high as it will go.

What a day. What a week. What a *year.*

Who knew turning eighteen could change the very course of your entire existence?

Even though I've just learned the most earth-shattering news about my family's history, that's the furthest thing from my mind. Instead, it's Felix I'm thinking about. His face floats across my mind as I pick at the edges of the blanket. It's hard to fathom how he can go from so hot to so cold. It makes me wonder, since he *has* been amplifying for most of his life, is it possible he's picked up on too many energies? Energies he's somehow absorbed that perhaps don't even belong to him? But then that might mean . . . that I don't really know him at all.

I refuse to dive any further into that can of worms.

Next thought.

Braxton momentarily pushes against the corners of my mind, but I manage to block him out. The Tymonds are the *last* thing I want to think about right now. In fact, they may be the only thing worse stewing over than where my relationship with Felix currently stands.

Much to my surprise, a memory of Rydan resurfaces. A happy one, that's somewhat recent, too—specifically, when we'd been swimming in the waterfall at the edge of Orihia without a care in the world. I've always felt so safe with him. So understood.

And then . . . a not-so-happy one. That fated day in the Soames's house. The murder of fellow illusié, unbeknownst to us at the time. My stomach turns as I recall bagging up the heads of the deceased just after knocking him—*my partner*—unconscious. I just . . . left him there.

I thought he'd deserved it.

Maybe he had.

The thought alarms me. After everything that's happened, I'd assumed I'd forgiven him. That I'd forgiven *myself.* We hadn't known any better. We were just following orders—an iron-clad decree that meant life or death not just for our targets . . . but for us, too, should we fail or disobey.

Sadly, I'd made the choice for the both of us, leaving Rydan to suffer the consequences. I'd chosen *life* and fled, but, in doing so, I'd simultaneously chosen death for Rydan. Had the Caldari not gotten to Trendalath in time, he would have been executed. How's *that* for a guilty conscience?

But I *did* go back. That's what counts.

And Rydan is okay.

And I'm okay.

And we're all here together in Orihia.

Funny how things always seem to have a way of working themselves out. Knowing that I've let that mistake eat at me for the better part of the year, it feels good to finally let myself off the hook. Rydan's forgiven me, so what's the point if I don't forgive myself?

I roll over onto my side, bringing my gaze to the window. Even though a tree is blocking most of my view, the dim lighting from Rydan's cabin provides a shimmering outline of the trunk. I briefly wonder what he'd been so keen on talking to me about, but figure that

I'll just ask him tomorrow. I've done enough thinking (and feeling) for one evening.

I blow out the candle in the lone lantern on my bedside table, noticing that Rydan's cabin lights flick off just moments after. I smile knowing that once those parallel lines of thought are established, there's no going back. I shift onto my back and tuck Juniper underneath my arm before climbing beneath the covers completely.

An effortless night of sleep whisks me away.

CERYLIA JARETH

DESPITE HER BEST efforts, sleep has managed to evade the queen. Cerylia stifles a yawn as she reaches for the curtain, pulling it aside. Nearly dawn. The others should be waking soon.

Pulling her cloak taut, she glides down the narrow hall until she reaches the only other room in the cabin. The door is halfway shut, but through the crack, she can see Opal—still fast asleep, still young as ever. Given all the poor girl's been through recently, she decides to let her rest a little while longer.

She makes for the kitchen, eyeing the black kettle and canister of loose-leaf peppermint tea sitting idly on the counter. A quick glance out the window at a newly lit fire reveals that Avery's already up and moving about.

Perfect.

She scoops both the kettle and the canister into her arms, snagging a small teacup along the way, before heading out the door. Avery, the gentleman that he is, sees her coming and quickly rushes over to greet her.

"I'll get this started for you," he says as he takes each item and sets them down. He kneels by the fire, his outstretched hands nearly *in* the flames. Cerylia watches as the fire grows bigger and brighter from the deep violet that's radiating from his fingertips. "That should speed things up a bit."

Cerylia gives him a polite nod before taking a seat at the wooden table. The surface is scattered with miniature glass bottles, no larger than the palm of her hand, ranging in color from cobalt to burgundy to jade to black. As she picks one up to examine it further, she realizes that some of them are full, others are empty. Avery seems to be preoccupied with preparing the tea, so she removes the cork from one and wafts the scent. "Do you mind if I ask what these are?"

He glances up at her, mid-pour. "Tonics, tinctures, herbal remedies. I suppose you could say I have an affinity for healing."

"Does your family own an apothecary?"

"Oh, how I wish." He hands her the tea with a steady grip, only letting go once he's sure she's got a firm hold on it. "No, my father's in the shipping industry—textiles, foods, silks, spices. Mostly from the Isle of Lonia back to Chialka."

"Where did you learn all of this, then?"

He smiles, as if recalling a pleasant memory. "In my spare time, mostly. When I wasn't at the docks. I visited neighboring towns, like Miraenia, as often as I could. The merchants were quite gracious with their time. I asked questions, they answered them. Eventually, I picked up enough knowledge to actually do something worthwhile with it."

The words warm her heart. To know that he still trusted his neighbors in other towns, even after Tymond's attempts to keep everyone separate and everything pulled apart . . . Hearing such a story immediately reminds her of simpler times, of when she'd met Dane. Having been born into royalty, her love affair with an Eliri, a family of non-royal blood, had sparked outrage amongst her family—but he'd certainly proven them wrong. In the time that they'd ruled Aeridon together, *before* the lands had been split into kingdoms, there had been complete harmony amongst the people. Dane, as power-hungry as he'd been, had never let his personal desires affect his empathy and kindness for others. As far as *worthy* non-royal blood goes, the Eliris certainly top the list.

Lost in thought, she picks up one of the jade-colored bottles, tilting it back and forth. "Might I ask why the different colors?"

"Helps me remember what's what. I only use certain herbs in certain colored bottles. Even after washing them, I wouldn't dare risk mixing some of them together." He starts replacing the cork she'd pulled out earlier. "The one you're holding is a healing tonic for illusié-inflicted harm. I gave some to Opal last night and made a couple different versions this morning."

Cerylia glances over her shoulder at the cabin. "She was still asleep when I left, but I did check on her. She looked peaceful as ever, so whatever you've given her must be working."

Avery boasts a proud smile at the compliment.

"And what about the others?" Cerylia asks, gesturing to the rest of the tinctures.

"The cobalt bottles contain water-based solutions, mostly for igniting-related injuries." A shy smile. "These are to make transporting a bit easier on the stomach," he says, pointing to the burgundy bottles. "And these . . ."

She holds up one of the black bottles. "Are heavy."

"They're more of a paste, not so easy to get down."

"Their use?"

Crimson crawls across his cheeks. "Between you and me, I'm hoping they'll prove effective in defense against the Mallum."

She raises a brow, her curiosity piqued. "Is this something you were taught in Lonia?"

He shrugs. "I suppose it's more of a collection of my own knowledge being put to practical use—or, at least, hoping that that's the case."

Cerylia runs her thumb along the smooth glass, tempted to pocket the vial. "Does it work?"

"I wouldn't know. I haven't come directly across the Mallum, but during the times it's been in close proximity, like when I was on the ship with Arden, well . . . I still have my abilities. So, I suppose that's something."

Cerylia sets the vial down. "If only it could *restore* illusié abilities—now wouldn't *that* be something?"

"I can't say I haven't tried."

Cerylia gives him a warm smile, realizing that she's hardly even touched her tea. "Thank you for indulging me. And might I recommend making plenty more of those transporting tonics? I have a feeling once we enter the Veil, it's going to take some time to fully adjust."

He gives her a one-handed salute. "Already on it."

"Right," she says brusquely, suddenly feeling like she's intruded on his time. "Well, I'm going to start gathering the others and check in with Estelle—"

"Good morning," a cheery voice says. "Did I just hear my name?"

"You sure did," Avery responds.

Cerylia turns to greet her. "Is the pocket watch in proper working order?"

Knapsack strewn over her shoulder, Estelle gives a quick nod. "As long as Opal's up to it, we're ready to go."

"I suppose there's no point in delaying the inevitable," Cerylia says as she swipes one of the green bottles from the table. "I'll be back shortly." She waits until Avery and Estelle have turned away and are engrossed in conversation before heading back to the cabin—but not before pocketing one of the black vials.

Because she'll be *damned* if that's how she goes out.

RYDAN HELSTROM

THE MOMENT HE sees Arden roaming about her cabin, he's out the door. Thankfully, Vira's busy gathering her things and barely even notices, offering only an absentminded wave as he shouts from over his shoulder. With the journal tucked securely underneath his arm, he makes the journey over to Arden's.

She answers on the third knock, looking slightly disheveled and a little crazy-eyed. "Oh, Rydan," she says, clearly noticing that dawn is just breaking behind him. "A little early to be knocking on doors, isn't it?"

"This couldn't wait." In an attempt to skip further pleasantries, he brushes past her and tosses his journal onto the table. It lands on the exact page he'd hoped for.

She follows him across the room, brows furrowed in confusion. "Am I supposed to know what that is?" she asks as she examines it further. "*Who* that is?"

He'd warned himself to expect this, but even so, his hopes are dashed all the same. "This is the man I saw in Opal's memory. In the Void."

Arden sits at the table, turning the notebook toward her. The charcoal smears slightly as she traces the outline with her index finger. "I'm not following. What memory? And why does this man have only half a face?"

Like she always does, he can tell she's trying to lighten the mood, but he doesn't crack even an inch of a smile. "Arden, I have reason to believe we're in imminent danger."

She looks up from the page, her grave expression in stark contrast to the one she'd worn just moments ago. "You know I need more than that, Rydan. Start from the beginning."

He takes a deep breath, begging his mind not to jumble the two memories together. "Just after Vira, Avery, and I arrived in Orihia, there was an . . . incident. I still don't know exactly how or why it happened the way it did, but Xerin suddenly appeared one night, in our cabin, soaked in blood and marred in scratches. We tended to his wounds, but he was curt with us, even more so than usual." He pauses, wondering why that particular detail sticks out to him, but continues, "That was just around the time I'd found the waterfall and went back to the Soames's house to look for the crest." He flips back a few pages to the sketch of the crescent fire. "I was certain that Xerin was the one who took that piece of fabric I found, the one with this very symbol, but in Opal's memory . . ."

Arden's leaning forward now, her eyes wide with curiosity. "In Opal's memory *what*?" she presses.

"It *wasn't* Xerin." Hearing the words out loud makes him question his own sanity, and from the look on Arden's face, perhaps he should. He shakes his head as the thoughts begin to tumble. "What I mean is that it wasn't Xerin who was bleeding out onto the floor that night." He flips forward a few pages. "It was this man. *This* was the man in Opal's memory. This is all I can remember of him."

Arden looks from him to the sketch then back at him again. "How is that even possible? That's a *completely* different person."

Oh, thank the lords. "That's exactly what I'm saying! It doesn't make any sense."

"Have you asked Vira? Or Avery?"

"I told Vira, but I can sense her disbelief. Honestly, I don't blame her. And Avery, well . . . Avery was a little more than inebriated that night, so I doubt he'd recall."

Arden leans back in her chair, crossing her arms over her chest. While she may not realize it, the question she asks next is the crux of it all. "Why would Opal be accessing a memory of something she wasn't even there for?"

"Precisely." He chooses his next words carefully. "I know she's an Inverter and travels through time and what not, but this is . . . questionable."

Arden chews on her lower lip. "So, what do we do?"

"I don't know," Rydan says as he slowly slides the journal back across the table. "But I'm concerned that we're about to travel into unknown territory with someone who can't be trusted."

"Are you suggesting that we leave Opal behind?" Arden shakes her head. "Cerylia would *never* allow it, given everything we've just been through to get her back."

Before their conversation can go any further, there's a knock at the door. Arden isn't even out of her seat when it swings wide open to reveal Queen Jareth. "There you two are," she says in an exasperated tone. "Come along now," she beckons. "We've been waiting on you."

ARDEN ELIRI

IT ALL HAPPENS in a blur. One minute I'm questioning our safety and the next, I'm leading everyone—including Opal—to the waterfall where the cave is. More accurately, *Rydan's* leading the way, but I'm just steps behind him.

I glance over my shoulder, noticing that Opal is last in line, just behind Cerylia. She seems to be keeping up with the group no problem—completely healed and as spritely as ever. Truthfully, I can't even begin to fathom the intricacies of time travel and *inversion*, but Opal's sudden return from crone to maiden is one I really can't figure out. And with what Rydan's just told me, I can't help but feel suspicious.

My eyes land on Felix, who seems to notice just how deep in thought I am, but I avert my gaze before he can amplify to confirm that theory. I pick up the pace, jogging the next few steps until I'm stride for stride with Rydan.

"We have to be getting close, right?"

He answers without looking at me. "Not much farther. I'm surprised you don't remember."

"I do," I say, my mouth suddenly going dry, "but only because I was following you."

He lowers his voice. "I'm still not sure about this."

There's no need for him to clarify. I know he's talking about Opal. And, in all honesty, I'm not so sure about it either. "Look," I say, keeping my voice quiet, "knowing what I know now about Cerylia being my aunt, I can't imagine she'd put me or Haskell or *any* of us in harm's way." I pause, hoping that if I say the words aloud, it'll make them true. "I trust her, Rydan."

"And I trust you," he says, finally looking at me and flashing a small smile. "But there's always a chance Cerylia doesn't know. She might be in the dark about all this, just like the rest of us."

I'm about to tell him that he might be right when we suddenly reach the edge of the waterfall. *Already?* Rydan turns to face the group and announces that we've arrived.

The queen is the first to step forward. She looks less than pleased as she peers over the edge, no doubt considering the long way down. "*That's* where we're headed?" I nod in the direction she's pointing. "And how do you suggest we get there?"

Hadn't quite thought about that. Informing royalty that we expect her to jump off a cliff isn't exactly bound to go over well.

"There's a pathway that leads directly to the cave," Rydan interjects. "Arden and I have taken it before, but it's long, treacherous, and slow. If you want something quicker, however . . ."

"You two jumped."

I look at Felix. Just as I'd expected, the scowl on his face matches his harsh tone. There's no use denying it because it's the truth. "You're right. We did. And before you ask, yes, the water's deep enough." My eyes flick to Opal, who seems entirely preoccupied with something no one else can see. "If you need Opal to verify, I'm sure she can."

At my icy tone, she snaps back to. Her gaze settles on me. "No need, seeing as there *is* another option that hasn't been suggested yet."

The way she says it sends a chill down my spine. Like she's been here before. *Done* this before. Like she already knows everything.

A smirk touches the corners of her lips as she gestures to my brother. "Haskell can transport us."

At the mention of his name, Haskell makes his way to the front of the group. He stands next to me, no doubt assessing the long way down. "Indeed, I can. I just have to get down there first before I can transport here and back."

"I'll go with him," Felix says a little too quickly. "We'll jump. Together."

With the way he looks at me, I can feel the fresh wound reopening, but I don't dare show it. "Be my guest."

He takes my place as I step out of the way. I keep my expression as neutral as possible, but inside, I feel like my heart is being ripped to shreds. Seeing the two of them standing at the edge of the cliff, together . . . it once again reminds me of that night at the tavern. I shake away the memory, trying to keep my emotions at bay.

"Ready?" Haskell asks as they back up a few steps.

Felix nods. "Ready when you are."

Without so much as a countdown, they take off at the exact same time and catapult off the cliff. I race forward so that I'm standing next to Rydan, praying to the lords above that they make a safe landing. A wave of relief washes over me as I hear a deafening splash and the loud whooping that follows. Haskell and Felix swim to the edge of the bank, the pale pink sand shimmering in the rising daylight.

I immediately notice Rydan's nostalgia. "You should jump, too. I'll wait with the others."

"I don't mind," he says, securing his bag a little tighter over his shoulders. "I can wait. Although, I will say, I'm not looking forward to transporting."

Right on cue, Avery pulls some burgundy vials from his bag and passes them around. "This should help with the nausea," he says.

Estelle passes one to me, along with the bag Haskell had left behind, and I try to ignore the fact that she's carrying Felix's. I force a smile and clink my vial against hers, downing the tart liquid.

"Good lords, what's *in* this?" Vira asks, puckering her lips. "It tastes like burnt cherries. And . . . basil?"

"Sure," Avery says. "Let's go with that."

Vira rolls her eyes at him, knowing that it's unlikely she'll get an actual response.

"Believe me," he says, "it's better if you don't know."

Just as we're returning the empty vials to Avery, Haskell, who's still dripping wet, appears in a flash of blinding green light. "Who's first?" He looks to Rydan and Vira, which, for some reason or another, hits me with an unwarranted spike of jealousy.

Noticing my unease, he clarifies, "I prefer to take two at a time." Then, with a shrug, "New location. Don't want to mess it up."

I can feel Rydan's eyes on me as I step back and let Vira take my place. I fall in line beside Estelle, watching as my brother disappears with the two of them before reappearing almost instantaneously. Cerylia and Opal go next. Then Estelle and Avery. And then . . . me. And Juniper. But I might as well be solo.

As if I don't already feel rejected enough today.

But, if I know Haskell—and I *do*—there's a reason for him singling me out. "Is everything okay?"

Even I'm surprised at the fact that his question throws me off—it makes me realize just how terrible I am at hiding my feelings. "I'm fine," I lie, holding Juniper tight. I raise his bag in my free hand before tossing it to him. "Seems we've got everything we came with. We shouldn't keep the others waiting." I go to link arms with him, but he takes a step back.

"You've been acting strange all morning." He raises a brow. "Tell me what's going on."

I make a silent promise to myself that I'll fill him in on everything later. But for now, we just need to get to Midvale. This journey has already been turbulent enough, and I don't feel like adding to that. So, I use the one thing at my disposal, something I *know* he'll understand and won't dare question. "I guess I'm still a little shell-shocked at everything. Our family history. Cerylia. The Tymonds." I let out a giant exhale. "It's just been a lot."

Not exactly the truth, but not a lie either.

He matches my sigh, releasing the tension in his shoulders. "It may not be the news we expected, or wanted"—he cracks a smile—"but at least we *know*."

I nod, realizing that it's the only thing that's been said today that's given me any kind of reassurance. "I suppose I've gotten exactly what I've asked for."

"And what's that?" Haskell asks as he takes my arm.

I look at him in earnest. "Answers."

RYDAN HELSTROM

FROM WHERE HE stands, it's hard to see exactly what's going on, but it seems Haskell and Arden are taking their sweet time at the top of the cliff. He reaches into his bag, digging around its contents for his canteen. When he looks back up, he's startled to see Opal standing right in front of him. Slowly, he maneuvers the bag back over his shoulder, not wanting to scare her off— treating her as if she's a frightened doe.

The expression on her face tells a different story. She doesn't so much as blink as she says, "I'm pleased to see that you're faring well."

Rydan's sure he fails in trying to hide the noticeable gulp that makes its way down his throat. "I suppose I have you to thank for that. For coming back for me, I mean."

She narrows her eyes. "For future reference, you should never make physical contact with an Inverter. Unless, of course, you're willing to travel great depths into the unknown." Her tone grows even icier. "But I suppose you'd know all about that, wouldn't you?"

As formidable as she seems at present, Rydan struggles to suppress the urge to ask about what he saw in her memory. *How* she saw it. *Why* she was there. And, most importantly, *who* the man was.

But he doesn't get the chance.

With impeccable timing, as always, Haskell appears with Arden and Juniper. "Looks like we're all here and accounted for," he says as he scans over the group.

"And in one piece with all former contents of our stomachs still *inside,* where they belong. Thank the lords for that." Avery flashes a toothy grin before downing yet another burgundy vial.

Estelle pulls Haskell's watch from the pocket of her cloak, Opal fading into the background as she takes her place behind everyone. "This is the spot?" Estelle asks, shooting a sidelong glance at Rydan. "You're sure?"

He can hear the doubt in her voice—and it *is* warranted, to say the least. "I know it doesn't look like much," he says, gesturing toward the enormous stone wall, "but this is where we entered the Veil." He glances at Arden for confirmation.

She nods. "It is. I'm sure of it."

Estelle takes a breath, then flicks open the watch and turns the small dial at the top. "Everyone, gather round in a circle. And join hands."

"And now we pray," Avery says mockingly, taking Vira's hand in his right, Opal's in his left.

Estelle shoots him a warning glance. "Oh, shut your mouth, would you? And your eyes, too, while we're at it." She takes her place in the center of the newly formed circle, still turning the dial.

Rydan does as she says but manages to peek out of one eye as she begins to murmur in a language he's never heard before. Suddenly, it grows very cold and very quiet. The waterfall's stopped. So has the chirping. He can't help but open both eyes, recognizing the silver-blue mist that's rising from the pocket watch. It drifts toward him, covering his head, his chest, his legs, his feet. He watches in familiar wonder as it does the same to the rest of the group, until it just barely lingers at their feet—like it had every time he'd unknowingly entered the Veil.

"Well, would you take a look at that?"

At Avery's remark, Rydan turns over his shoulder at the same time Arden does. There, no longer disguised by a solid wall, is a clearly marked entrance, just like they'd claimed. Arden's eyes lock on his and, for a fleeting moment, it feels like it's just the two of them again. He's about to squeeze her hand when Cerylia slides right between them, forcing them to break their grip. Arden's hand falls but her gaze lingers.

"It's darker than I remember," Cerylia says, mostly to herself, as she steps closer. And then, in a much louder tone, "Ignitors!"

Avery appears within seconds, completely blocking Rydan's view of Arden. He's barely heard what's been asked of them when he notices Avery lighting the torches he'd brought with his bare hands.

"Care to lead the way?"

Rydan looks to the queen, catching a glimpse of Arden as Avery makes his rounds. Without the slightest bit of focus, his hands burst into flames. He catches Arden's smirk, knowing that she just saw his own.

"Follow me."

CERYLIA JARETH

THEY'RE NOT EVEN halfway across the cave when Cerylia feels a rising panic. Is it insane that she's come here? What's to be expected? Will they welcome her back with open arms . . . or exile her?

Perhaps these are all questions she should have considered *before* taking Estelle up on her offer—especially since Opal no longer needs the assistance of an Arcane Healer. She tries to calm her nerves by reminding herself that she's agreed to come in order to fully regain her extracting abilities—an important task if they hope to stand a chance against the Mallum.

For the Caldari. For illusié. For Dane.

She repeats the mantra in her head, over and over again, but still, the nerves remain. She stays close to Rydan. Not meaning to, she's nearly walking on top of him. He turns over his shoulder and, even in the dim lighting, she can see the irritation etched all over his face. She falls back a few steps, again reminding herself that they're in no hurry.

Eventually, they arrive at another familiar cliffside, but this one contains an entirely different view—different, but spectacular. Cerylia sucks in a breath at the same time the group does, no doubt in awe at the magnificent structure that stands before them.

She notices Rydan's hesitation as he seems to recall something about their last visit. "Haskell, we may need your abilities again."

Haskell's head perks up from the back of the group. He finishes his conversation with Opal before jostling his way forward. He whistles as he looks across the cavern, mostly at the journey *down* into it.

"We need to get to that walkway, there," Rydan says, pointing.

"Well, you all know how this works," he says somewhat glumly. "I have to physically get over there first before I can take anyone else with me." He brings his attention back to the group. "Does anyone have any rope?"

"I do," Felix and Arden answer at the same time.

"The more, the better, I suppose," Haskell says, ushering them forward. They empty the supplies onto the ground, waiting for his direction. Rydan and Felix offer to tie the knots before securing the rope. "You're sure the two of you can hold me?" Haskell angles his head at the giant boulder sitting just behind them to indicate another alternative.

"We've got you," Felix affirms, wrapping the rope once more around the outside of his hand. "Let's get this over with."

"Be safe," Cerylia says to her nephew. She steps back to give them space, noticing that she's now standing right next to Arden.

"Every time he goes to do something alone, I can't help but wonder if that's how everyone felt about me," Arden whispers so that only her aunt can hear. She casts her eyes toward the ground. "I know I've already apologized, but I'm sorry I fled. I can't even imagine how worried you must have been."

Cerylia takes her niece's arm in hers, crossing it protectively over her chest. "You've grown into a strong, dependable, oftentimes *intimidating* young woman. I've never doubted that you would turn out more than okay— even if the majority of your life was spent with the Tymonds. As difficult as that must have been, I believe it made you stronger."

Arden lifts her gaze, her eyes damp with tears. "I hate to admit it, but I think you might be right," she says quietly, a small laugh escaping.

Cerylia squeezes her niece's arm. "What matters now is that we're all here, together. Your father would be so proud. Your mother, too."

Arden beams.

Cerylia lovingly pats her on the hand before releasing it to point to the bridge that leads to Midvale. "Looks like your brother made it just fine." Not a second after she's spoken the words, a flash of emerald light appears, disappears, then reappears right before them.

"You know the drill," Haskell says cheerily, ignoring the vial Avery's trying to offer him. "Two at a time. Who's up first?"

ARDEN ELIRI

I OFFER TO go last, despite how I'd felt about it the first time around. I stand by as my brother takes the group in pairs of two, just like before. Juniper won't stop squirming in my arms, so I finally set her down, urging her to stay close.

When I'm the last one remaining at the cliffside, I look over my shoulder at the dark tunnel we've just taken. For some reason or another, the edges of my vision begin to grow hazy as I hear something . . . something *familiar.* The tunnel grows lighter, but not in the way I'm used to—not like torches being lit or sunlight peeking through.

Like a sort of fading . . . from black to gray.

Confused—and inextricably mesmerized—I take a step forward and reach out in front of me, although I don't know what it is I'm reaching for; but there's something here, *someone* here. I'm certain of it. And . . .

They're lost. Hopeless. Distraught.

In my mind's eye, I'm suddenly brought back to the night we'd helped Opal find her way out of the Void. My hand on Felix's shoulder. The strangeness of it all. But then again, not strange at all. Because I'd felt that same feeling before. With Felix—when I'd been certain I'd been amplifying somehow.

The haze pulses, growing darker and then lighter, making it even harder to see. I'm not sure what I'm looking for because I can't *see* anything, but I feel it. Like *I'm* the one who's stuck there. Lost. Hopeless. Distraught. And then, I see something. It's faint, but recognizable.

A tree. There's something, or rather, *someone*, crouching next to it. While I can't make out who it is, what I *can* hear is the name that's being whispered over and over again, like a broken record. *Opal. Opal. Opal.*

My blood runs cold.

FELIX BARLOW

EVEN FROM A distance, he can see her aura—the deepening golden glow shifting to a murky gray until eventually. . . it becomes an inky black.

But that hasn't happened yet.

And he won't ever let that happen, despite the agreements he's made.

With his eyes locked on Arden, Felix slinks along the bridge, away from the incessant chattering of the group. He and Arden are connected, they always have been . . . ever since they'd crossed paths in the Thering Forest. He'd known it then and so had she, no matter how hard she'd fought to deny it. He'd expected the connection, yes, but what he hadn't expected was the strength of it. The sheer immensity of her willpower, her determination, her *being* . . . it's been overwhelming in the best possible way.

His gaze trails to the opening she's standing in, on the verge of disappearing. While he may not be able to see much, he can *feel* that she's latched onto something—or rather, something's latched onto *her*.

Some time back, he'd promised not to amplify . . . to never use his abilities on her. And he hasn't. He's kept his word, which has honestly surprised him as much as it would probably delight her if she knew. But when that *feeling* comes—one of imminent danger—he can't resist. He needs to feel what she feels, see what she sees, *know what she knows.*

There's so much she's still in the dark about, but too much she's already caught onto. And right now, in this very instant . . . is no exception.

He focuses all his energy on her, on that pulsing, hazy aura, his heart racing in his chest as he links up with her.

Gray. She sees gray. *A tree. A figure, crouching.*

Despair. She feels despair. But why?

His heart immediately sinks in his chest, dropping down, down, down into his stomach. This is low, even for her. This is . . . hopelessness. It's desperate. It's pure desolation.

Where are you, Arden? Where did you go?

Sensing her feelings *without* amplifying them has only gotten trickier over the months. As much as he wants to pull her out of the barren wasteland she tends to wander into, he's had to (patiently) learn the art of waiting, of surrendering. In order to see what's there, he has to go there himself—so long as he doesn't get lost along the way. But this . . . this is too dangerous, even for him.

She's a loose cannon, especially right now.

So, while he may be desperate for information, keeping her safe is his biggest priority. Because without her, they're all doomed—and what a burden that's been, carrying such a heavy secret with no reprieve in sight.

He grips the railing for support, scanning her aura for a glimpse of any other emotion besides fear. He can work with feelings of overwhelm, with disappointment, even. But not fear. It's far too strong to try to manipulate.

"Come on," he grunts under his breath, eyes searching. "Give me something, anything." Her aura's growing darker by the second, and as much as his own fear threatens to prod at him, he finds a way to push past it without breaking focus.

He may be a decent distance away, but even from where he's standing, he can tell that whatever's latched onto her isn't going to let go without a fight. He continues to scan the glow around her body, the one that only he can see, searching for just one tiny semblance of color. A pop of pink. A stroke of purple. A dash of yellow . . .

And that's when he catches it. A speckle of red. Yes, he can work with anger. It'll have to do. He softens his gaze, leaning into the sensation until he feels it pulling at every remaining ounce of peace within him. His breathing grows labored, muscles tensing, back stiffening in defense. It's interesting how anger and passion evoke nearly identical feelings, but the labels with which they're used depend solely on context.

Immersing himself in blind rage is never a simple feat, but it's easier with her because they have the memories together to do so. He can pull and tug at those moments of frustration, irritation, and annoyance because laced between them all is passion. Thirst. Desire.

He braces himself once more against the side of the railing, watching with satisfaction as her aura begins to change, the gray dissolving into a river of red. Her anger is on its way to becoming a distant memory as he dives deeper into their collection of private moments. They emerge with ease, reigniting within him what he's always felt for her, what he always *will* feel for her. It's the confirmation he's needed to know she feels the same.

At this point, Arden's aura is blooming red. Hardly any gray remains. His work is almost done.

I've got you I've got you I've got you

But then Haskell steps right in front of her, blocking his view and thereby severing the connection. A shock to his system, Felix groans and falls to his knees. He may be dizzy with emotion, but that doesn't stop him from lifting his head, even though his entire body feels as though it's made of lead.

When he's finally able to focus his eyes, he can see that Arden's mouth is moving as she talks with her brother. *She's okay.* His shoulders sag with relief.

Footsteps sound from behind him, drawing closer until Avery is crouched in front of him. "You okay, mate?"

He produces a vial from his pocket and Felix takes it from him without question. "All good over here. Must be the change in altitude," he lies, downing the tonic in a single gulp.

"You've got that right," Avery says, hoisting him to his feet. "And that's coming from someone who lives below sea level."

Felix chuckles. "Thanks for looking out."

"No problem," Avery says, clapping him on the back and leading him back over to the group. "You know, I was thinking . . ."

But Felix doesn't hear another word as he takes another glance over his shoulder. The sight is reassuring. He can breathe easier seeing that Arden and Haskell are still talking, because that means she's okay and that whatever had had its hold on her is no longer in the vicinity. Crisis averted . . . for now, at least.

ARDEN ELIRI

I'M YANKED FROM the strange encounter the moment a hand lands on my shoulder.

"What are you doing?"

Startled from my daze, I snap my head up at my brother. There's concern written all over his face. "Waiting," I say, not able to find the words to convey what I've just seen. "For you."

His mouth rigs to the side, even more confused. "If that were the case, why didn't you respond after the sixth time I called out your name?"

A knot begins to form in my stomach. "How long have you been standing there?"

"Long enough to call out your name six times."

I didn't hear anything. I didn't see anything. I didn't even know he was here.

Even with my mind reeling, I force a smile. "Must have been lost in thought, I guess."

He snorts. "Happens a lot."

More than you could possibly know.

"Come on," he says as he picks Juniper up. "Our aunt seems rather keen on entering Midvale as soon as possible."

"Understood," I say, linking my arm with his. As much as I want to, I don't dare look back at whatever bizarre reality I'd just wandered into. Perhaps some things just aren't meant to be explained.

"I'll count down from three."

"Oh, just go already," I say as playfully as I can.

A whisk later and I'm plopped in front of the group, thankfully on my feet. Avery hands me a vial, which I graciously take. As I drink it, I can't help but notice how closely Felix is watching me, looking rather pale himself.

Upon returning the empty bottle to Avery, I manage to catch Opal's menacing stare, which is directed straight at me. I try to shake it off as I walk over to Rydan, but I'm not surprised that it lingers.

Cerylia clears her throat. "Arden, Rydan, would you two care to do the honors?" she asks, gesturing to the monstrosity of an entrance.

I look to Rydan, noticing that his expression mirrors my own. We're about to tell her that the last time we were here the doors just *opened* on a phantom wind, when the sound of creaking does it for us. I can sense the group collectively take a step back as the inside of the haven slowly comes into view. But this time, something's different. This time, there's someone here to greet us.

I hear Estelle before I see her. "Lane?" She rushes past me in a flash and embraces the girl in the doorway in a heartfelt hug. "What are you doing here?"

"What are *you* doing here?" the girl exclaims.

I can tell I'm not the only one who's confused, so I clear my throat loud enough for Estelle to hear. She looks at me, then at the rest of the group. "Oh, right," she says with a grin. "Everyone, this is Lane. My cousin. Who, if I remember correctly, is supposed to be in Trendalath."

First off, I had no idea Estelle had a cousin, but the last part is what gets my attention. "Trendalath?"

For some reason, Lane's face falls the moment she looks at me, like she *knows* me, or has seen me before. I find it odd, seeing as I'm only just now meeting her.

"Inside job," Lane says. "A Caldari infiltrating the Cruex." She shrugs. "Someone had to do it, seeing as you two left on a whim." She points her fingers at Rydan and me.

The insinuation she's making is clear as day, and I don't appreciate it one bit. Before I can rebuke her, she does something entirely unexpected. She approaches me, then wraps her arms around me. My arms hang at my sides in confusion, but I push her away the moment I hear her say, "Braxton is supposed to be here, too."

I open my mouth to respond, but words fail me like they never have before.

Having heard everything, Estelle swiftly arrives at her cousin's side. "What do you mean? What happened?"

By the look on her face alone, I can tell that whatever she's about to tell us isn't good news. I'm also trying to wrap my head around the fact that she *knows* Braxton.

"We had a . . . *confrontation* with Darius," she says, her voice cracking. "I thought I could take him with me, to Midvale, but something went terribly wrong." She turns to me then, and I can see the immense strain that's pulling at her eyes. "He wanted to come find *you*, his cousin. We'd only just discovered the truth, Arden. It was my idea to go back to Trendalath. It's *my* fault." Tears rain down her smooth mocha-colored cheeks, pooling at the bottom of her chin. "I thought I could bring us both here safely. I thought—"

The knot in my stomach twists into a full-blown coil, expanding and contracting with each shallow breath I force myself to take. When I finally speak, my voice doesn't sound like my own. "Where *is* he?"

Lane hangs her head, sobbing even harder.

"Where is he?" I say again, harsher this time.

"There's only one place he can be."

My skin prickles the moment I hear Opal's voice.

"He's in the Void."

I don't dare look at her. Instead, I exchange a knowing glance with Rydan. And it's in that moment, deep in my gut, that I just *know* . . . that bringing Opal here is perhaps the most dangerous, careless thing we've done yet.

ACKNOWLEDGMENTS

This is the first time I've written a "fourth book" in a series and all I have to say is *wow*. We're in those moments where everything is starting to come together and, as a writer, I'm constantly questioning when the right time is to reveal things I've been foreshadowing since book one. Writing this book was an *experience*, to say the least. Growing alongside these characters over the years is something that will stay with me for the rest of my life, this I know.

First and foremost, I'd like to thank the Divine Force that flows through and connects us all. When you understand your power as a co-creator, life becomes limitless and full of wonder. I truly believe that creativity is the magic of this lifetime, and I am so grateful for the story ideas that I get to nurture, develop, and share.

To my sister, Erin, for always talking books with me and for keeping me updated on allll the bookish things. It's no surprise that we have a librarian in the family—and it's even less surprising that it's you! I'm so proud of you for pursuing what makes you happy. I love you so much, sister!

To my Mom, for always checking in on me and for offering support in more ways imaginable. Thank you for being so open, loving, and accepting of my creative path and spiritual journey. I love how much our connection has deepened over the years and feel so grateful to have you as my mother. I love you!

To my Dad, for reading all my books and for the thoughtful and unexpected texts about the characters in this storyline, specifically. As someone who wouldn't traditionally call themselves "a reader", I feel honored that you find my books interesting enough to keep reading them. I love you, Dad!

To Anna Vera, for literally being one of the best friends I ever could have asked for. Honestly, I had almost given up on thinking that someone like you even existed! I thank my lucky stars every day that I get to know someone like you in this lifetime. You are truly one of the most talented, witty, caring, and beautiful people I've ever met. My soul would seriously be lost (and devastated—no joke!) without you. I love you so damn much, bb!

To the incredibly talented cartographer, Deven Rue, for bringing The Lands of Aeridon to life, and to the cover designers at Damonza who continuously stun me with their artistry and professionalism. Thank you for being such a pleasure to work with!

To Sammi Davidson, Edward Gray, and Krista Olsen—okay, for real, I think about you guys ALL THE TIME. Whenever I need to go to my "happy place" (which is quite often in this pandemic), I think of Canada. My trips there were some of the best of my life, thanks, in large part, to you three! I'm so incredibly grateful for all the time we got to spend together. Just know that I love you and that I'm missing you terribly!

To Jonathon—I still remember the look on your face when I told you I'd be writing a character after you… and how you'd walk by whenever I was writing, see the character's name, and go, "Hey, that's me!" This goes without saying but I'm so proud of you and the person you've become. Thank you for really *seeing* me before anyone else did. And thank you for reminding me to always look for the silver lining. Oh yeah, and… BAHBAH COACHAHHHH!

To my furbabies—you are simply the best. The snuggles, the loves, the zoomies, the belly and ear rubs… I don't know how I got so lucky to deserve such sweet little companions. I remember the first time I read about spirit animals and nothing has ever rang more true. I love you more than life itself, my sweet, sweet, girls!

And finally, to my YouTube fam, readers, and fans—you are all so wonderful. Seriously. Thanks for sticking with me, for reading my books, for tagging me in your heartfelt posts, and for sending me emails that literally have me tearing up throughout the day at the sheer thought of them. I'm so grateful for the opportunity to connect with so many of you, and I'm honestly still floored that there are people out there who care enough to follow along on this journey. Your support has truly been life-changing. I love you all!

Don't miss the fifth installment in the
Shadow Crown series:

ARCANE HAVEN

TURN THE PAGE FOR A SNEAK
PEEK OF CHAPTER ONE

ARDEN ELIRI

THE NEWS OF Braxton certainly comes as a shock. And Opal's assuredness in the matter?

Even more so.

Rydan and I fall back behind the others, watching as Lane ushers everyone into Midvale. Opal is the last to join them. She brushes by us without so much as a glance or a smile, and it takes everything in me not to reach out and pin her to the ground.

From the front of the group, I notice Felix glance over his shoulder at me. I give him a small nod, and I can tell he's about to smile . . . until his eyes land on who's standing next to me. With a sharp jerk of his head, he turns back around and swiftly follows Lane inside.

"I suppose we shouldn't straggle too far behind," I mutter, pulling on Rydan's arm.

He follows me without saying a word. Honestly, he doesn't have to. I know exactly what he's thinking, because it's exactly what I'm thinking.

What have we done?

"We need to talk about this—"

I shake my head as if to say, "later", but deep down, my blood is boiling, my heart is pounding, and every inch of me feels on edge.

We shouldn't have brought Opal here.

I should have told Cerylia.

I should have delayed this trip as much as possible.

Because now, not only have we endangered ourselves; we've also endangered everyone in Midvale.

"Come on, you two!" Lane calls from the giant doors.

Rydan and I pick up the pace. When we finally cross the threshold, the rest of the group is standing in the center of the haven, staring up and around in awe, just as we had.

"I take it you've been here before?"

Lane directs her hazel eyes right at me. "Yes. Many times." She tilts her head, ebony ringlets falling alongside her face. "You haven't?"

"Only once." I force a smile. "Our trip here was cut short."

"An accident?"

"More or less, yes. But a happy accident, I suppose."

I follow her around the corner of an ancient-looking desk, its legs secured deep in the ground, as if they were the sturdy roots of a tree themselves. She opens a few of the drawers until whatever she's looking for floats out. A yellow orb. "Let's see," she says, referencing something I can't quite make out. "How about the northeastern wing, chambers three through seven? Once we get you all settled, we can talk about what's happened with Braxton." She nearly chokes on his name, and I can feel the guilt that's currently gripping her as if it's my own.

I feel for her. I really do. I know what it's like to feel entirely at fault for someone else's fate. I want to say something, but words fail me. So instead, I watch as the yellow orb closes in on itself before splaying out in what appears to be a map. "I assume you don't mind pairing up?" She moves the images of the chambers around with her hands, zooming in, then back out, checking to see what's available and what isn't.

Confused, I say, "I thought this was a school?"

"It is." She stops what she's doing as a small smile tugs at the corners of her mouth. "An *illusié* school, mind you."

"So, there's housing?"

"Mmhmm."

"And there's . . . *more*? Of *us*?"

"Honestly, you didn't believe you were the only ones, did you?"

I'm about to tell her that it'd certainly started to feel that way, what with all we've been through as a group, but I think better of it. "Believe me, I've hoped. I just figured, well, isn't that what Orihia is for?"

"Oh, don't get me wrong. Orihia is lovely. But it's more for leisure. Midvale is, how do you say, better *equipped* for illusié. To further hone our abilities."

"At a place where not even illusié *know* they have access?" My question comes out sharper than I'd intended, but I don't regret it. In fact, if I've gathered anything from this brief interaction, it would be that the people here have been *hiding*. And that's infuriating.

Her answer is clipped. "They know when they need to know."

"I'm not sure I can agree with that. Sure would have been nice to know about Midvale *months* ago."

Lane's gaze doesn't leave mine as she blatantly ignores my remark. "Pairs, then?" she repeats as she gestures to the glowing outlines of the open chambers floating before us.

"That should be fine." I glance over at my friends. "I assume Estelle will stay with you?"

"That would be wise. Especially if we have any late arrivals." She sizes up the group. "Will Queen Jareth prefer her own quarters?"

"Opal and I will stay together," Cerylia calls out, somehow having overheard our conversation from clear across the room.

Vira's head whips toward me then, her eyes shooting daggers. For some reason, I'm the one who's being tasked with rooming everyone. *Great.*

"So, Cerylia and Opal will be in one room, Rydan and Vira in another," I say, gesturing in their direction. I try to ignore the pang of discomfort hearing their names paired together, yet again. "I suppose Haskell and Avery can stay in a room."

"Which leaves you and Felix," she finishes.

I hesitate before saying, "Yes. That'll work just fine."

Lane catches my trepidation. "Will it, though?"

For someone I've only just met, the girl's sharp.

"Yes," I say bluntly, readying to turn away from her.

"Don't forget your keys." She holds out two gigantic brass keys, engraved **M.V.** at the head.

Amused, I take them from her. "What, no incantation to open the door?"

"Oh, don't worry, everything here is enchanted. Once you open the door and the room recognizes you, the key essentially disappears."

"Essentially?"

"Yes, in that *you* become the key itself." She gathers the remaining keys, nearly tripping over herself as she leaves to distribute the rest to the group.

It only takes a second to catch Felix's gaze from across the room. I flash the two keys at him and offer him a small smile, hoping it'll lighten the mood some—but from the bleak look on his face, it seems this unwelcome tension between us is here to stay.

Kristen Martin is the International Amazon Bestselling Indie Author of the YA science fiction trilogy, THE ALPHA DRIVE, the YA dark fantasy series, SHADOW CROWN, the metaphysical standalone, BEYOND THE STARS AND SHADOWS, and personal development books SOULFLOW and BE YOUR OWN #GOALS. A writing coach and creative entrepreneur, Kristen is also an avid YouTuber with hundreds of videos offering writing advice and inspiration for creatives and aspiring authors everywhere.

STAY CONNECTED:
www.kristenmartinbooks.com
www.youtube.com/authorkristenmartinbooks
www.facebook.com/authorkristenmartin
Instagram @authorkristenmartin
TikTok @authorkristenmartin

www.ingramcontent.com/pod-product-compliance
Lightning Source LLC
Chambersburg PA
CBHW051159190726
48288CB00006B/1721